D0436811

RUPTURE

RUPTURE

A NOVEL

A. SCOTT PEARSON

Oceanview Publishing

IPSWICH, MASSACHUSETTS

ISBN: 978-1-933515-23-6

Published in the United States of America by Oceanview Publishing,
Ipswich, Massachusetts
www.oceanviewpub.com

2 4 6 8 10 9 7 5 3 1

PRINTED IN THE UNITED STATES OF AMERICA

To Robin, always

ACKNOWLEDGMENTS

A book, the toil of one person for years, takes a small army to send off. For that, I thank everyone at Oceanview Publishing. First, I am grateful to Bob Gussin and Susan Greger for their vision. My publicist, Maryglenn McCombs, has promoted the book from day one, literally. I also thank John Cheesman, Gayle Treadwell, Susan Hayes, and Mary Adele Bogdon. I appreciate the artist George Foster for tweaking that cover one more time. And I want to give a special thanks to Patricia Gussin for sharing her remarkable talents with me. Every book needs a shepherd. Pat, you're the best.

I want to thank Penny Tschantz, my college English professor, for answering my call twenty years after graduation and agreeing to read a mound of rough pages. I thank Suzanne Clark and Stephanie Dorr for reading my early work. My academic colleagues, Nancy Reisman and Kate Daniels, have encouraged and supported me. I want to thank Chris Roerden for her wisdom.

My love for words on the page began with my grandmother, who read *Treasure Island* to me the year I skipped kindergarten, when I typed the opening chapters on my father's Remington typewriter. I cherish Bonnie Mae Stoots, "Nanny," who taught me, by example, always, always, to be working at something.

I thank my parents, Norma and Wilder Pearson, for their ceaseless love and dedication and for providing me with an idyllic childhood. I'm thankful to my brother, John, for spring planting and a harvest each fall and for his family, Denise, Andrew, and Rebecca, the Summerhouse crew.

This book would not have been possible without the unwavering, selfless support of my wife, Robin, loving mother, incredible physician, and caretaker of our own little version of a writer's paradise. I thank Will and John for the deep joy they bring every day.

And finally, I am inspired by the fields and fencerows nestled in the Forked Deer River basin, a slice of earth guarded by a small, country church, a place that holds my soul.

RUPTURE

CHAPTER ONE

GATES MEMORIAL HOSPITAL
MEMPHIS, TENNESSEE
MONDAY, JULY 10
12:03 A.M.

Dr. Eli Branch stood at the scrub sink and looked through the window into Operating Room One. He slung soap across his arms and hands while counting blood-drenched sponges that lay on the floor in piles. From the looks of the room he was about to enter, sterility was not a prime concern. Inside, a nurse hustled with bags of warm saline while another scrambled in with more sponges. The anesthesiologist hung two units of blood at the head of the table and forced the transfusion with a white-knuckled grasp. A figure gowned in blue bent over the patient, working frantically, deep in the abdomen, to quell the flow of blood.

Just twenty minutes earlier, Eli's beeper had pierced his sleep.

Dr. Korinsky needs you in room one.

A difficult case.

Cold water splashed off his arms and soaked his scrubs. His pulse quickened. As the newest member of the surgical staff at Gates Memorial, Eli knew to come running when paged, no matter what time of night. Even when he wasn't on call.

From the operating table, a pair of anxious eyes met his—a summons from Dr. James Korinsky, chief of vascular surgery, ten years his senior. On the other side of the table, a surgery intern stared into the wound. An orderly rushed through the room with a cooler of blood, little packets stacked together like summertime drinks waiting to be spiked.

Eli held to one more quiet moment, as if watching a silent movie unfold before him. He closed his eyes briefly, a preoperative routine that had developed not out of principle or theology but from a sense of necessity. Then, with water dripping from his elbows, he bumped the door open with his butt and walked on stage.

"I've got trouble here, Branch," Korinsky said before the door fully closed. "Dumb shit over here doesn't know an aorta from his asshole."

Above his mask, intern Landers rolled his eyes and discreetly shook his head.

Although Eli was a board-certified surgeon, he felt closer in rank to Landers. An awkward, sympathetic twinge grabbed him as the verbal barrage continued.

"I've seen monkeys with better hands."

Eli approached the table and peered over Korinsky's shoulder. Then he looked at Landers and winked. The intern took his first full breath since the start of the case.

"Damndest thing I ever saw," Korinsky said, lifting a matted wad of intestines out of the wound as if handling a tangled ball of Christmas lights.

The scrub nurse draped a towel across Eli's open palm. He quickly dried his hands while studying an X-ray of the patient's abdomen that hung from a lighted view box on the wall. The culprit was immediately apparent, a metallic device embedded in the center of the patient's abdomen, thin metal spikes projecting from the top of a cylindrical cage tilted at a deadly angle.

"Get over here!" Korinsky yelled. "If I needed a radiologist, I'd have called one."

Eli lingered at the view box. He had not scrubbed with Korinsky before and wanted another moment before fully committing himself with bloody hands.

Why does the top vascular surgeon in Memphis need my help on an aortic aneurysm? Especially when he has an assistant?

Then Eli considered the time of year.

July.

The first half of the month, no less, when attending surgeons took vacation just to avoid the new interns who knew only enough to be dangerous, and the naive medical students in shock from sixteen-hour days that started with four A.M. rounds. A man has only so many Julys in him, one of his mentors used to say.

"What kind of endograft is this?" Eli asked, referring to the biomedical device.

"Hell if I know," Korinsky said. "Some older model." And then, as a disclaimer, "Not one of mine, I can tell you that."

Eli peered closer at the X-ray. Surrounding a radiolucent inner fabric tube was an expandable steel mesh visible as a latticework of small V's connected and stacked on one another, like a tube of interlocking paper clips. The device was used to replace the aorta at the site of ballooning or aneurysm, a newer innovation that could be deployed within the vessel itself, avoiding the morbidity of an open abdominal incision. The device was designed to prevent aortic rupture, to save a life. But, as with any medical innovation, this one carried its own set of complications.

And this one is killing the patient.

"Some bastard from St. Screw-up put it in," Korinsky said.

Though the design was outdated, there was something familiar about the device, a recognition that Eli could not fully identify. The metallic image lingered with him as Roberta, the scrub nurse, snapped his gloves into place.

The overhead monitor buzzed with a rapid heart rate and showed a hypotensive pressure of seventy-four. Eli's waist met the patient's arm tucked deep beneath the drapes and he submerged his hands among warm loops of intestine floating in blood.

"Can't see a damn thing," Korinsky said as he wrestled with the matted wad of bowel. Blood welled up from the retroperitoneum and he jammed the wand-shaped sucker deep in the rising pool. The tubing turned bright red from the column of blood snaking its way toward multiliter canisters hanging on the wall.

The temperature of the room had been warmed to combat the

patient's progressive hypothermia, his abdomen an open medium for the escape of heat. The air above the operating table was thick and stale, compressed by another boggy southern night. Korinsky's paper cap was plastered against his forehead, moisture forming a pool in the center. A drop of sweat dangled from the cap's rim and threatened the open wound. Eli glanced at Roberta, who shook her head as if the situation was a lost cause. When Eli looked back at Korinksy, the drop was gone.

"Every time I retract to get a look, blood wells up and I can't see shit." Korinsky demonstrated the maneuver by tugging the small intestine to one side.

Eli watched as a crimson lake swelled and obscured any detail of the anatomy. "Is it ruptured at the device or has a second aneurysm blown?"

To Eli's surprise, Landers answered the question. "There are holes at both the proximal and distal end."

Korinsky looked at him with an ice-cold stare. "He's not asking you!"

Roberta handed a second sucker to Eli and both he and Korinsky evacuated the wound, blood gurgling so loud it rendered the rapid beep-beep of the patient's heart barely audible.

"Look what I found," the anesthesiologist said, shuffling through the patient's chart. "A spec sheet for this device you're after."

Korinsky looked up and snarled. "Damn it, Kanter, run the blood in, will you? No one asked you for information."

Kanter ignored him. "It's from our very own RBI," he said, referring to Regency Biotech International, the biopharmaceutical giant that had relocated to Memphis and was world renowned for its innovative medical devices.

"Who cares?" Korinsky shouted. "Just pass gas and hush."

"That's weird," Kanter said, continuing to examine the sheet. "The bottom half of the page is missing, like it was ripped off."

"RBI will be sorry to hear about this," Roberta chimed in. "Device failure can take a company down."

"Oh, they'll cover it up," Kanter said. "Trust me. They've got teams of people waiting to bury an adverse event."

Korinsky acted oblivious to this transaction. "How old is this son of a bitch?" he yelled as he allowed loops of intestine to slip through his fingers like strands of spaghetti plopping into a colander.

Kanter found the date of birth, 1937, and did the math. "Seventy-two."

"An exercise in futility is what this is," Korinsky said. He glanced at a clock above the anesthesia machine.

It was near one A.M.

"I've got three more operations in the morning."

Eli stared at Korinsky. *Are you finished?*

"And I meet with Dr. Fisher at nine," Eli said, then wished he hadn't.

"The big boss, hmm?" Korinsky raised his eyebrows at Eli's meeting with the chairman of surgery. "You'd better suck up while you can. After your first month here, the honeymoon's over."

"Excuse me, doctors, this isn't bridge club," Kanter said. "His pressure's sixty — and dropping. He's going to arrest."

Nurse Virginia Brewer stood near the head of the table and called out identification from the next unit of blood, a maneuver required to prevent a transfusion mismatch.

"39-11-972 — Gaston, Mortimer."

The medical record number was background noise, but when Eli heard the name, it resonated.

"Who?" Eli peered over the drapes to see the patient's face, but it was wrapped in a towel. He saw only the endotracheal tube sticking out. In an urgent whisper to the anesthesiologist he said, "Show me his face, please."

Kanter peeled the towel back, releasing a tress of matted gray hair. Although the patient's eyes were closed, Eli saw familiar sockets, deeply embedded with years of pain.

"Gaston," Kanter said, reading from his clipboard now.

Eli felt paralyzed and he looked again for confirmation. The man's pale, withered skin and unkempt beard were unmistakable. A collage of images rushed from his childhood, each dingy and out of focus. A boy following the disheveled, gray-haired man among rows of cadavers in Anatomy Hall. The unstoppable image of Gaston alone one night on top of the body, pulling himself, and writhing, over and over.

"His name is Gaston," Kanter repeated.

"Yes." Eli, stunned, fought the insistent memory. "I know him."

Blood-filled suction tubing hung from the side of the table like red tentacles, twitching under the pull of vacuum. Eli took a breath and said, calmly, "We need proximal control to see the tear."

Korinsky held his hand out toward the scrub nurse. "Richardson retractor."

From an array of instruments, Roberta selected an instrument shaped like a large spatula and bent at a right angle on the end. Even though she moved quickly and precisely, Korinsky yelled "retractor" twice more before she slapped the handle against his gloved hand. He slid the instrument along the central diaphragm beneath the left lobe of the liver and pressed hard, collapsing the aorta against the spine like a garden hose caught under a tire.

Korinsky looked at Eli. "See what we got, hot shot."

You want me to take this case? This is your turf.

Korinsky seemed content to hold the retractor, a task usually demanded of an intern. Eli moved the sheath of mesentery to the side of the abdomen and placed Lander's hands over the tissue to hold it in place. He grabbed a pen-shaped instrument, the Bovie electrocautery, and yanked the cord connected to the mobile floor unit to obtain more slack. When Eli incised connective tissue overlying the aorta, plumes of smoke floated out of the wound, the aroma of seared flesh. He cut through the final layer and partially clotted blood burst forward like cherry Jell-O under pressure.

"Lap pads and keep them coming," Eli ordered.

One by one, Roberta tossed absorbent white sponges into Eli's hand and he scooped out blood into a plastic basin.

"Suuuck!"

With his free hand, Korinsky reached for the sucker. But the retractor slipped off the spine and jabbed the base of the patient's liver, ripping its left triangular ligament from the man's diaphragm. Blood spewed from the wound like a fountain, and Eli batted it down with a hand to keep the deluge from covering his face.

"Damnation to hell," Korinsky yelled, scrambling to reset the retractor. Eli plunged the suckers in and with both hands scooped blood onto the floor, bailing a sinking boat.

"I don't have a pressure up here," Kanter yelled. "No pulse."

Korinsky shifted his weight down on the retractor. "He's not going to make it, I'm telling you."

Eli reached toward the anesthesiologist and released the clamp that held a blue drape suspended between the open abdomen and Kanter. As the sheet fell, Eli leaned over, breaking the sterile field, and lingered a moment close to Gaston as if whispering into the ear of an old friend. Then, in one swift move, Eli grabbed a pair of Mayo scissors from the tray of instruments, jammed the tips through the left diaphragm, and opened the muscle in a circular motion as if it were a piece of construction paper. Gaston's heart lay still, with only an occasional quiver of cardiac fibers. Eli inserted his hand into the left chest and began CPR with direct cardiac massage.

"He's exsanguinating," Korinsky yelled at the circulating nurse. "Get the whole damn blood bank in here."

"Three-0 Prolene on a vascular needle — with pledgets," Eli ordered, continuing to rhythmically squeeze the heart, pressing his thumb into the left ventricle, and wedging his hand against Gaston's spine. In a blind move of desperation, he submerged a vascular clamp above the liver.

Kanter was peering over the drapes. He wasn't looking at the patient but at Eli. As if his eyes weren't disparaging enough, he slowly shook his head.

Eli turned to Korinsky. "Throw some sutures in the hole," he said. "That's all we can do."

CHAPTER TWO

Applause filled the opulent banquet hall of La Belle de Marigot Resort from eager supporters who had dished out a thousand dollars per plate. Bernard J. Lankford gave a double thumbs-up and winked to his wife in the front row as attendants escorted the distinguished scientist off the stage. Lankford planted his steps with hesitation, testing his weight on the ramp of stairs as the men held firmly to his arms. What he lacked in agility, he more than compensated for in his command of an audience. The clapping had congealed into a rhythm, and a chant of "Ber-nie, Ber-nie" erupted. His wife joined him backstage and they were whisked toward a waiting limousine.

With his closing address, the International Conference on Embryonic Stem Cell Therapy (ICESCT) officially ended after two days of speeches, rallies, and sun-soaked cocktails on the tropical island of St. Martin. The agenda had been crafted to wine, dine, and lull supporters into breaking out their wallets as they popped a complimentary bottle of Dom Pérignon to celebrate the opening of the first embryonic stem cell infusion clinic. Prohibited on American soil, the International Clinic for Embryonic Cellular Therapy was a revolutionary facility. A young woman with a rare neurologic disorder had been selected as the first patient to receive the potentially life-saving embryonic cells. During the conference's opening plenary session, a riveted audience watched a live interview with the patient on a thirty-by-thirty-foot screen. She was scheduled for the treatment in less than a month. Behind the scenes, but in command of it all, hovered Regency Biotech International. RBI stood ready to watch its stock soar.

"You've still got it," Fran Lankford told her husband, sliding across the shiny leather seat until her hip pressed into his. For over thirty years, he had devoted his career to the cellular-based therapy of disease ranging from diabetes to Parkinson's to cancer. And he had reached the pinnacle as the chief medical officer (CMO) in charge of RBI's innovative, world-renowned Division of Stem Cell Therapy.

"Did I . . .?"

"No," she said, gently squeezing his knee to reassure him. "No stammering, no stuttering, not any of that. This time."

Lankford smiled, leaned forward, and removed two glasses from a miniature bar carved in the lush interior. "The hard stuff?"

"Yeah, why not."

He plopped a single cube of ice into each glass and poured a round of the island's best sparkling water.

"Now, home to that grandbaby," Fran said.

"I'm sorry, the timing of this conference was awful."

"We've been traveling as a team for what, twenty years or more?" Fran said, as if she needed to convince him of her loyalty. "They'll be fine." But as she said this, her new grandmother voice cracked. "Probably just out of recovery now."

They clinked their glasses in an awkward toast as the limo accelerated toward the airport.

They had landed on the French side of the island barely ten hours before. Upon boarding the company jet in Memphis, they received an urgent call from their son-in-law.

"They're taking the baby. Stat C-section."

Now, Bernie and Fran Lankford stared out the window of their chauffeured car into a black Caribbean night. Each had the same thought. *Taking the baby. Our little Celia. We've waited for years to be grandparents. And now we're off on an island in the Caribbean Sea.*

Minutes later outside the airport in Marigot, Bernie Lankford stood beside the limousine, stretched his arms, and watched the flare of a commercial jet overhead. The night air was fresh with an island breeze that wafted the fragrance of jasmine under a heavy sky pulsating with stars. As the roar of jet engines peaked, pain ripped through his abdomen as though he had been shot.

Fran Lankford stepped out of the car without assistance. Both the driver and a bodyguard were at the side of her husband, who was bent over at the curb. "Dr. Lankford. Sir?" They called to him but the man was on his knees, hands cupped against his chest, retching.

"Bernie?" Fran said softly, thinking he had slipped. Then she knew otherwise. "Bernie!" she screamed as she lunged to see the face of her husband.

His eyes were unfocused. An increasingly blue face, lathered in sweat. He moaned and pressed hard against his abdomen with a balled fist.

"Call an ambulance," Fran shouted.

While the driver punched numbers into his cell phone, Bernie Lankford toppled forward. As though in slow motion, but before Fran could catch him, his face smacked the dull edge of the curb.

Fran knelt by her husband and bathed his face with a cloth doused in the sparkling water. He was unresponsive, only shallow, wispy breaths indicating life. But at least he was alive. She talked to him, just inches from his left ear, with the life-sustaining words that only a wife of thirty-seven years could offer.

"Your grandbaby is waiting for you. You hear me?"

Fran placed her hand on his abdomen and noticed it tight and tense as if fluid had come from nowhere and was expanding under pressure. An airport attendant came out to assist them, but he could do nothing. A family of tourists gathered, quite disturbed at this scene on their first day of vacation. The father ran into the terminal to call an ambulance, again, while the mother held on to three small children and watched.

After twelve agonizing minutes of the slowest possible island time, an ambulance pulled up beside them. No siren, no flashing lights. The passenger exited the vehicle, dreadlocks flowing from beneath a red cap that announced Island Medical Transport. The driver remained inside, smoking a cigarette.

"What we got here, man?"

"My husband, he collapsed," Fran said. She was crying now for the first time since her husband went down, either from relief that help had arrived or her sense that she would soon be completely alone. "Please help him, he's barely breathing."

The driver got out, walked casually to the back of the ambulance and swung the doors open.

"Hey, Mars, throw me a blanket, man," the dreadlocked partner said. "This guy's bluer than Orient Bay."

Mars rolled out a stretcher parallel with Lankford and lowered it to the ground while Fran continued to caress her husband's forehead and whisper into his ear.

With Mars at the feet, they secured a hold on Lankford's body and lifted as his large, grotesquely protuberant abdomen folded in toward the pavement. "Here goes my back," Mars said as they swung him onto the stretcher like a sack of mangos.

Fran Lankford insisted that she ride in the back with her husband. When she climbed into the ambulance behind them, Mars looked at his partner and shrugged. "Whatever she wants, man."

Once the ambulance was moving, they drove like it was a real emergency with lights flashing, siren blaring, and racing through turns at full speed. Fran Lankford was thankful for the speed but feared they would turn the ambulance over, or worse, flip Bernie off the stretcher. She looked again at her husband, his abdomen hugely swollen, face the color of ash.

At a medical facility in Marigot, Mars and his partner rolled the stretcher into a receiving area, where they were met by a young woman. A name tag that read Miranda, R.N. was displayed on her pink floral sundress.

Fran hoped that the emergency team had at least called ahead about her husband.

"Who's this?" the nurse asked Mars with a frown.

Neither paramedic had called the hospital.

Miranda pointed to a curtained bay with a stretcher, an emergency cart, and a cardiac monitor overhead. "Take him over there. I'll wake Dr. Francisco."

A male orderly helped them transfer Lankford to the bed and minutes later a short doctor appeared sporting a goatee and wearing a leather vest over a tie-dyed tee shirt.

"Vitals?" he asked, in the final stretch of a yawn.

No one answered as Miranda scrambled to hook him up to the monitor.

He looked to Mrs. Lankford. "You his wife?"

She stepped forward, hands folded in front of her as if in prayer. "Yes."

"What happened?" the doctor asked as he cleared his throat and swallowed hard.

"We stepped out of the car at the airport and he collapsed. You've got to help him."

Dr. Francisco looked at a blank screen on the monitor and took Bernie's wrist to check for a pulse. "Medical problems?"

"Just diabetes, I mean, controlled by diet and he has — "

The doctor moved from Lankford's wrist to his neck, searching for a pulse while Fran completed her husband's history.

"—an aneurysm." She pointed to her own abdomen.

"Aneurysm!" Francisco repeated, his hands now on Lankford's distended abdomen. "Oh, shit. He's ruptured a triple A."

"But he just had it repaired a few months ago." Fran's voice pleaded, her hand cupped over her mouth in disbelief.

The cardiac monitor blinked to life and a flat tracing confirmed Francisco's exam. "Okay, here we go folks," the doctor said, "he's coding." Then quietly to the nurse, "Get her out of here."

As Fran Lankford was escorted away, she turned to see the orderly crouched over her husband, pounding his chest.

"A round of atropine, epinephrine, the works," Francisco called out, as if ordering drinks at a local bar. "Continue compressions." He yanked the portable ultrasound machine close to the table, ripped open Lankford's shirt, and squirted a glob of gel onto the mound of abdomen. "Oh yeah, here it is," he said as he ran the probe along lubricated skin and watched snowy shadows dance across the screen. "Blood everywhere. Damn, it's blown to hell."

The nurse pushed epinephrine into the IV and turned to face the machine.

"See," Francisco said, as if seeking confirmation. He pointed at the screen. "All this here? Blood. Liters of it." He slammed the probe into a rack on the ultrasound machine. "Ain't no way. Ain't no freaking way. We can go through the motions but that's it. He's a dead man."

CHAPTER THREE

Intern Landers stood over the body of Mortimer Gaston. The volume of the man's blood was divided between steel basins on the back table and sheets thrown over a thin lake, which spread across the floor and drained Gaston's skin bluish-white. Poised in Landers's right hand, a needle driver clamped a three-inch curved needle with black suture thick enough to sew elephant skin.

"Just baseball stitch it," Roberta, the scrub nurse said, coaxing the intern to close the dead man's abdomen.

Landers grabbed a thick plug of abdominal wall with heavy forceps but stopped before he drove the needle. He looked again through the door at his attending surgeon, Dr. Branch. Eli bent over the scrub sink and held to its side with both hands.

Virginia, the circulating nurse, tossed a bundle of blood-soaked linens into a hamper. To Landers, she said, "He'll be back in. Just needs a second."

Korinsky had stormed out of the OR during the final minutes of a failed resuscitation, leaving Eli and the intern to decide the time of death and make the declaration. But the senior surgeon continued an eloquent oration during his exit.

"Would you mind closing for me? I'm going to watch the back of my eyelids."

Like a kid shooting a rubber band, the chief of vascular surgery flung his bloody gloves against the wall. They were still in Gaston's chest when Korinsky added, "Just remember, doctors, all bleeding eventually stops."

That bastard, Landers thought, still feeling harassed by Korinsky's invisible presence. He threw in the sutures, over and over, like sewing a seam, and pulled them tight. As Landers jerked the needle through the tissue, it jammed deep into the joint of his left thumb.

"Damn it." He threw the needle driver against the cover drape.

"Did it get you?" Roberta asked, as if she didn't know that the point had penetrated Landers's skin.

He stepped back, pulled off his glove, and squeezed the entrance wound. A large drop of blood formed and ran down his hand. The dangers of a needle stick flooded his mind.

Eli reentered the OR and Roberta told him what had happened.

"Scrub out and wash your hands with alcohol," he told Landers. "Go. I'll finish."

Virginia led the intern well away from the electrocautery machine and poured alcohol over his hand, letting it run into a waste can before he washed at the sink.

When he came back in the room, Landers had pulled his mask down to his chin and his face looked washed out. He had had enough of this case. Needle sticks, although infrequent, were the dreaded risk of a surgical career. Hepatitis B, Hep C, not to mention HIV. "Well, at least he's an old man, probably harmless."

"You need to get tested, Landers. I'll draw his blood and send it for everything. Occupational Health is closed this time of night. Go down to the ER and get your blood drawn."

"I'll get the paperwork started," Virginia said. "You can take it with you."

"Listen," the intern urged, "this old guy doesn't have any risk factors. It'll take two hours to get through the ER mess."

"No, you listen," Eli said, and everyone in the room stopped. "I know this man and . . ." Eli hesitated. "He had a risky lifestyle. You need to get checked."

Landers gathered the paperwork, muttered "Thanks," and left.

•   •   •

Eli placed the final stitches and tied the two ends together in a bulky knot at the pubis. He knew that this was a temporary closure that would be reopened soon for the autopsy. He hadn't wanted to scare the intern, but Eli was the only person in the room who knew the history of Mortimer Gaston. And he knew it all too well.

He tried to suppress the crazed images of Gaston. It had been late at night.

Dark.

Maybe too dark.

The ten-year-old's mind was probably playing tricks on him. What did a child know about such things?

"Virginia, give me a spinal needle on a twenty-cc syringe," Eli requested.

A senior nurse who had been at Gates forever, Virginia could guide even a junior surgical resident through major abdominal operations.

Eli remembered her from his time as a medical student eight years ago at University of the Mid-South's School of Medicine, before his near decade of surgical training.

While he waited, Roberta stood nearby, curiosity crinkling her face. She asked in a near whisper, "What *was* his lifestyle?"

Virginia handed the syringe to Eli. "I'm not sure he has any blood left. I should've squeezed some out of the laps."

Eli knew that he was reopening a deep wound that had taken years for him to heal. He turned to Roberta. "Mort Gaston worked with my father in the anatomy lab at the medical school. For over thirty years, he prepared the cadavers for dissection."

"So you knew him as a medical student?" she asked.

Eli held the syringe in a vertical position, the five-inch needle pointing to the ceiling like a spire.

"I knew him since I was a kid hanging out in the anatomy lab. Gaston lived in the basement of what the medical students called Cadaver Hall. I learned more anatomy from this old man than all my professors combined."

"Doesn't sound like a risky lifestyle to me," Virginia said, while she finished counting the instruments.

The needle pierced Gaston's skin just to the left of the xyphoid process. Eli angled it to forty-five degrees and plunged it toward the man's heart.

"Eli," Virginia blurted, "your student just got stuck by a dirty needle. We need to know what this man's risk factors are."

What does it matter now? he thought, watching Virginia pull a sheet over the greyed head. Eli unscrewed the needle and handed the blood-filled syringe to his nurse.

"Just send the blood. Trust me."

All the doors to Gates Memorial Hospital were locked at night except the exit from the emergency room to the parking lot. Eli approached the sliding glass doors and nodded to the guard.

"Evening, doc." The guard checked his watch and the motion pulled his blazer open, revealing a holstered pistol. "Morning, rather."

The outdoor oven that greeted Eli made him stop momentarily under the neon emergency room sign for his daily readjustment to Memphis in July. The combination of sultry air and the site of the weapon recalled a similar night when he was a medical student on emergency room call.

A prisoner from a maximum-security facility was brought in with complaints of abdominal pain. Eli's resident assigned him the case. When Eli entered the exam room he was skeptical, knowing that prisoners often faked symptoms to go on hospital field trips. They were notorious for ingesting foreign objects—pencils, watches, packs of cigarettes, even razor blades. These they wrapped in tape to prevent laceration of the gastrointestinal tract. Yet the presence of a razor blade on an X-ray won them an operation and a week's vacation.

The first thing Eli noticed was the guard who accompanied the prisoner—a frail man in his mid-sixties. The prisoner was a forty-two-year-old male. The man opened his bright orange jumpsuit to reveal a scarred landscape of stab wounds, surgical incisions, and a tattooed fist in the middle of his chest with the middle finger extending up his sternum.

During the abdominal exam when Eli pressed on the prisoner's right side, the man groaned and bent his right leg.

The guard came to Eli's side. "Be still and let the doctor examine you."

Eli moved his hands to the prisoner's left side but got no pain response. Back to the right lower quadrant. At the location of the appendix, the man grimaced and tensed his abdominal muscles.

"I need to bring in my chief resident," Eli told the patient and confirmed this with the guard. But his chief resident was busy in a trauma resuscitation, so Eli returned, alone, two minutes later. As he approached the examining room again, he heard the rattle of handcuffs, the crash of a metal tray against the floor. The blast of a gun ricocheted through the emergency department. The prisoner burst from the room, his shackled hands gripping the pistol and aiming it up and down the hallway. Nurses and technicians scattered. Eli found the guard lying face down in an enlarging pool of blood.

He picked up a phone in the hallway to notify hospital police, when the man aimed the gun at Eli's head.

"Hang it up," the prisoner demanded.

For a moment, they stared at one another. Without looking away, Eli dialed the number as the man walked toward him, sighting down the barrel.

"Code Black, emergency room," Eli said.

Immediately, an alarm sounded and the prisoner took off down the hall toward the pediatric wing. Eli drew a deep breath and rushed to attend to the injured guard, but he was already dead. A few minutes later, the prisoner was apprehended in the hospital parking lot.

Later, when it was all over, the ER staff applauded Eli for acting so quickly and calmly. Eli remembered the fear as nearly incapacitating.

"Hey, Doc, you okay?"

Eli shuddered and wiped sweat off his face. His skin fluoresced green under the neon ER sign.

"I said, are you okay?" An ambulance had backed up to the bay and a paramedic opened the back doors. He stopped and watched Eli.

Eli nodded and started toward his car. After ten years, the memory occurred less often now, but seemed to grow even more vivid.

•   •   •

After a full day in the OR, Eli usually lingered in the lounge, signing operative notes or reading the day-old news, a mindless routine that facilitated his transition from surgeon to civilian. But after the Gaston debacle, he changed from scrubs to street clothes and left the hospital as quickly as he could.

Mist blurred the windshield, wipers missing a swath, but smearing an accumulation of bugs. He had not washed his '96 Ford Bronco since heading west from Nashville. Along Interstate 40, insects night bombed like hail from the flatlands of cotton and soybeans. The odometer was stuck at just over 116,000 miles, but Eli knew the vehicle had traveled well over two hundred thousand.

He took an unusual route through the grounds of the medical center and found himself driving past Anatomy Hall. Moonlight reflected off the crest of a gargoyle that stared from the corner of the roof with a wide ceramic grin. Eli slowed at a stop sign in front of the century-old structure. A row of ground-level windows, barely visible beneath scrubby boxwoods, outlined the foundation of the two-story building. The embalming lab was tucked away in the basement, where Gaston had spent his life preparing the dead for the next group of medical students.

Eli turned off the wipers as condensation fogged the glass. An anatomist, Professor Elizer Branch had wanted nothing more than for his son to be fascinated with how muscles inserted into bone and how the liver hung from a canopy of ligaments to form the roof of the abdomen. Summers and after school, little Eli spent his time at the anatomy lab, where his father ignited sparks of curiosity that he had hoped would propel the boy into the career of medicine.

As Eli looked toward the dimly lit building, he pictured himself at ten, sitting high on a stool next to Gaston, watching him pump a new body full of embalming fluid to replace stagnant blood. The medical students called their mascot "little E." He remembered, with a surprising pang of fondness, being lowered into an open abdomen, his ankles held by two laughing first years as he picked a spilled gallstone from the cadaver's retroperitoneum.

Gaston was not so bemused by the students' antics. He would sneer from behind his grey curls that dangled across his face and fell on bony shoulders. To Eli, the man seemed ancient even then, over twenty years ago.

Along with his oddities, Gaston appeared deeply committed to Eli's well-being even though he resented the presence of a young boy among the bodies of those who had made the ultimate donation to medical science. Over the years, Eli questioned whether this commitment was a form of psychological blackmail, an attempt to prevent the unwitting witness from divulging the secret that haunted them both. Now it was Gaston whose body lay in waiting, his soul called beyond.

Eli pulled the Bronco forward so he could see the back of the building, where the slope of the ground revealed a single window pane, illuminated. He imagined the bare bulb hanging in a stone-encased room, pipes along the ceiling hissing and bucking with the pressure of steam, a cold dwelling furnished with only a low cot in one corner, a cupboard holding canned food in another. *Gaston must have left the light on in a rush to reach the hospital.* Eli tried to imagine the intense pain that must have pierced Gaston's body as he lurched the quarter mile across campus to the emergency room.

Eli drove down Union Avenue wiping condensation off the inside glass with the back of his hand. He passed the Mesquite Chop House, which was formerly Sleep-Out Louie's. Through the window, he caught the glimpse of a couple sitting off by themselves at the bar. The girl sat sideways on the boy's lap. A tassel of blonde hair stuck out the back of her baseball cap, her arms draped around his shoulders and her head nestled in the crook of his neck.

A car pulled up beside him, the latest rave blaring out of open windows. Eli thought of the money he had saved in high school to buy two ear-splitting speakers that he mounted behind the seat of his short bed Chevy pickup. Today, Eli couldn't name one song in the top ten. What ever happened to Molly Hatchet and southern rock?

He passed St. Jude's Children's Hospital and a linear array of lights outlining the triangular face of the Pyramid Arena, first home of the NBA Grizzlies. An avid baseball fan who always pulled for the Pirates, Eli had never been to an NBA game. In his recruitment package, however, Eli had requested season tickets to the Memphis Redbirds, triple A affiliate of the St. Louis Cardinals. To sweeten the deal, he received not only two seats in Autozone Park, but also prime seats behind the basket in the Grizzlies' new home, the FedEx Forum.

At the beginning of his final year in medical school, he was invited to a Fourth of July celebration in Harbor Town at the home of one of his radiology professors. From the second-story balcony, as fireworks lit the sky over Tom Lee Park, Eli was intrigued by the homes that lined the eastern bank of the Mississippi River. In contrast to the frenzied pace of medical school, the massive river had a calming effect on Eli and he considered it a refuge.

After crossing Auction Bridge to Mud Island, Eli turned onto Island Drive and drove toward his new Harbor Town home. He passed the gazebo and followed an inland channel that snaked its way past villas and condos of orange brick, alternating with wooden homes of light yellow or Caribbean blue. Fountains shot tentacles of water that glistened in the sunlight during the day and kept the stagnant muddy water moving at night. Willows hung over the channel with drooping limbs that accentuated the serene landscape.

His bungalow was a small rental unit, but Eli had plans. After knocking down his medical school debt, he would buy a plantation-like home that faced the river. He pulled into his driveway, cut the lights so as not to wake the neighbors, and coasted into the garage. He turned off the engine, let his head fall back, and yawned. The pulsating screech of his beeper shattered the moment. His body jerked as if the beeper hadn't gone off a thousand times before. He glanced at the number.

Now what? From his cell phone he thumbed in the number to the OR.

A tired voice answered. "Front desk."

"Dr. Branch," Eli said in a tone meant to discourage further paging.

"Anyone page Branch," the voice yelled, as if calling an order back to the fry cook.

Too tired to shake his head, Eli imagined the scene, a couple of nurses at the desk flipping through mail-order catalogs, orderlies cleaning Room One after the bloodletting, a spotless floor being readied for the next victim: some youngster shot in a crosstown brawl or a dozing factory worker from West Memphis, Arkansas, slamming into a concrete abutment.

Eli heard the phone bounce across the counter and another voice answering, "This guy has no family."

It was Korinsky, calling about Gaston's autopsy. Eli was surprised the surgeon was still there. Why did he care about the autopsy? Then Eli remembered. Just before Korinsky left the OR, he stressed the need to obtain autopsy consent from the family. "This device killed him and I want to know the hell why." Eli could have saved Korinsky the trouble of searching for family that Gaston didn't have.

"But I talked to the medical examiner," Korinsky barked into the phone. "They'll have to do an autopsy since he died on the table. It's set for seven tomorrow morning, if you care."

Hell yeah, I care. But Eli suppressed the urge to jab Korinsky for his behavior in the OR. "Thanks for the call."

"Sure."

Eli knew that Korinsky wouldn't show for the autopsy. His presence would, in effect, acknowledge defeat. Something to which the chief of vascular surgery was surely unaccustomed.

Eli did wish that Korinsky knew about Gaston. That he wasn't just another case off the street that nobody cared about. That Eli had spent hours looking over the man's back at cadavers. But he hid what he knew would be seen as touchy-feely crap and ended the conversation with "I'm sorry we couldn't save him."

Before he hit the end call button, Eli heard Korinsky again.

"Hey, Branch."

"Yeah?"

"One more thing. Hope it goes well this morning with Fisher."

CHAPTER FOUR

The night mist turned to rain just as Eli opened the rear gate and sprinted across his deck, barely large enough for an outdoor grill and two small chairs. He headed straight for the refrigerator, grabbed a beer, and flipped on the television from a leather chair that no longer reclined. He had saved money by furnishing the unit himself, which meant loading his worn-out furniture and appliances into a U-Haul the same day he finished surgical residency at Vanderbilt before leaving Nashville.

At least some things you can count on, he thought, watching a female meteorologist on the Weather Channel predicting highs near one hundred for the next three days and a humidity level about the same. *Good ole Memphis summers.*

He changed to ESPN and caught the last minute of a beer commercial, a cold bottle snatched from a bucket of ice. *Sports Center* came on and highlighted the top ten plays of the day. He sipped from the can and watched a two-run, upper-deck homer, then a bone-slapping collision in the outfield with the left fielder snow-coning the ball. ✗← *evidently not a baseball fan!*

It's never as good as the commercials. He swallowed the tepid brew from his outdated refrigerator that barely kept milk from spoiling.

At nine A.M. he would meet with his chairman, Karl Fisher, head of the Department of Surgery. To support Eli's goal of becoming a surgeon-scientist, Dr. Fisher would pour money into his laboratory as start-up funds while Eli applied for external grant money from the National

Institutes of Health. Until then, patients would be diverted from Dr. Fisher's practice to Eli's clinic to provide a source of early income. Eli had barely started in this position and already he felt in debt, a tremendous pressure to see patients and operate successfully without complications while simultaneously conducting state-of-the-art molecular research.

The layered structure of the medical school imposed many bosses to whom Eli would have to answer, from the president of the university to the Medical School dean and on down. But Dr. Fisher had recruited Eli, steering him away from the lure of high-income private practice offers and into the trench of academia, one that ran deeply in the Branch family, having been dug over the career of his father.

Elizer Branch had been the medical school's professor of anatomy for twenty-seven years before his death. That event, two years ago, had left Eli unmoored from the rock of his life. Although his father never complained about it, Eli knew the man felt isolated in the old anatomy building, an obscure anatomist on the fringe of the medical profession. And since Eli's return to Memphis, no one had even mentioned his father. How soon the dead are forgotten.

Although his father held none of the power or prestige of the physicians in the medical school, Eli had still distanced himself from the man, almost to the point of rebellion, to ensure that not a hint of favoritism or leniency was perceived by his fellow medical students. Toward the end, when his father lay ill and Eli was too busy to visit, he realized that his self-imposed distance had been costly to them both.

In a few hours, after having witnessed the death of an old friend, Eli would watch the man being filleted open, his organs cut away one by one. Then he would attend the first official meeting with Chairman Fisher since his arrival at Gates Memorial. Possibly the most important meeting of his career.

Eli turned off the television and walked into the kitchen where the day's mail lay on the counter. The events of the evening still swirled in his head and he could not make sense of them. He knew that he wouldn't be able to sleep.

The mail consisted of two bills and a missing person card. He glanced at the age-progressed face of a ten-year-old girl next to another female he assumed was her mother. After twelve years in emergency rooms and indigent clinics, Eli always felt obligated to look.

The first bill was a friendly note from his consolidated loan agency that reminded him, monthly, that he could no longer defer his medical school debt and must start payments now. With his new address, he had hoped for a month's reprieve, but they had wasted no time in tracking him down. He slid the bill behind the coffeemaker, out of sight.

Eli held the other envelope in front of him with both hands. He would pay this one before the Harbor Town management or his loan officer ever saw a dime. Along with the statement was a brief note.

Dear Dr. Branch:

This letter is addressed to you as legal caregiver of Henry L. Branch. As indicated in an earlier correspondence, you will notice an increase in the monthly dues. We trust you will understand that this allows us to give the best care to your loved one. Please note that this increase is in response to recent renovations of Green Hills State Home required by the State of Tennessee.

Renovations? What, you decided to mop urine off the floor? Maybe got some soap for the bathrooms?

Eli removed a check from the drawer, filled in the figure of $3,157, and slipped it into the enclosed envelope. He took the check out again to confirm that he had written the correct amount, signed it, and put it back in the envelope.

The digital clock on the microwave showed almost three A.M. "This is crazy," he said aloud as he inverted the beer can in the sink and climbed the stairs to a loft bedroom.

As unrehearsed as breathing, he slid a pressed blue button-down shirt to the middle of the closet rack, then a pair of dark green slacks beside it. A pair of socks on the banister, underwear and tee shirt thrown on the bathroom counter. He selected his favorite tie, dark blue with a crisscrossing array of bright red diamonds. Eli reconsidered the meeting with Dr. Fisher as a time to look respectful, conservative, and needy. He replaced the flashy tie with a brown one, diagonal thin tan stripes, barely visible. He clicked the switch of his alarm, set to hard-driving classic rock at his standard 5:14 A.M., and lay on the bed. He imagined his meeting with Fisher, step by step.

First, he would go to the pathology suite to follow-up on Gaston's autopsy. Not good. He'd smell like the morgue when he shook hands with the boss. He dragged himself out of bed to get a pair of blue scrubs from the piled collection he had "borrowed" over the years from a dozen hospitals. He'd carry his real clothes in on a hanger and change after the autopsy.

The beat of raindrops against the skylight kept pace as his mind raced through Gaston's operation; his first operation as an attending surgeon at Gates Memorial.

A stellar debut, he thought. One hundred percent mortality. His next ninety-nine patients would have to sail through their operations for him to achieve an acceptable mortality rate of 1 percent. It didn't seem fair. Korinsky had called him in after it was too late. Given all the blood loss, Gaston had already crossed the line — a Wigger's prep, his physiology teacher had called it, when a lab animal was bled to irreversible shock and could not survive.

That's it! That's why Korinsky left the operation early. Some of the mystery surrounding the case was becoming clear. *I would have to pronounce the time of death, and the mortality would be charged to my record. So that's how it works in big-time academia.*

Lightning flashed over the skylight, closely followed by the rumble of thunder. The rising humidity smothered the loft and a sweaty shiver rippled over his skin.

Gaston's death was troubling beyond the mere fact that Eli knew him. It was the timing. The blood. Then the needle stick exposure of his intern and the sordid history of Gaston that Eli had never been able to get his mind around but was again forced to confront.

But it was the device that most bothered him now.

The failed device.

Out of bed once more, his heart racing, Eli removed a dusty, oversized folder from behind the dresser. Of the hundreds of radiographs he had seen, he had a formidable aversion to viewing an X-ray from his own family. He slid a single film out of the jacket and turned on the reading light above his bed. Holding the newspaper-sized plastic sheet at the bottom with a cupped hand, he lifted it to the light. A sharp crack of thunder shook the house and the lights blinked off.

Damn.

Eli leaned back against the headboard. The cool pillow felt good against his neck and he thought of the girl in the baseball cap, of a pleated skirt that framed long brown legs. He wondered about the couples he'd seen inside the Chop House and what it would take to sustain a long-term relationship.

At the next rumble, he raised the X-ray and the next flash through the skylight was enough to illuminate the metal device centered on the abdominal X-ray, confirming his suspicion in the OR. He closed his eyes and the bright outline of the device remained, as though burnt against his retina. He recalled Gaston's X-ray from a few hours before and the configuration of the old man's aortic device. When he looked again at the film in his hand, he realized that the two metallic devices were near identical.

CHAPTER FIVE

The floor was wet with a thin film of slime, as though moisture oozed from the concrete. Along the ceiling, rusty pipes twisted around a corner and led Eli down a long hall to a set of double glass doors. AUTOPSY was lettered on one, SUITE on the other. He hadn't been to this part of the hospital since his second year as a medical student. He whispered the popular name for the place: "The dungeon." It hadn't changed a bit.

He glanced at his watch and thought of Korinsky's call. *Maybe I'll be surprised and he'll be here too. Maybe he'll delay his first case to attend the final ceremony of this patient, whom he knew so intensely yet so briefly.*

Not a chance.

The doors reflected his image like a mirror, blue scrubs under a white coat. Carrying a hanger with his shirt over a pair of pants, he parted the doors and entered the void of the autopsy suite.

The suite was no more than a square room with cheap wood paneling and rows of filing cabinets. The stringent smell of formalin flooded him with memories of Anatomy Hall. The noxious chemical had seeped from his skin and anointed his clothes during the entire first year. Before him sat an empty desk with a bulky computer and brass nameplate that signified Ms. Conch, the occupant. *How, in a six hundred-bed hospital, with patients and families and visiting students, can a place exist so completely and absolutely alone?*

A six-foot-long steel tub, positioned at waist level by four metal legs with wheels, hugged the opposite wall. A blue felt blanket covered the bin like a flag over a casket. *Only in Pathology would they park the customers so close to the front door.*

Mixed with the odor of formalin was a pleasing aroma, rich and alive. Behind the reception desk, on top of a file cabinet, a half-full carafe of coffee rested on a hot plate. Eli tested it with his knuckles and found it still hot.

He filled a Styrofoam cup and looked in the drawer for cream, but decided he was pushing his luck. His stomach felt irritated from the late-night beer and no breakfast. It growled as he sipped the coffee. A clock radio, the old kind with rotary numbers, buzzed, then flipped to 7:13.

The only sound in the room was a remote hum, like the drill of a dentist, underwater. He walked to the metal tub. *Surely it's empty, just parked here, waiting for the next mortal pickup.* Eli peeled back the corner of the felt blanket.

Not empty.

"Anybody you know?"

Eli flipped the cover back and patted it smooth, as though making a bed. Mrs. Conch, he presumed, occupied the doorway, five foot tall, just as wide, squinting at him through dark-rimmed glasses.

"I was just —"

"Who you here to see?" The woman crossed the floor and squared up behind her desk, a mother elephant claiming territory.

Eli hesitated, assessing the situation. "Autopsy. Gaston's the name."

"Done started." Mrs. Conch pointed down a narrow hallway. "Probably got him peeled back like an oyster by now." She flicked her wrist as if cracking a shell. "You the surgeon?"

"Not exactly. I was asked to —"

"Good. Got some paperwork for you to sign." She produced a legal-sized document three pages thick, carbon paper between each sheet.

Since Eli had pronounced the time of death, he was left the duty of signing the death certificate, which required the immediate cause of death and the correct diagnoses leading up to the event. But Eli had not had contact with Gaston since leaving medical school for surgical residency, and he had no idea of Gaston's health during those eight years.

"Isn't it the law that the death certificate has to be signed before the autopsy starts?" Eli was trying to delay what he knew was inevitable.

"Well, technically yes, but . . ." Ms. Conch hesitated and looked back toward the autopsy room. "This new doctor, Daily, she don't exactly follow the rules, best I can tell."

Guess not, Eli thought. Who starts an autopsy before 7 A.M.?

Eli gave it one more try. "His actual surgeon is James Korinsky. He's the one who —"

"Look doctorrrr . . ." She squinted to see the name embroidered on his coat, "Branch." She emphasized the "ch" as if it ended a hard sneeze. "We don't want no legal trouble now, do we? Just put something down here and sign it." She scooted the form across her desk and drew out a long "Pleeeease."

Eli removed a pen from his coat pocket and leaned over the form. Ms. Conch's stubby hand held firm to the corner of the page. He surmised by the presence of an endograft that Gaston had suffered an aortic aneurysm, although there was so much blood that the aortic wall could not be visualized. Landers had been correct; the leak seemed to be at both the upper and lower edges of the aortic graft. Eli pressed hard against the page with his pen:

Events Leading to Death—*Abdominal Aortic Aneurysm*
Immediate Cause of Death—*Aortic Device Failure*

"There you go," Eli said, and released the pages.

"Thank you, Dr. Eli Branch." Ms. Conch swiveled in her chair toward a file cabinet. "How's my coffee?"

She was all smiles now.

Eli looked down at the black syrupy brew. With Ms. Conch's raw oyster visual still in mind, Eli raised the cup as if toasting. "Best I've had in a while." He used the cup to gesture in the direction of the autopsy room.

"Sure, go on back."

Eli hung his change of clothes on the handle of a filing cabinet. He paused by the body bin, out of respect and a bit of curiosity.

"Don't worry," Ms. Conch said, smiling like a witch. "He'll keep me company."

The drilling sound became louder as he parted a set of swinging doors, and a cold front hit him as if he'd entered a meat packing plant. Eli passed four deep metal chambers, with a handle on the front of each. Lined up on shelves were sealed opaque plastic buckets holding tissue specimens floating in juice, like a chunky fish stew.

An observation window to his left revealed the procedure in progress. Gaston lay naked on a metal bench, rectangular and dipping toward the corners, an eerie pool table collecting fluid in the pockets. The corpse's legs were bluish white, with the knots of his knees falling back disjointed against steel. Between Eli and the old man's face stood the pathologist, back toward him, leaning near the head. A line of sprayed bone spat against the table. The buzz of the Stryker saw stopped and a gloved hand lifted the skull like a halved coconut suspended by long gray hair. Placed on the table, sideways, it rolled forward like a bowl.

Eli stepped closer to see Gaston's head supported by a wooden block under his shoulders, neck extended as though hanging off a table. The glistening inner surface of his scalp was peeled down and sagged on his face in redundant pockets, a ghoulish Halloween mask.

As if aware of his presence, the pathologist turned to face Eli in a graceful pirouette. Not the awkward butcher he had expected. Her face was protected by clear plastic, like a welder's shield. A paper mask had been pulled tight across her nose. In this room of cold, mottled flesh, the only promise of life was condensed and magnified in her brown eyes.

She held a knife of sorts, long and blunted at the end, and with two quick flicks she motioned for him to enter. She turned again toward her patient and Eli kept his eyes on the twist of a gathered white smock, tied in the small of her back just above a perfect pair of tight blue scrubs.

"Gown and mask, please. On the corner table."

Eli removed his white coat and slipped his arms through a yellow protective gown. She watched him for a brief but intense moment.

As a surgeon, he was comfortable with warm bodies lying on the table. But here, Eli felt strangely out of place, even though as a boy he was familiar with the dead lying cold. He tied his mask and approached the corpse sprawled between them.

With the top half of the skull removed, Gaston's brain lay exposed revealing fissures and deep ridges like a shelled pecan. The pathologist pressed the brain posteriorly to expose the cranial nerves at the skull base. With a pair of Metzenbaum scissors, she clipped the slender white cords. They popped, like tight ribbons on a Christmas present, as the distal nerve ends retracted into the neck. Swiftly, she divided both vertebral arteries and delivered Gaston's brain, seventy years of wisdom and pain plopped into a metal pan.

"I saved the abdomen," she told Eli. "Figured you'd been there."

Eli glanced at Gaston's ashen face. A contorted left cheek pulled his upper lip in a snarl.

"Thanks."

"Dr. Branch, I presume."

"Yes. Eli. Please."

"Most surgeons just read the report." She looked up for his reaction. "We don't get many visitors down here."

"In the dungeon?" He hoped for familiarity, then wondered if she considered it an insult.

Above her mask, barely perceptible, the brown eyes narrowed in a playful squint. "Yeah, the dungeon."

Behind his mask, Eli smiled, as though he had broken through the code. Then he looked down at Gaston and Eli's transient delight evaporated. Gaston's torso had been opened with a V-shaped incision that started at the shoulders and came to a point at the bottom of his breastbone. The ribs were cut on both sides, the marrow-filled ends sticking out like a rack of barbecue. The chest plate had been removed to expose the lungs, two large sponges framing a lifeless heart.

"And you are—?" he asked.

She extended her gloved hand across Gaston's chest and Eli accepted it with an impersonal, latex-on-latex shake.

"Meg Daily." She quickly retracted her hand and cupped it around Gaston's heart as though holding the head of an infant. With a pair of scissors, she zipped open the pericardial sac.

The silence grew louder as he pretended to look around the room.

"You don't have much help here, do you?"

Dr. Daily continued her examination, now dissecting the descending coronary artery off its groove in the cardiac tissue.

"The muscle is intact," she said calling out her findings as she went, "but bruised."

Eli thought of his cardiac massage and the damage it must have done in a futile attempt to force blood to Gaston's brain.

"There's a tiny puncture mark in the left ventricle. Did he have an intracardiac injection?"

Eli studied the muscle closely. *Oh, she's good,* Eli thought as he tried to find the tiny hole created by his needle when drawing blood. *She's very good.*

Meg moved to the lungs and began to open the left pulmonary artery, totally absorbed in her work. Two long minutes of silence passed.

"Ms. Conch, she seems nice," he said, hoping this would engage her again, maybe get a laugh.

Dr. Daily looked up at him. "It's quiet and lonely down here, just like I like it. Can get my work done. Usually."

With this, Eli focused his attention on Gaston. He imagined the man at his work, hovering over the medical students, calling attention to every detail. And now he was a cadaver, a delegate to medical science. Just like those bodies he had attended in Anatomy Hall for all those years.

Eli looked at the hasty closure of the old man's abdomen, whip-stitched together with thick sutures that cut through edematous tissue. He removed a pair of trauma sheers from the instrument tray and cut the first stitch just beneath the breastbone. Then the second. The third snip was followed by a ripping sound, and tissue burst open like an over-ripe melon.

Meg Daily stood with her arms crossed, watching him.

He cut the remaining sutures, extracting the ends with a pair of heavy forceps. With the incision fully opened, Eli slid a finger inside to separate a film of congealed blood that covered loops of cold intestine.

"Here," Daily said, presenting a self-retaining retractor to Branch.

Eli inserted the finger-like metal hooks along each side of the abdominal wall. He spread the instrument with a ratcheting force that transformed the linear incision into the shape of a diamond, a move that allowed the abdominal organs to be viewed at once.

"Thanks."

"You're welcome."

He felt a current pass through him, light and rapid, like the fluttering of moths. He tried to ignore it but looked at her again. Something about her eyes, a sadness that beckoned and suggested to him sorrow in her life, just as there was in his. He had come to the autopsy in search of closure in the life of this man, Gaston. Not only to learn the cause of his death but to bury the memory of his impropriety with the dead. Now, over Gaston's body, Eli tried to resist a slight, untimely attraction he felt for Meg Daily, despite her removing, at that moment, clots of old blood from the abdominal cavity.

"Ruptured aortic aneurysm?" she ventured.

"I wish it was that simple." Eli was beginning to mobilize the sheath of small intestine, a move that would expose the exact cause of death.

They moved in tandem, a preordained rhythm of hands searching violent lands, perfect pressure on tissue, giving, taking, vying for command, then submission, an electric brush of knowing, experienced fingers retracting from illicit contact, but wanting more as they pushed deeper toward a synchronous destination.

There it was. A perfectly cylindrical tube interposed in the aorta, expandable mesh cage intact and structurally competent.

"The endograft looks fine," Daily said, her fingers spread and stretched over mounds of clot to hold the exposure. "Don't you think?"

"Appears to be."

Above and below the graft, where the native glistening white aorta should have been, Eli saw only shards of tissue, like the aftermath of a grenade. "But," he added, "the aorta's blown to hell."

"Hold this," she said as she released her hold on a shelf of clot and Eli slid his hand over hers.

Tiny electric shocks.

"It's moth-eaten," she said.

Eli looked at her but saw her focused elsewhere. "Come again?"

"Little holes, everywhere." With DeBakey forceps, Daily lifted from the wound a torn portion of vessel wall, like a flat noodle, and held it at a mutual focal point between them. "See?"

"Okay," Eli said, studying the tissue. "Moth-eaten."

Unaware of time, until now, Eli found a clock on the wall.

"Damn it," he said, "sorry."

"What? Damn it, sorry."

The clock read 9:06. Eli removed his hands from Gaston's belly as if it were on fire and ripped off his gloves. "I'm late."

Dr. Daily looked up and Eli sensed a hint of disappointment at his leaving.

"Operating room?"

"No, worse," Eli said and held his arms above his head to mimic an imposing figure. "Chairman of the Department of Surgery."

CHAPTER SIX

Eli pushed the button to the seventh floor three times, rapid fire. He would have taken the stairs but he was already winded after a brisk four-block run from the Pathology building to the administrative offices of Medical Center South. He needed a moment to collect himself. Eli buttoned his white coat to conceal his scrubs, but this seemed only to highlight a fan of black hairs on his chest. He pictured his starched shirt and tie hanging next to Ms. Conch's desk and glanced at his watch for the tenth time. 9:14.

Scrubs and fifteen minutes late were definitely better than a tie and twenty-five.

The elevator opened to a reception desk and a face that Eli remembered from his recruitment interviews. The young woman wrinkled her forehead in a sympathetic gesture. She looked at Eli like she was watching a car about to crash. "You better go straight back," she said. "He's kind of waiting."

Of all the times Eli had waited patiently to meet with senior staff, this had to be the day when all appointments were running smoothly and on time. The secretary closed the door behind him.

"Dr. Fisher, I'm sorry."

"Have a seat."

Eli knew this wasn't a request; it was an order. Karl Fisher was a large man with shoulders that started somewhere on his back and rounded over like the hood of a Volkswagen Beetle. No neck. And from the looks of his reddened face, he'd been idling on simmer. Eli settled immediately into the straight-backed chair.

Centered on the wall, above a thick mahogany desk, hung the chairman's prize kill — the head of a rhinoceros. Eli let his eyes fall along the curve of its slick head, downward, until Fisher occupied his view. The resemblance was striking.

"Been operating this morning, have you?" Fisher asked, eyeing Eli's scrubs.

Their last interaction had been at a recruitment dinner earlier in the spring. Fisher had smoked a Partagas cigar, drunk straight Kentucky rye whisky, and laughed like jolly Saint Nick. It was a joyous, carefree night.

Deceptive as hell.

Fisher hunched over Eli's personnel folder. Eli knew immediately this was a bad sign. He wished he had a fifth of Kentucky's best to serve Fisher, to lubricate the next few minutes.

Fisher flipped a page and began to recount Eli's academic pedigree.

"Summa cum laude from the University of Mississippi." He cleared his throat, pretentiously. "Ole Miss."

He continued.

"Accepted to a prestigious comparative anatomy fellowship at University College London." He glanced up at Eli as if to confirm this account. Beefy eyes peered over a set of diminutive glasses, perfectly balanced on his horn.

Eli nodded in affirmation but remained silent. The chairman of surgery went on. "Ranked number three out of a hundred nineteen students in an exceptional medical school class. Chief administrative resident, Vanderbilt University."

Fisher's voice was gaining speed like the charge of a rhino.

"Sixteen peer reviewed publications on Matrix Metallo — blah, blah, blah, and a teaching award from the sweet little medical students in Nashville."

He ripped off the glasses and flung the chart across his desk. "What the hell is going on?"

Eli had been lulled into the singsong verse of all his accomplishments. He tried to rebound from Fisher's sudden change.

"Sir?"

Fisher released a lung full of air. "James Korinsky called me at six this morning."

Eli said nothing. He had no idea what this was about, but the tone of his superior suggested it wasn't in his favor.

"Look, Eli." The big man folded his hands over his abdomen like he had just finished a large meal. "I like you. We rolled out the red carpet for you. I can't remember recruiting someone harder." Fisher picked up a pen and sawed it across his thumb, like he was cutting a steak. "I mean, dinner at Folk's Folly, a Lakers' game at the Forum."

He stopped and tilted to one side as if passing inaudible gas.

"This is not a good start. All you really need to do is show up when called, do your operations, and publish some papers out of your lab. Can you do that?"

"Yes, sir." Eli still didn't know where he was going with this. "I don't understand."

Fisher rolled forward. "Korinsky said he called you to assist. You didn't answer your beeper for almost an hour and then complained like a wimp that you weren't on call. When you finally came in, you insulted the nurses and the brand-new intern."

Eli could feel his mouth opening and his chin drop. He balled his right hand in a fist, quickly recounting the early morning hours. He had come in immediately, greeted the nurses, and put Landers at ease. *This was preposterous.*

Fisher continued as he read from notes scribbled on a sticky pad. "Then, just as Korinsky started to repair the aortic rupture," Fisher looked at Eli, like a judge about to deliver jail time, "you tore the liver and the patient exsanguinated."

Before stopping the impulse, Eli struck the top of Fisher's desk. "That's a damn lie." The impact propelled a stream of coffee from Fisher's cup, splattering across a stack of neatly arranged papers.

Oh shit, Eli thought, his face burning with rage. He reached for the cup, to steady it, while trying to salvage the papers.

"Leave it," Fisher demanded as he pressed an intercom on his phone. "Julene, come in here please."

Fisher's secretary entered the office with a wad of paper towels, as if she already knew.

Fisher eased back from the edge of his desk, removed his glasses, and began to clean them with a white cloth from the drawer. Eli settled in his chair and tried to regain control, but rage still boiled inside.

As Julene leaned over the desk, coffee dripping from the stack of papers, her tight blue skirt slid well above mid-thigh. She blotted and wiggled around until everything was tidy again. Eli glanced at Fisher. He seemed to be enjoying the show.

Questions raced through Eli's mind. *Why had Korinsky called him in the first place? Why not one of his vascular surgery partners? And why concoct this absurd story for the chairman?* Eli had faced fierce competition from surgeons before, a group always looking for an edge, more money, a promotion. But he had never faced an outright lie from a member of his own department. A falsification that ruined his reputation with his chairman, jeopardized his position, possibly his job, and had malpractice implications that he couldn't even fathom at this point.

Julene finished with the spill and left the room. Fisher's eyes followed her backside until it disappeared behind the door. Then he growled, "Branch!"

Eli's attention snapped back to Fisher.

"James Korinsky has been at Gates Memorial for over two decades. He is head of the Division of Vascular Surgery and chairs our committee on credentialing and privileges. I could go on and on." He rotated a thick forearm to check the date on his watch. "You've been here, what, a week, barely? I would rethink your position on calling Dr. Korinsky a liar, and go hide in your lab while the smoke clears. Don't you think?"

Eli had no idea what to think. Only that he had come to the meeting to get a blessing from the chairman to start his clinical practice and his research laboratory. After sixteen years of school and training, the last eight spent in one of the finest surgical residencies in the country, all that anyone in his position could want was to have his own patients, decide who got what operation when, and reap the financial benefits, yes, but mostly enjoy the pure satisfaction of finally becoming a surgeon.

Sure, he wanted his own laboratory; it was part of his dream of becoming a surgeon-scientist. But the research would take time, years even, before he was funded on his own through the National Institutes of Health. And until that happened, the last thing he wanted was to be banished to the laboratory, a move that would instantly brand him "rat doctor" among his colleagues.

Fisher was still waiting for him to say something when Korinsky's words struck Eli like a spotlight.

"Got a meeting with the boss, do you?"

He'd been set up. No doubt about it.

Korinsky knew about the meeting because Eli, in the rush of Gaston's operation, had volunteered the information. Now, the whole night was backfiring against him.

"I've asked my secretary to cancel your clinics. That'll free up some time. And you'll still be in the call rotation, every third. I'll add you to the trauma call so you can keep your hands wet, literally." At this, Fisher made himself laugh.

"Of course, without the clinical income of an elective practice, your salary will be cut. We'll still fund a lab tech at the lowest salary level."

Eli could see his whole recruitment package dissolving before his eyes. At night, he would be surgeon to the local knife and gun club, a busy organization with an expanding membership. And during the day? Rat doctor with some inexperienced technician and barely enough money to buy a petri dish.

"Are you getting all this, Eli?" Fisher asked, staring into his protégé's glazed eyes.

Eli couldn't believe what he was hearing. Though his head was spinning, he sucked it up, military style.

"Yes, sir."

"We're not talking forever. Let's reevaluate in six months, maybe a year, see how things are."

Fisher glanced at the door to indicate the meeting was over and Eli stood.

"We've put a lot into you, Branch." The chairman straightened the papers on his desk and Eli felt as if more was coming. He was reaching for the doorknob when Fisher looked up with an icy stare.

"Don't screw this up."

CHAPTER SEVEN

Meg Daily was seated behind the microscope, just ten feet in front of him, balanced on a stool with rollers that forced an inward curve to her back as if she were racing a motorcycle full throttle. Black hair fell over her shoulders in a straight shot before a sassy upward flip on the ends. She inched forward, just slightly, to realign her vision through the scope, a pair of blue scrub pants fitting snug and cinched tight at the waist.

How long can I just stand here and stare?

The previous afternoon, when he wasn't throwing imaginary darts at Fisher's head, Eli had wondered about the face hidden behind her surgical mask. He took a few steps to his right and leaned forward while trying to stay out of her peripheral vision. The silhouette of her face was obscured by strands of black hair that brushed olive skin, full lips poised in perfect concentration.

"Can I help you?" she said, eyes still focused without so much as a twitch.

Eli cleared his throat. "Oh, yes, Dr. Daily."

At this, she swiveled to face him, hands on her knees. The black pen in the pocket of her scrub top jiggled with animation.

"I'm wondering if you had a chance to look at the aortic specimen."

"Good timing, Dr. Branch. I'm looking at it now."

"Eli, please."

To this she said nothing and returned her gaze to the scope.

To his right, a Formica table was pushed against the wall. In the center of the table sat a metal tray about the size of a cookie sheet with a yellow slab of wax coating the bottom. Meg had washed the device and pinned it to the wax much like a frog readied for dissection in a middle-grade science class. It was a cylindrical cloth tube reinforced with a metallic mesh. Meg had left a cuff of native aorta at each end of the graft, their inside layers smooth and glistening like macaroni.

"The device is intact, the steel matrix sound, no warping or fracture. I've examined the lining — no signs of sheer."

While she remained buried in the microscope, Eli looked around her office. Her small desk had a metal top with a stack of papers in the center. A single picture frame off to the side showed a girl — four, maybe five years old — a gray tabby cat snuggled close to her face.

He glanced at Meg's left hand.

No ring.

Maybe, as a pathologist, she doesn't wear one. Formalin and diamonds? Not a good combination.

But her hand was soft and slender, poised with a flesh-toned polish, not one of years dipped in preservative. With feline swiftness, she refocused the scope and stood, with an open-hand gesture toward the instrument. Eli leaned over the eyepiece into a hint of perfume.

Or maybe she just smells that good, all natural, like when she first wakes up in the morning, like when she —

"Eli?"

"Yeah, what?" He realized he had been staring through the double lens as though an endless tunnel.

"What do you see?" she said with a half smile that made his face burn.

"Oh, very interesting," he offered at last. Eli bent over the microscope again until his eyelashes just brushed the lens. He focused on the slide and wished now that he had attended all those microscopy labs in med school.

"Here, let me show you something," she said.

Eli stood, and in the process of switching places, a tassel of Meg's hair brushed his cheek.

She selected another glass slide from the collection in a metal tray, slid it under the microscope, and searched for a preselected image.

"Yes, here it is."

She looked up from the instrument and motioned Eli to another eyepiece connected to the main microscope directly opposite hers.

"Use the teaching scope so we can view at the same time."

Awkwardly, Eli bent toward the view piece. He had viewed cells in his lab hundreds of times, always sitting at the machine, his hands at the controls. Not since his second year of medical school had he been instructed to watch through the teaching scope. He preferred to switch places with her each time, more opportunities for accidental contact.

"I marked it for you," she said.

Eli focused on a small blue smudge made by the tip of a marking pen. It isolated a colony of cells arranged in a rosette pattern.

"Do you see it?"

Eli diverted his eyes off the lens and across at Meg. The eyepiece blocked his view of her face, but Eli watched the tiny movements of her eyebrows and long dark lashes. There was a glance from large brown eyes, up quickly and then back to the eyepiece.

"Sure, I see it," Eli said, attempting to recover. "The big blue dot."

"And the cells beside it."

"Yes."

"I scraped them off the graft."

Eli knew it was common for native cells to migrate and stick on a prosthetic device. In fact, endotheliazation was a requisite process. Surgeons depended on it to keep the graft open.

"Endothelial cells?"

"Very good, Sherlock. But not just endothelial. There's a second population of cells. Bizarre shape. If I didn't know better, I'd say the cells look malignant."

Eli examined the cells more closely. Each nucleus appeared dark against a light cytoplasm speckled with densely packed granules. "They're turned on," he said.

Silence.

He looked at her, above the scope, and decided to wait her out.

Finally, she rephrased his description. "You mean mitotically active?"

Eli took a moment to choose his words. "If you wish, but I say they're packing a load and about to blow."

Meg shifted in the seat and crossed her legs, tightly, toes hooking her calf. "It's interesting you say that because some cells have already blown. Let me find them."

Back to the scope, Eli watched as high-powered fields blew past in a blur until his equilibrium was shot and he had to look away. A clock above a stainless steel sink showed 8:55. He had a cholecystectomy on a middle-aged schoolteacher at nine o'clock, the only operation remaining on his elective schedule since Fisher, his chairman, had cut off his private practice.

"Here," she said, somewhat louder, as if her words were held under pressure. "These cells lying just on the edge of the native aorta."

Eli located a group of cells in the center of the field. He tried to discern the difference in these cells before Meg told him.

"The granules are disrupted, gone," she said emphatically, in a higher pitch. "Do you see that?"

Eli tried to raise his level of enthusiasm to match that of Meg's. *Speaking of turned on.* But he didn't yet understand the significance.

"It's like these cells have shot their —" She stopped and cleared her throat, "The cells have unloaded their cargo, as though programmed to burst upon contact with the intimal layer of aorta."

Although Eli felt a new level of interest, he responded, "So?"

Meg Daily had obviously planned the sequence, this escalating series of molecular clues, taken the time to build the story, the characters choreographed a few microns apart on a world of glass. Now Eli felt it building to a climax.

"See these tiny holes in the aortic wall?" she asked.

Eli found the section of riddled aorta, moth-eaten as Meg had described it.

"There are more," she said, "not quite full thickness though, like something had eaten through or was eating through the aorta."

"Like a little alien," Eli said with a laugh.

"No, these are not the holes of mechanical failure."

No sense of humor. "I was only kidding."

"More like a chemical dissolution."

Eli thought about how serious she was, so completely into her work. The more technical terms she used — detailed morbid description — the more endearing she became. The moment was rudely interrupted by the high-pitched wail of his beeper.

The OR.

"Something doesn't make sense," Meg continued, listing her observations as she tried to fit the story. "The graft is intact. There was no migration. No thrombus that may have increased the intraluminal pressure. And the rupture occurred at both proximal and distal implantation sites."

Eli took over.

"So, the barbs on the graft poked holes, weakened the wall, and it ruptured. Makes sense to me. All these patients have diseased aortas. Looks like cheese a rat's chewed on."

"But the barbs didn't cause these holes. They were intact and in the proper position."

"What are you getting at?" Eli asked. He knew that if he delayed any longer, he would be late to the OR. Punctuality was tracked and recorded for each surgeon; Big Brother always watching.

Meg looked through the scope again as if for confirmation. "These cells, the funny-looking ones, are attached to the aorta just above and below where the graft was, and where the holes are, but not in any other location." She stopped and looked at Eli to make sure he was listening. "As though the cells were put there, implanted. I've never seen anything like it."

Eli thought her last statement was a little pretentious. *She couldn't be more than thirty-five. How many had she seen?*

"Dr. Daily," Eli said with great conviction to finish the discussion. "This was an old man with a bad problem. His time had come." As he said this, Eli was surprised at how quickly he could formulate such a cold, clinical solution.

"What do you know about this patient, really?"

As he thought of Gaston, Eli began to wonder just what he did know about the man. His beeper went off, the OR calling again.

"Is she on the table?" he asked after answering the call from a wall phone. "Be right there."

He hung up the phone and said, "There's quite a story behind the man, actually."

Meg's full attention turned to Eli. He secured the top button of his white coat and said, "I'd be glad to tell you about it sometime."

But Dr. Daily was peering through the scope again, absorbed in cells and holes and rat cheese.

Eli walked toward the door. Just before opening it, she stopped him.

"And Dr. Branch," she said, brown eyes cresting over the scope. "I prefer Meg."

CHAPTER EIGHT

"Dr. Daily, there's a phone call for you." Ms. Conch spoke through a barely cracked door in the autopsy suite.

She could see that the doctor was midway through the autopsy; a fifty-four-year-old man found dead in his apartment, the body decomposing over the past week, the smell eventually seeping under the door. She had removed the abdominal organs and was weighing the liver, a glistening brown slab swinging on the tray like an order filled by the butcher.

"Take a message, please."

Ms. Conch paused a moment to consider the life of this new female pathologist who had been at Gates Memorial only two months. She knew virtually nothing about her except that Dr. Daily was a single mother who rushed in after dropping her four-year-old diabetic daughter at day care each morning and rushed back home in the evening.

As the chief anatomic pathologist, Meg Daily was called routinely throughout the day, mostly by residents and medical students needing autopsy results. Although this phone call originated from outside the medical center, it was not the first call Ms. Conch had received from the day care. The tone of the caller's voice let Ms. Conch know it would not be pleasant.

"It's the day care lady. Says Margaret isn't feeling well, blood sugar's low."

Meg placed the liver in a plastic bucket and looked at Ms. Conch, who had her full attention. "Transfer it in here, please."

A moment later, with a gloved hand streaked in blood, Meg removed the receiver of the wall phone. Ms. Conch heard her say, "How low is it, Ms. Williams?"

Ms. Conch watched her reaction through the observation window. Dr. Daily closed her eyes and her body became rigid.

"Thirty-six! Well, give her some juice, please." The doctor's eyes shot wide open. "What's she doing right now?" She took a step forward. "Okay, Ms. Williams, you need to call an ambulance. Call nine-one-one, right now!"

Ms. Conch continued to listen as the doctor began to pace, flipping the phone cord like a whip.

"Yes, you have to. I'll meet her in the ER."

Meg slammed the receiver down and ripped off her gloves.

Ms. Conch cracked the door again. "What can I do?"

Dr. Daily looked at the body on the table, the abdomen and chest splayed open with individual organs waiting to be weighed and examined. "Bring me a large drape. I'll just have to cover him until I get back."

"How bad is it?"

With this question, the situation seemed to overcome Meg Daily. She closed her eyes and cried briefly into her mask.

Margaret's insulin regimen was just not working. Countless doctors. Countless admissions to the hospital. Something had to be done. They just couldn't go on like this. It was too dangerous. If it wasn't too late already.

"I'll do this," Ms. Conch said, unfolding a large blue plastic drape. "You go on."

"Hand me the end," the doctor said, composed.

Together, they pulled the drape to full length and let it descend on the corpse, a bed sheet floating down. The pathologist pulled off her mask and cap in one quick motion. She ripped her protective gown off without loosening the tie and ran out of the autopsy suite.

·   ·   ·

Using a pair of Adson forceps, Eli Branch closed the skin incision as intern Landers fired a straight line of metal staples with a handheld gun. After the last staple was placed, Eli examined the incision and gave a tug to a crooked one that lay crimped within the umbilicus.

"Sorry about that one," Landers said.

"Of all the work we did," Eli said as he wiped Betadine scrub off the skin with a wet laparotomy pad, "the incision is the only part the patient will see, right?"

"Right."

"If the incision isn't perfect, she'll wonder what we forgot inside."

After a sterile white bandage was placed and the anesthesiologist had begun extubation, Eli held out his hand, a ritual he did with the medical students and residents after completing each operation.

Landers took it in a single congratulatory shake of gloved hands.

"You did a good job today."

"Thanks," Landers said.

Eli nodded to the scrub nurse. "I must be living right to get you for two cases in a row.

Roberta blinked. "It was a pleasure."

After the edict passed down from Fisher, Eli knew he would be seeing much less of the operating room, at least during daylight hours. But there was no reason to inform the nurses of this yet — especially after such a smooth case. He stepped back and removed his gloves, and Landers took down the drapes.

"Heard anything from the tests?" With the whirlwind of events over the past thirty-six hours, Eli had almost forgotten about Landers's exposure to Gaston's blood. He could remember well the agony of waiting for the results after one of his own needle sticks.

"No," Landers said. "Should be back tomorrow."

A beeper went off in the back of the operating suite, a common occurrence for the interns and residents, who received a barrage of calls from the floor nurse for discharge orders or dosage clarifications. But this time, Eli recognized the specific tone as his beeper.

"Will you take her to recovery?" Eli asked Landers. "I'll talk to her family."

The intern applied a bandage to the wound. "Sure thing."

"Dr. Branch, is this your beeper?" the circulating nurse asked. She held the small black box in the air.

"I believe so. Could you answer it please?"

As Eli wrote a brief, two-line operative note in the patient's chart, the nurse handed the phone to him.

"Eli?"

He recognized the voice and immediately closed the chart. "Yes, Dr. Daily."

"They're bringing my daughter to the ER. She's a diabetic."

Eli thought of the little girl in the picture. And by the tone of her voice, he knew Meg was scared.

"She's unresponsive."

"I'll be right down," he said. "Meg?"

"Yeah?"

"They'll take care of her."

CHAPTER NINE

Kinder Day Care was less than two miles from the hospital. Dr. Meg Daily waited at the entrance to the ambulance bay and listened to the siren approaching from Jefferson Street. The ambulance backed in and Meg stood within inches of the back door, peering through the windows to see a disheveled man strapped to the gurney. The man's arms were folded across his chest and he mumbled incoherently. He appeared very comfortable for someone in an emergency.

As the paramedics unloaded the gurney, the man raised his head and said, "Hey, you my doctor?"

Meg stepped back in disbelief. Her daughter was still out there without her mother. *I should have driven,* Meg thought, dazed with guilt. *I could have been there by now.*

As the man wheeled by, he turned his head toward Meg. His eyes were unfocused in an intoxicated glaze.

"I want her to be my doctor," he said, reeking of alcohol. "Yeah, baby, you're my doc. Come over here, honey."

Acknowledging her medical attire, the paramedics stopped when they saw her approach the gurney. She stood next to the man, her composure dissolving and her right hand shaking uncontrollably. He tried to speak again.

"Hey baby, you wanna —"

But his words stopped abruptly.

Before she realized it, and to the amazement of the paramedics, Meg Daily, M.D., slapped the man's face so hard that the gurney shook from side to side.

Eli bounded down two flights of stairs from the surgical suite to the first-floor emergency room. He punched the five-digit code into the box and the doors opened to madness. Two police officers sat on metal folding chairs in the hallway beside an open door. Eli was greeted by a familiar sound in the ER, the clang of handcuffs against a gurney.

A quick scan of the patient board informed him that she was already there — Margaret Daily, Bay 4E. At least she's on the opposite hall, Eli thought, where it's quieter, away from the criminally insane.

He parted the curtain to find a flurry of white coats over the four-year-old girl. Meg stood to one side, arms folded, hands clenched, trying not to jump into the fray.

Margaret's body lay still. A nurse was attached to each of her arms, trying desperately to get an IV started. A resident poured Betadine across her left shin in preparation for an interosseous line.

Eli walked behind Meg and placed his hands on the slope of her shoulders. He tightened his grasp when he felt her give way, welcoming the support. She reached back and cupped her hand over his. Eli felt short, blunt nails indent his skin.

"I've got a twenty-gauge right antecubital," a nurse called out in triumph.

"Good," said Dr. James Felding, the pediatric ER attending. "Start D-ten infusing at fifty cc an hour."

Dr. Felding approached Meg. "She should respond to this, but we don't know how long she's been down."

"They said she was jerking her head back and forth at day care." Meg spoke in short gasps, forcing back tears.

Felding nodded in confirmation. "Her blood glucose was undetectable when she arrived. I'm sure she had a seizure."

As he said this, the little girl moved for the first time, turning her head to the side to vomit.

Meg rushed to her daughter and wiped the stream of yellow fluid from her mouth. She pushed fine dark curls away from Margaret's pale face.

Dr. Felding addressed the team of doctors. "Let's get her to the ICU for monitoring. To Meg, "She'll make it through. This time."

CHAPTER TEN

Harvey Stone sat at a picnic table waiting for his associate. He felt the weather-beaten wood on his fingers, deep ridges cut by a thawing freeze that lifted flat splinters, poised to pierce. He tested the point of one against his finger, pressing harder and thinking of the implications of the deaths.

Two in less than twenty-four hours. Coincidence? Sure. Had to be.

Then the wood punctured the center of his fingerprint and drew blood.

The meeting was arranged for one o'clock in the afternoon, but not in a smoke-filled chamber lined with oak paneling and a long table from which to sip dark roast coffee. This meeting would take place in the middle of two acres of preserved greenery in a concrete world, research hospitals on one side and a parking lot on the other. The boardroom would have implied the necessary involvement of other company members, employees who didn't have the "need to know" at this point. And the subject of this meeting could be classified as premature knowledge that, among the uninitiated, would at first alarm, then spread like fire in an oxygen-saturated tent.

It was ten minutes to one and Stone was early. He was always early, one of his trademark virtues. First to arrive each morning at company headquarters, at his desk, always, by six A.M. Harvey Stone, the CEO of

GlobeVac International for over two decades, had reached a point in his career when he could take chances. Big chances.

GlobeVac had its standard line of drugs ranging from antireflux to chemotherapy, which boosted the bottom line quarter after productive quarter. But it was the company's vaccine development that had garnered worldwide attention. From campaigns to vaccinate Third-World children to the production of a consistent supply of flu vaccine for U.S. citizens, it was this aspect of his company of which Harvey Stone was most proud.

He had weathered the storms of acquisitions, lawsuits, and last year's merger with the state-of-the-art biomedical device firm, Regent Biotech, to form Regency Biotech International. A sexy new name and global appeal. And with this merger, one of the largest in biopharmaceutical history, RBI's stock soared to an unprecedented level. While the credibility and worldwide acclaim came from the company's history of vaccine production for Third-World care, the profit margin was largely based on a single device, the AortaFix graft, predicted to revolutionize the treatment of aortic aneurysms.

In the early years, Stone's company had conducted experiments on an endovascular device, the forerunner of what would ultimately become the AortaFix developed by their sister company, Regent Biotech. The eventual merger benefited both companies. Regent Biotech needed the marketing support of well-known GlobeVac International and Stone's company needed a financially lucrative product. The device was a windfall for the company, placing RBI in the upper echelon of biotech power. Now, Stone was ready to take his company to an even higher level.

Embryonic stem cell therapy was the next biomedical frontier. These earliest cells, taken from a several-day-old human embryo, had the potential to grow into any type of human cell. Careful manipulation in RBI's research facility could transform these immature cells into functional adult cells that could be ultimately transplanted to cure human disease.

Stem cell therapy using adult cells from the bone marrow had been used for years to treat hematologic malignancy such as leukemia. While there was no moral controversy surrounding the use of adult stem cells in medicine, these cells did not hold the same curative potential as embryonic cells that could be "told" what kind of cell to become. But adult stem cell therapy did not require the destruction of human embryos. Undaunted by this obstacle, Stone had vowed, at a recent shareholder's meeting, that RBI would be the first to conquer what many believed to be the future of medicine.

Many of RBI's top competitors had ratcheted down their embryonic cell research and were focused instead on engineering adult skin cells to mimic the embryonic stem cell. While this approach garnered federal funding and tempered the moral debate over the destruction of human embryos, the research with adult stem cells had proceeded slowly, with mixed results. Some early genetic manipulation experiments had produced embryonic-like cells from adult cells. But a proportion of these induced stem cells lacked important internal regulatory signals, the cells ultimately dividing out of control, like a cancer.

Stone had grown impatient waiting for this embryo-preserving approach to result in curative therapy. While both pharmaceutical companies and academic centers withdrew resources from human embryo research, Stone diverted every possible dollar into RBI's embryonic stem cell program. He told the investors that when RBI claimed the medical revolution of embryonic stem cell therapy, no bio-pharma-tech company would come close to their stratosphere. The plans were in motion. If he could just keep the right-to-lifers off his company's back long enough to collect a freezer full of human embryos.

His thoughts plunged back to the two deaths. Harvey Stone had never doubted his decision to merge with Regent Biotech.

Not until now.

Through a stand of oaks, he could see the Confederate Civil War general atop his horse looking south across Union Avenue, a manicured marble beard and mane of hair falling heavily around his ears. Stone considered the irony of Union Avenue forming a barrier to Nathan Bedford Forrest's reign. But his attention was diverted away from history to the figure of a man ambling toward him, a burlap sack slung over his right shoulder.

"Spare some change mister?"

Alarmed at the suddenness of the man's appearance, Harvey searched his empty pockets and removed a five dollar bill from his wallet. This appeased the man, and he stumbled away toward a racing green Jaguar that pulled to the curb at Manassas Street.

Alexander Zaboyan, RBI's first vice president, exited the vehicle carrying a black briefcase that matched a full-length overcoat. He certainly looks the part, Harvey thought, admiring the northeastern wear that Zaboyan had brought with him a few months before from New York, Regent's home for the past seven years. Even though Harvey wore a short-sleeved golf shirt and sat in the shade of tall oaks, he was sweating in the humid park, where nothing stirred except a couple of squirrels in a garbage can. He looked again at the figure in black approaching. Black coat, black pants, Memphis summers. *He'll learn.*

As he walked, Zaboyan stroked the sides of a finely trimmed goatee. Stone had observed this gesture, this stroking, petting motion of his, any time that a power move was at hand — which included whenever Alex Zaboyan had a lot to lose. He sat down on the bench across from Stone and flipped back the wings of his coat like a gunslinger.

"Quite an auspicious setting for a conference."

"Just wanted you and me on this one," Stone replied.

Zaboyan looked at the empty bench beside him. "You got me," his hand stroking his face. "What's the agenda?"

"Two items." Harvey Stone slid a plain manila folder along the corrugated wood between them, removed a sheet of paper, and handed it to Zaboyan.

"First is a Mr. Bernard Lankford; some of us knew him as Bernie."

Zaboyan examined the paper, which displayed a picture of Lankford with a description of his biomedical device below.

"Yes, tragic. It was all over the TV. Overseas wasn't it?"

"St. Martin."

"Ah, yes." Another stroke of his beard.

"Uncanny that he died just a few months after having his aneurysm repaired with one of our own grafts."

Zaboyan did not respond to this.

"For the past five years," Stone continued, "Bernie has been developing our Stem Cell Division. We had investors pouring in money from all over the world. We were right on the cusp of the first stem cell transplant." The CEO leaned forward as he made his conclusion. "Now, we're dead in the water."

Zaboyan exhaled and leaned away from Stone. "I didn't know him that well, but they say Lankford was a superb scientist. A very likable man."

Stone ignored Zaboyan's accolades as if they were unworthy. "The second is a fellow named Gaston. . ." Harvey hesitated until the sheet of paper was in the hands of Zaboyan. "This one didn't make the nightly news. Just an old man."

Zaboyan cleared his throat and pinch-rolled his chin hair as he looked at the information before him. The spec sheet listed Gates Memorial as the institution that had placed the aortic device in 1975. It was the first model and was placed in Gaston even before the experiments in animal models using pigs were completed. Besides Stone and Zaboyan, only a handful of people knew about Gaston. Most of those-in-the-know were dead.

"Harvey, you know as well as I that device failure can occur. It's on every device label — in plain English."

When the device was first approved by the FDA for the treatment of abdominal aortic aneurysms at risk for rupture, vascular surgeons were skeptical. Could threading the device through the vasculature and allowing it to expand inside the aorta replace the traditional method of sewing in a synthetic graft through a large abdominal incision? But when patients on the trials showed fewer complications and were able to leave the hospital after a day or two, use of the device became common, and patients began to request the less invasive method. Since the approval, thousands of aortic aneurysm patients had been walking around with confidence that they were safe from the catastrophic event of aortic rupture. For the CEO of RBI and its vice president of device production, maintaining that confidence was paramount.

Zaboyan continued to make his case. "And besides, who says it's the device? These patients all have a plethora of diseases that could kill them — diabetes, coronary artery disease, or a recurrent aneurysm. I'm confused, Harvey. What's the big deal?"

Harvey Stone handed a third sheet to Zaboyan. "I misspoke. There are three items on the agenda."

Zaboyan read the handwritten, paragraph-long memo from the company's chief legal counsel. "This surgeon —" Zaboyan stopped to find the name again. "— Branch. He is asking questions." Again at the memo, goatee twisted in a tight twirl. "Based on one case? This old man, Gaston? What the hell, Harvey?"

"I'm not sure he knows all the questions to ask — yet." Stone cleared his throat for emphasis. "You see, Branch knew Gaston. He worked in his father's anatomy lab on campus for three decades." Stone looked behind him at the medical school, and for emphasis he pointed in the direction of Anatomy Hall. "Then, as surgeons are apt to do, Branch operated on the old man. Pulled out the AortaFix when his aorta ruptured around the device."

"But I thought this first patient, Gaston, didn't have an aneurysm," Zaboyan said. "I was told that the device was placed after he volunteered for the experiment.

"This was well before your time, Alex." Stone cleared his throat. "I wouldn't say he volunteered. He agreed to the device to prevent being reported to the police."

"The police? For what?"

"Improper contact with a client."

Zaboyan considered this for a moment. The man was basically an undertaker for cadavers at the medical school. "Improper what?"

Stone glanced at a squirrel a few yards away. "Let's just say his sexual persuasion drifted toward the nonliving."

Zaboyan raised his eyebrows. "So he was blackmailed?"

"Let's don't go there," Stone said quickly.

"In any event, device failure is a known complication," Zaboyan said, repeating himself.

"I understand that, Alex." Stone leaned forward abruptly. "But there's another reason we don't need this Eli Branch to be snooping around. Do you remember hearing about a child, in the early years of

RBI, who had a graft placed in him as the final human subject before FDA approval?"

Zaboyan leaned away from his CEO, uncomfortable with the closeness. "Don't tell me we tested the graft on kids?"

Stone acknowledged this with a single nod. "The graft recipient was a retarded boy."

"That's bullshit, Harvey. No way someone approved the graft for pediatric placement."

Harvey Stone remained calm. "Who said anything about approval? Anyway, it happened." He took the memo and held it up facing Zaboyan.

"What does this have to do with Branch?"

"You won't believe it. The retarded kid was Branch's brother."

"You're right," Zaboyan said. "I don't believe it."

Stone stared at him. "I don't care if you believe it or not, we had better retrieve the graft from this doctor's brother before he links it back to us. If someone finds out the graft was illegally placed in a human subject, not to mention a child, our whole company will be destroyed."

That statement got Zaboyan's attention. "You say 'retrieve it' like that's easy. We're talking about another operation, a big one."

Stone confirmed his understanding with a nod.

"Whatever it takes."

CHAPTER ELEVEN

The office Eli had been given adjoined his laboratory space in the old North Research Building. It was a square room just big enough for a desk pushed against one wall and a bookcase opposite it. No window. The bookcase held surgical texts that Eli had accumulated through his years of training: *Sabiston's Textbook of Surgery*, and *Schwartz*, revered names in the field and known around the world.

He propped his feet on the desk and looked in the bookcase across from him. He had kept textbooks from medical school, such as Stryer's *Biochemistry* and a less-than-current text on genetics. His favorite book was one his father had given him upon graduation from medical school —a rare, antiquated text of classical anatomical illustrations by the master, Vesalius.

The desk was pressed wood with hard-to-open metal drawers. Two framed pictures adorned the wall above an outdated computer. The first picture showed Eli standing in a row with six other Vanderbilt chief surgical residents, all wearing long white coats, together with their devoted mentor and friend, Dr. Tarpley Hopkins. Next to this photograph hung a three-by-two-foot aerial photograph, taken at night, of Vaught-Hemingway Stadium, with sixty thousand red and blue fans screaming for their beloved team. The photograph captured the Ole Miss Rebels taking a goal-line defensive stand against the driving Georgia Bulldogs. Staring at this picture always gave Eli a deep twinge of homesickness.

And now, the fist-in-the-turf stance of the linemen seemed to hold personal significance.

All his diplomas remained unframed in manila folders at his house. He had estimated the cost to have all of them framed, his bachelor's degree from Ole Miss, medical degree, Founder's Medal for service to student government, even the Coffey Award that was given to the graduating medical student who published the highest quality research paper. Given his meager salary as a surgical resident and monthly payments to his brother's facility, the cost of framing them all was an unnecessary luxury.

For a surgeon-scientist, there were distinct advantages in having one's office so close to an active research laboratory. The proximity allowed ongoing contact with the research personnel, who usually included technicians, medical students, and perhaps a surgical resident, if one was fortunate enough to be assigned one. Since his office was separate from the academic offices of his partners in the Department of Surgery, he was not subject to interruptions or drop-by visits and complaints from his fellow surgeons about salaries too low, malpractice insurance too high, and an administration that took them for granted.

Eli had envisioned being able to sit in his office and read the latest scientific journals while looking across bench tops layered with beakers and flasks, a new PCR machine, a dissecting microscope — all of this, while his minions labored to uncover the next big discovery in molecular oncology research.

In theory, and as elucidated in his contract, the vision seemed possible. But that was months ago. Now, Eli sat at his desk and looked through the office door at two parallel, waist-high benches of solid black Formica that stretched the length of his lab. The countertops held a fine layer of dust and little else except for a rack of test tubes and two glass beakers left by the previous lab occupant, a Dr. Pinkston, whose grant was rejected after being funded for over a decade. That forced Pinkston to leave the university. In the corner of the laboratory sat an open cardboard box. A tangled wad of plastic tubing wrapped around a metal rod flowed out the top of the box. *I had better equipment in my sixth-grade science class.*

In the back of the lab, a separate door led to the walk-in closet-sized incubator room. The only valuable resource that Eli possessed were cells he had engineered to express high levels of a naturally occurring, tissue-dissolving enzyme that enhanced the ability of cancer cells to invade. He had worked for two years at Vanderbilt to successfully insert the matrix metalloproteinase or MMP gene, isolate the colony of cells, expand the population, and characterize the enzymatic production using state-of-the-art molecular techniques. Before Eli left Nashville, he was told that after many previous attempts by his mentor's laboratory staff, Eli had been the first to be successful in establishing the cell line.

The cells were engineered to churn out matrix metalloproteinase, a family of enzymes that degraded the extracellular tissue, a foundation of sorts that normally kept cells in their proper orientation and position. Early on, Eli recognized the importance of this enzyme. When human cells go awry and become cancerous, they secrete MMPs to dissolve this matrix, an important step in the progression of cancer that allows cells to migrate, invade, and become metastatic. The cells that Eli constructed were crucial to cancer research and to understanding this enzymatic process so that anticancer therapeutics could be developed.

Since his return to the University of the Mid-South Medical Center, Eli had checked the incubator each day to ensure that the temperature was maintained at precisely thirty-seven degrees Celsius and that the chamber was clean without signs of bacterial infection or fungus that could kill the cells. He'd have to check that his lab was connected to the hospital's backup generator that would power the incubator in case of an outage. These cells were Eli's only hope for establishing a successful laboratory, publishing papers, and advancing in the academic world. He would do anything to make sure they were safe.

On a scrap piece of paper, Eli listed the items he would need to begin his research: a Western Blot apparatus to measure protein levels, a PCR machine to amplify DNA, a centrifuge, a freezer to stock antibodies. The list was long. But at the top he wrote what he needed most: an experienced and qualified technician.

Though his laboratory was lacking all these needs, at least he had the space — three hundred square feet. Not bad for a start-up. And as part of his recruitment package, he had inherited Vera Tuck, the lab technician who worked for Dr. Pinkston during his twelve years at the university. Eli knew that good technicians were an invaluable asset to a successful laboratory. From ordering supplies to running experiments and maintaining the laboratory notebook, a research effort would come to a screeching halt without the work of a good tech. And when one was available, especially a technician with a decade's worth of experience, they were usually hired within a few days by a basic scientist from one of the many labs on campus.

Eli pulled open the top drawer of his desk and removed the employment contract. He read it, again, and wondered why Ms. Vera Tuck had not been employed during the six months since the lab was vacated by the unfunded Dr. Pinkston.

We're holding a lab tech for you, Dr. Fisher had emphasized during Eli's recruitment. *She's got over ten years' experience.*

Eli had been to his lab every day for the past week, but he was yet to see this Ms. Tuck with so much experience, who was being held from all the other labs on campus, just for him.

He reached across to the bookcase. The latest issue of the campus phone directory had just been distributed. He flipped to the T's and found Tuck, Vera, research lab assistant. The address matched that of Dr. Pinkston's lab and was obviously wrong. But at least Vera Tuck existed. He turned back to the front of the directory, curious about his own existence. He found three employees with the last name of Branch but Eli Branch was not listed — anywhere.

Great. I've moved back home and am virtually unknown.

He flipped to the D's, then the Da's, to the spot where Dr. Daily's name would be listed. She wasn't there either. He thought about her daughter in the ICU and made a mental note to go by and see her.

He tossed the directory onto his desk and pushed the chair into a reclining position. He had been out of residency for only two weeks, after eight years of not sleeping every third night of call, and with just three hours of sleep since Gaston's emergent operation, already he was fatigued. His head met the back cushion and he closed his eyes.

Moments later he heard the rattle of a cart pushed over uneven tile in the outside hallway. One of the wheels screeched with each revolution. Eli sat up and stretched his facial muscles to appear awake. The screech grew closer, the cart banged against the door of his lab.

He remained still, hoping that whoever it was would continue to another lab down the hall. But the struggle at the door continued, metal ramming into wood.

"Damn Jew Baptist Obesities," a woman's voice blurted out, accompanied by more cymbal-like crashes.

Eli eased from his chair and peeked into the lab. The shopping cart was wedged in the door frame, a petite woman of forty, maybe fifty years, at the helm. She wore a dress covered in bright yellow daisies, so long that it dragged on the floor. Strands of peroxided blonde hair, in desperate need of shampoo, hung over her eyes.

"Sanctification of Mary. The bastards." She repeated "bastards" over and over as she jerked the cart and banged the wheels against the floor.

Eli backed up a step into the safety of his office.

It couldn't be. Please. No.

She was silent now, the cart still.

"Dr. Branch?"

Eli said nothing.

"Dr. Braaa-anch, is that you?"

Eli froze. *How could she know?*

"Need a little help out here." Then, under her breath. "Jew Baps. Jew Baps. Jew Baps," and she banged the cart some more.

Eli emerged with a surprised expression as though just noticing her presence. "I'm sorry," he said, "let me help you."

She was even shorter than Eli first realized, a diminutive presence for such an outburst of racial and religious curses. The bright colors of her dress contrasted sharply with moldy gray skin and dark neck hair that crept toward her ears like a web. When she spoke, her head twitched and pulled to the left.

"My equipment transporter is wedged in the door, Dr. Branch."

Equipment transporter?

Eli looked at the shopping cart. The name of its owner, Piggly

Wiggly, was stamped in plastic on the side. The cart was filled with standard equipment needed for any molecular research lab. Glassware, an electrophoresis unit, Western Blot, a state-of-the-art PCR machine, even a small centrifuge that made the bottom rungs of the cart sag.

"Just lift up on the front, Dr. Branch."

Eli wished she would stop using his name so frequently, as if they had known each other for years.

She lifted the cart by the handle and Eli saw rope-like veins protrude from her neck. Together, they maneuvered the cart across the threshold and into his lab.

"Where did you get all this stuff?" Eli asked, as though talking to a college roommate moving into the dorm.

"Them Jew Baptists down the hall." She said this with a proud smile and an extra tic for emphasis.

"Excuse me?"

"Dr. Branch, they don't need them, got more supplies than ever they'll use. Now *you*," she said, emphasizing her reference to him with a crooked finger, "*you* ain't got no cash." This last phrase was enunciated with streetwise slang and a cocky tilt of her head.

"How do you know who I am?"

"You my new boss man. Dr. Elizer Montgomery Branch, says right here on my contract." She reached into her flat bosom and pulled a folded sheet of paper from her dress. He realized she was not wearing a bra.

"Okay, okay," he said, in hopes of avoiding any further exposure. "And you must be Vera."

"In the flesh." She curtsied like a schoolgirl and flipped her skirt, revealing knobby, purple-mottled knees.

Eli ducked his head to hide a silent laugh, charmed by this daisy-dressed woman with her bag-lady shopping cart.

"Now help me with this equipment, will you?"

Eli looked at the jam-packed "equipment transporter" before him. In the past twelve hours, he had contributed to the death of an old friend, discovered on an X-ray that his brother harbored a defective, life-threatening medical device; and been demoted to a position of rat doctor by his chairman. Now he was being asked to stock his lab with what appeared to be stolen equipment—a felony. Meeting a feisty pathologist named Meg Daily stood out as the absolute highlight of his day.

Eli looked at Vera, her knuckles clenched white on the cart's handle. She wasn't going to budge, and Eli was nearly out of fight.

"Sure," he said, with a wink at Vera. He grabbed the PCR machine. "Let's get this place looking like a lab."

CHAPTER TWELVE

Eli stood at the end of two long bench tops and admired his newly stocked laboratory. What impressed him most was not the amount of equipment, but rather how quickly and expertly Vera had assembled it all. He watched her tapping numbers into the PCR machine, calibrating it to run successive cycles while amplifying a sample of DNA. As she did this, she repeated a new phrase, over and over, one that Eli was not familiar with.

"Rich Bitch Ink."

"Rich Bitch Ink."

She turned the words into three-syllable soup and rocked her head back and forth as she sang it. He could not stop watching her, a perplexing combination of mental illness and scientific savvy.

Vera keyed in the final sequence of numbers and turned to face him. She lightly tapped her fingernails over the top of the centrifuge and twirled around with the hem of her dress in her hand. Like a game show hostess, she danced along the row of stolen equipment, her free hand poised to display each item. As abruptly as she began, she locked a pose and stated, "Dr. Branch, you're ready for the Nobel Prize trophy."

At first reluctant to entrust Vera with access to his lab's only commodity, Eli unlocked the door to the incubator room and escorted her inside. Eli showed Vera the cells and told her, in exact detail, how to culture them — what media to use, how to trypsinize the cells gently, which antibiotics would prevent infection. Eli examined the cells under the microscope, then had Vera take the seat and carefully move the plate to examine both single cells and those growing in colonies.

"These cells," Vera said, looking up from the view piece, "very special."

"Yes." Eli was surprised and pleased to find that Vera was not only proving competent, but also falling immediately into the proper hierarchy between a principal investigator and technician.

Carefully, she examined the details of cellular architecture, how the cells attached to plastic, which looked healthy, and which seemed near death. Eli took the moment to study her. At first she appeared disheveled, hair matted, sundress barely covering her chest, its hem dragging on the floor. Nothing could be more inappropriate laboratory wear. Yet she carried a certain sophistication that somehow peeked through her appearance and vocal outbursts. *How had she maintained the same job for so long?*

Was she medicated?

Probably not. Probably couldn't afford it, since she had been unemployed for the past six months. Or had the department maintained her health benefits during that time? Just for him?

Eli realized that, as of now, her health insurance was his responsibility.

Vera remained intent on observing the cells, her posture awkward as she bent toward the scope. Eli leaned closer to see her face. Her eyes were fixated and glazed, and she had tongued a clump of hair into her mouth, chewing vigorously.

He stepped back and closed his eyes. *What am I getting into?*

A moment later, Eli heard the hallway door open into the lab and a deep voice call, "Hello?"

Oh great. Here it comes. An investigator from the nearby lab. The lab we've been stealing from.

Vera held her head cocked to one side like a dog pestered by a high-pitched whistle.

"Quick," she said. "Hide."

Eli held up his hands in disbelief and pretended to look for a place in the closet-sized room. "Hide?"

"Hello, is this the Branch lab?" The voice was coming closer.

Glass pipettes, the size of drumsticks, were stacked in a rack inside the cell culture hood. Vera had armed herself with one in each hand and acquired a ninja-like pose.

"Deny it like hell, Dr. B. We ain't going down."

Eli wanted to wring her neck.

"Put those down and stay behind me."

They stepped into the main lab, Vera crouched behind Eli like a schoolgirl. He saw that the pipettes were still clutched in her fists.

Eli tried to prepare an alibi. *Should I deny any knowledge of the stolen equipment or just blame the whole thing on this nutcase from the start?* He suffered from great inexperience when lying about stolen property.

The best dressed scientist Eli had ever seen extended his hand with an expensive click of gold cuff links. "Hello, I'm Harvey Stone." His black suit looked tailor-made.

Eli gripped his hand firmly. "Dr. Stone." Eli decided on a wait-and-see approach.

But Vera stepped from behind Eli and wedged herself between the two men facing Harvey Stone.

"I'm the alfalfa and the omega," she said in a ninja-death pose, pipettes pointed at his eyes.

Stone glanced at Eli, bewildered.

How easy it would be to blame a lab full of stolen equipment on this crazy loon.

Stone stepped back to a more comfortable distance, but Vera met his move with a forward lunge.

"Methodist Eskimo bitches did it."

Stone pointed to the hall and said to Eli, "I think I'll come back at another time." He reached over Vera's head to display a business card between two fingers.

Vera watched his arm move above her, a snarling dog ready to bite.

Eli took the card, and Stone exited to the hallway.

Vera looked around at Eli with a victorious grin. "Baptist Jew Whore Daddy. Think?"

"Don't say anything," Eli said, and he quickly read the card. "Please. Just shut up."

HARVEY STONE
CEO
REGENCY BIOTECH INTERNATIONAL
ONE RBI DRIVE
SAND DOLLAR REEF
731-325-2104

This guy isn't a scientist from down the hall. He's CEO of one of the leading biotech companies in the world. He came to find me?

"Get your smelly rags out of here," Vera yelled, loud enough to travel down the hall.

Eli stared at Vera. She was quickly losing her charm, if she ever had any. "Hush, will you? Hush."

Eli sprinted into the hallway, Vera yelling behind him, "Rich Bitch Ink, Rich Bitch Ink."

Harvey Stone was waiting for the elevator at the end of the hall, arms folded across his chest.

"Mr. Stone," Eli called to him. "Wait just a minute."

The elevator arrived and Stone disappeared into it. Eli stuck his hand in the crack of the doors as they were closing.

Harvey Stone had his back flat against the wall.

"I'm very sorry, sir."

"I thought surgeons always protected their paws," Stone said, holding his hands as though scrubbed for surgery.

"I usually stop elevators with my head," Eli said, "but right now it's up my ass."

Slowly, the stern expression on Stone's face melted into a gentle smile. "I want you to come see me," he said and pointed to the card in Eli's hand that was braced against a nervous door. "Call that number and a limo will pick you up."

The elevator beeped in revolt and Eli released the doors to Stone's final words.

"We need to talk."

CHAPTER THIRTEEN

Alexander Zaboyan pushed back from the edge of his desk and reclined deeply in a black leather chair. He tapped a pen against the armrest, methodically sliding down the shaft with each tap before flipping it to the other end. The vice president of RBI had been sitting like this for almost an hour, replaying his conversation with Harvey Stone.

These events were just confirmation of what he had expected all along. After building one of the most successful biomedical device companies in the world, he felt now that he'd been suckered into this merger. For the first few months, the merger seemed successful, causing wide exposure in the press, a prominent cover article in *Forbes*, and resulting in a sharp rise in the price of the company's stock. All it would take was one crafty reporter to link the deaths to RBI for everything to go to hell.

During visits from New York before his company's relocation, Zaboyan had been shown only the best of Memphis. Except for passing through the Atlanta airport on his way to other destinations, he never had a reason to visit the South. Before the merger, he couldn't imagine a reason that might take him there.

Bunch of rednecks in pickup trucks shooting helpless ducks and anything else that moved.

But it was becoming clear to him now. He had been carted around in an air-conditioned limousine down select streets to penthouse receptions with views too high to expose the decay. And the RBI compound itself was a like a city, with a restaurant, salon, even a post office. Every convenience needed that would prevent the 237 employees from having to leave the premises except for their trip home at the end of the day.

He rotated his chair to a floor-to-ceiling window with a panoramic view of the Mississippi River and looked upstream at a rusty barge loaded with pyramids of barrels.

Moonshine, most likely.

He smiled at the thought.

The AortaFix is my baby. Stone doesn't care about it. He just wants the profit to fuel his stem cell therapy. And he'll drop the device in a second if the media picks up a problem.

The majestic river view spiraled when he looked down, just beyond the six-foot barrier wall that surrounded the RBI complex. Kudzu and poison oak entangled every scrubby willow in a thick web.

Two deaths is nothing. I'll sweep them both under the rug.

Zaboyan pictured the skyline view from his beloved office in New York, a billion lights above the East River. He shook his head.

I have moved to hell.

CHAPTER FOURTEEN

"It was the Episcopalians, you know."

"What?" Eli asked. He was trying to get his mind around Harvey Stone's surprise visit.

Vera smoothed the front of her dress with both hands and stopped at her pubic bone. She patted it twice.

"They kidnapped me in the basement and tortured me with holy water."

Eli told Vera to take the rest of the day off. The last thing he needed was one of her ludicrous stories.

She banged her empty cart through the door and kept talking ninety miles an hour using explicit terms about the Episcopalians who had kidnapped her in the church basement and tortured her with holy water, a drip-drip-drip on her private parts. Eli sent her down the hall and locked both the lab door and his office.

He pinned Stone's business card to the corkboard above his desk. It was the only thing on the board and he sat staring at it.

A limo will pick me up? Yeah, right. I'm barely hanging on to my job here and they're going to escort me for a chat?

He focused on the address. RBI Drive.

RBI?

Where had he heard those initials recently? Eli tried to bring his thoughts into focus through a sleep-deprived haze.

Runs Batted In?

No. Too obvious.

Then it came to him.

Kanter.

It was Kanter, the anesthesiologist, who called out "RBI" during Gaston's operation. RBI was the manufacturer of Gaston's device. A failed device was one thing. It happened rarely. Failure of even the best-made device was possible. But a fatal device was a disaster.

He knew that a major biotech firm had relocated to Memphis recently. His father had kept him in touch, during his years in Nashville, with the Memphis health care and business scene, sending clippings from the city's newspaper, *The Commercial Appeal.* He knew that the move had been ensnarled in controversy when the company decided to build on an obscure island in the middle of the river. He glanced again at the card.

Sand Dollar Reef

The computer on his desk was a mid-nineties model. The screen saver was the logo for the Memphis River Kings with a shot of a player slamming the puck. Eli looked closely at the jersey, a majestic crown-topped M, gold outlined in black. He remembered this version from the hockey team's '95 season.

Eli selected the early version of Netscape and typed in Regency Biotech International. After a full minute, the first ten hits appeared, including the company's home page. But another site grabbed his attention first. It was a headline from *The Commercial Appeal.*

RBI STUNS CITY OFFICIALS:
To Build Multimillion Dollar Complex on Sand Dollar Reef

He scanned the story. When GlobeVac International and Regent Biotech announced the merger and plans to relocate to the Mid-South from Washington, D.C., and New York City, officials in Memphis all but donated large tracts of land to house the biotech giant, a move that would propel a city once established on bolls of cotton into a frontrunner of biotech power. CEO Harvey Stone announced that he would move his company to Memphis and the business community assumed that other pharmaceutical-based companies would follow. They envisioned a booming industry that would make the city competitive with other giants such as Research Triangle Park in North Carolina.

But after RBI executives visited the city's prime real estate sites, the whole Mid-South and anyone who followed the biotech industry were shocked to learn that the new complex would rise on a no-man's-island between the lines of Arkansas and Tennessee, unclaimed by either state.

Then the company denied the city administration's plan to advertise RBI's choice of Memphis over other sites such as Seattle, Philadelphia, and Phoenix. The mayor was stunned when the advertising campaign, one that would have boosted the River City's commerce and invigorated tourism along Beale Street, fell through with a bang. The final blow occurred when the privately funded bridge to the island was built not from the Tennessee shoreline but from a peninsula of land protruding from Arkansas, so that employees would choose to live in West Memphis, Arkansas, effectively shutting the company off from downtown Memphis.

Eli closed the Web site and clicked on the company's home page. While the outmoded computer searched, he glanced at the clock. He could hear no one in the hallway or the building. With the relaxed schedule of summer, most of the personnel in the neighboring labs would have left by now.

The Web page displayed the letters RBI in bold silver, each rotating in a random, chaotic manner before realigning to form the trademark. After a couple of seconds, the letters began their dizzying rotation again. Eli clicked on the screen with no effect until the letters realigned once more. Eventually, a double click took him to the next page, which displayed three options:

- *Vaccine Development*
- *Biomedical Devices*
- *Stem Cell Technology*

He knew RBI was a leader in vaccines, and that the recent merger had incorporated an established medical device company. But it was the third item that attracted his attention. As a scientist, Eli understood the rationale of embryonic stem cell therapy. A no-brainer, as they say. With a bit of finesse, and the addition of human growth factors, these earliest embryonic cells could be coaxed to differentiate into a specific tissue.

Insulin producing cells for the diabetic.

Dopamine secreting cells to control the ravages of Parkinson's disease.

Spinal nerve cells for the paralyzed.

How could a country with the most advanced health care in the world not take full advantage of this resource?

Eli knew, however, that embryonic stem cell therapy was much more complicated than had been portrayed to the general public. What could be accomplished in a test tube was often vastly different than actual therapy in a human patient. The promise of gene therapy, followed by the disappointing results, had shown how the hype of medical breakthrough is much different than reality of cure. It would take years, a generation at best, for embryonic stem cell therapy to come to fruition, if it worked at all.

Eli thought of his mother, dead from cancer. His grandfather, devastated by Parkinson's before he died. And Henry, his own brother, a mental invalid from his neurologic condition. Who wouldn't want to eliminate these dreaded diseases?

But an issue that at first seemed so clear in Eli's mind quickly turned gray.

Is the sacrifice of human embryos the answer to the shortcomings of doctors and the medical profession? Allowing one potential life to save another? But then Eli remembered. These human embryos will be discarded anyway, the unintended surplus of our well-intended technology for infertile couples. What could be the harm? Unused, prediscarded embryos could furnish the much needed embryonic cells for research that could advance the field of embryonic stem cells into therapeutic reality.

But how many embryos would ultimately be needed for this miraculous healing? An experiment in a culture dish was one thing, the escalating demand and sheer magnitude of cells needed for human therapeutics was entirely different.

There was always one point on this issue that Eli could not get his head around. That point was Henry, his brother. Would defective embryos be specifically chosen for this purpose, the bad cells discarded, the normal embryonic cells harvested for therapy? If that had been the case years ago, Eli would have been an only child. He thought about that — no fights in high school for defending his brother, the retard. And now, he would not be responsible for the expensive bills that paid for Henry's care.

Considering these arguments, Eli wondered why he didn't use his position as a surgeon-scientist to advocate for embryonic stem cell research. But this same scientific acumen warned him this was not the path the profession of medicine should take.

Or maybe his scientific acumen had nothing to do with it.

Maybe it was simply his brother, with his kindergarten IQ, and his developmentally delayed, precious life.

Eli returned to the menu page of RBI's Web site and clicked on Biomedical Devices. No controversy here, he thought. The page was further divided to give the history of New York-based Regent Biotech before the merger and applauded the company's success as an innovator in the industry.

Eli scanned a series of pages until CURRENT PRODUCTS appeared. He skipped past *Pacemakers* and *Robotics* to the category that interested him most, *Endovascular*. He clicked on the subcategory *Aortic*, but after a few seconds of delay the following message appeared:

> We're sorry.
> This page is unavailable.
> Current updates being installed.

The same rotating emblem appeared and began to bounce from side to side and from the corners of the screen. Irritated and fatigued with a lengthy search that had taken him nowhere, Eli closed the Web page and shut down the antiquated computer.

He walked from his laboratory to the hospital and hit the fourth floor button on the elevator. The pediatric intensive care unit brought a flood of memories to Eli from his days as a third-year resident on pediatric surgery.

Stat call for a chest tube in a three-year-old. Perforated intestine from necrotizing enterocolitis in a premature infant no bigger than a squirrel.

He shuddered at the mental image.

Eli entered the unit and showed his badge to the clerk. She pointed to a soap dispenser on the wall.

"Scrub those hands, doctor."

Eli squirted a glob of alcohol-based gel in his hand and rubbed it in, acrid fumes from the evaporating gel filling his nose.

"I'm seeing Margaret Daily."

The clerk glanced at a clipboard on her desk. "Bed seven. Mom's in there now."

The rooms were arranged in a circle around a central nurse's desk and the doctor's workstation. Eli passed a group of pediatricians on their daily afternoon rounds outside room four. As he approached, they stopped their discussion and eyed his name badge. Surgeons ambling about in the pedi ICU either brought a sense of relief or great consternation. There was no in between.

Margaret's nurse was standing in the doorway.

"How is she?" Eli asked.

"She's not scheduled for any surgery, I can tell you that."

Eli put up both hands in surrender. "I know that, I'm just a friend."

The nurse smiled. "She's much better now. Might even go home in the morning." Then she held out a finger and made like a hook. "But she's scared enough already, doesn't need any more doctors."

Eli understood. He took off his white coat and dropped it over her hook.

Meg was sitting in a chair pulled close to Margaret's bed. The girl held a gift store teddy bear and was bouncing it on her stomach.

"How we doing?"

Eli could see the relief in Meg's eyes when she saw him. She started in with some formal introduction.

"Sweetheart, I want you to meet Dr. —"

But Eli came up beside the bed, took the bear, and used it to kiss Margaret on the nose.

"My name's Eli. What's his?"

Margaret grabbed the bear, hugged it close to her chest, and stared at Eli while she thought about it. "His name's Fuzzy."

Eli leaned over and opened his eyes wide.

"How fuzzy was he?"

Margaret giggled and kissed Eli's nose with the bear.

Eli turned to Meg. She was covering a smile with her hand.

"Glad things are better," he said.

Meg straightened the covers over her daughter. "Mommy will be right back, okay?"

Eli followed Meg into the hallway.

"A pediatric endocrinologist came to see us today. Says there's a new treatment that can help her diabetes."

"The specialists here are top notch," Eli said to reassure her. "I'm sure they can help."

"They have to do something," Meg said. "I can't work here and be worried constantly that this will happen again."

Eli nodded. "So, home in the morning?"

"That's what they say. Look, I have to come in tomorrow around noon to sign reports. I want to know more about that Gaston fellow."

Eli looked back in the room at Margaret.

"There's a nurse who lives on my block," Meg said. "She's coming over tomorrow afternoon for a couple of hours to watch her."

"In that case, let's grab some lunch in the cafeteria," Eli offered.

Before Meg reentered her daughter's room, she turned and said, "There's something very strange about Gaston's autopsy."

CHAPTER FIFTEEN

Eli avoided the physician's dining room, an area partially secluded behind a gourmet coffee stand that would be full of residents and attending physicians at lunchtime. Instead, he chose a table at the edge of the main dining room.

He placed their trays so that he and Meg could sit next to one another, and he sipped a Coke as he waited for her to arrive. After studying the seating arrangement, Eli scooted her tray to the opposite side of the table. *This is silly,* he thought. *It's just the cafeteria, not some fancy French restaurant like we're on a date or something.*

But when Meg arrived, he realized how conspicuous they must look, the only two white coats sitting among patients and their families.

"No scrubs?" Eli said, noticing Meg's attire, white blouse and burgundy scarf tied in a knot just above the top button of her coat.

"I try to clean up before dining with the customers," she said and winked at him. "I'd hate to have a chunk of spleen stuck on me."

Eli motioned for her to sit. "Caesar salad okay? It was that or mystery meat loaf."

"Caesar's fine. Thanks."

They began to eat in silence, Meg with her Caesar, Eli with a refried burger off the grill. Eli asked about Margaret and was told she was fine. After a couple of minutes, he reached beneath his chair and brought an oversized brown folder to his lap.

"What do you have there?"

Eli removed the film from the folder. "I know it's early for such an intimate look at my family," Eli said, delaying as though he was embarrassed. "I was going to show it to a radiologist, but since you made an A in radiology —"

"I made an A in everything," she said, cutting him off. "Give it to me."

She popped the last crouton in her mouth and held the X-ray up to the fluorescent light while she chewed.

Even at an angle, Eli could easily see the device's heavy white imprint in the mid-abdomen.

After a few seconds she asked, "Why's the name not there?"

"I don't know," Eli said as though it didn't matter, "cut off I guess."

Meg just stared at him.

Eli held out his hands with open palms and asked, "What?" He felt like a medical student on rounds getting quizzed about some obscure lab test.

"What's the first thing you do when you look at an X-ray?"

"Here we go, back to med school," Eli said and rolled his eyes. "Well, Professor Daily. I look at the clavicles to check the orientation, then I —"

"Wrong."

Eli stopped his act. "You're serious?"

"You look at the name to make sure it's the correct patient." She handed the X-ray back to him. "Whose film is this?"

Eli held it up against the cafeteria lights. "It's an X-ray taken of my brother, Henry, when he was a kid."

"Your brother?" Meg asked. "Why on earth would he have a graft device like that?"

Eli began the story. "When Henry was two years old, the doctors told my parents he had a critical stenosis of his aorta. They went in and fixed it with a new type of device. Supposedly, it was a very risky procedure, but it worked."

"For aortic stenosis?" Meg asked, trying to understand the indications for the operation. "Was he sick?"

"I guess so," Eli answered. "Henry is developmentally delayed. It's sometimes hard to know when he's sick or not."

The look on Meg's face told him that was a cop-out.

"I wasn't born yet, okay?" Eli said, becoming defensive now. "Henry's three years older than I am."

"But aortic stenosis usually presents much earlier, just after birth."

"I know. When I was in medical school, I tried to get more details about Henry's operation from my father. But he always said it was just a congenital condition that was repaired with surgery. My father was never one to give out much information."

Meg gestured toward the X-ray in Eli's hand. "I can tell by looking at the mesh configuration, it's the same make as the device we found in your friend Gaston. Are you sure that's your brother's film?"

Within the identification panel in the right upper corner of the film, Eli located the date of birth next to the medical record number. The top of the numbers were clipped off, as though someone was trying to exclude that information as well. But he could still read them.

11/23/71

"November 23rd, nineteen seventy-one?" He looked at Meg. "That's my brother's birthday."

CHAPTER SIXTEEN

Green Hills State Home lies eighty-eight miles northeast of Memphis, accessible only from a two-lane road that runs parallel to the Mississippi River. It was built in the late 1800s along the edge of the Reelfoot Bayou in the northwestern tip of Dyer County. A home for the disabled, both mentally and physically, its name conjured a vision of warmth and pleasantness. But every time Eli visited, he saw roaches under Henry's bed and smelled the reek of urine in the halls.

Henry had entered the home on his twenty-eighth birthday, the day after their mother died of breast cancer. Elizer Branch had neither the time nor the patience to deal with a son who required around-the-clock care. A familiar pang of guilt hit Eli whenever he calculated how long his brother had been a resident in that miserable place — over ten years.

When Meg returned to the morgue following their lunch, Eli took the rest of the afternoon off for the trip. He had no secretary to notify and no idea how to contact his nutty lab assistant. He was not on call again until Thursday night, and the fact that his superior, Karl Fisher, canceled his clinic patients made it much easier to leave the medical center.

His brother's X-ray, the device, and what he had been told about the operation years earlier — none of it made sense. *What he planned to do when he got to Henry?* Eli had no idea.

Outside of Dyersburg, he turned off the interstate onto a small road that angled back toward the river. Johnson grass that had gone to seed waved high along the asphalt's edge, and kudzu crept over the shoulder, beaten back by traffic.

Eli knew he was well out of pager range from the hospital, one of the few times that he could truly be unavailable. Out of reach of the nurses, the residents, the operating room, and especially the emergency room. But then his phone chirped.

"Damn cell phones," he muttered, remembering that surrendering all personal numbers was required for staff membership at Gates Memorial.

"Hello, Dr. Branch?"

"Yeah, speaking."

"This is Felicia from the hospital Credentialing Office. I'm calling you about Dr. Margaret Daily."

Eli hesitated before making the commitment. He had just been through the ringer with the credentialing people. They wanted every bit of information on him, from what he did during his college summers to his mother's maiden name.

"Yes, what about her?"

"Are you familiar with Dr. Daily?"

You can't even eat lunch with someone. "I know a pathologist named Daily. What's this about?"

"We need someone to, well, confirm or vouch for her credentials," the young female voice said, reluctantly.

"You mean, she's not credentialed?"

"Technically she is, but we received a phone call, a warning if you will, about her appointment here."

Eli's concern about why Meg was always alone and seemed to have no colleagues quickly surfaced. "Why are you calling me, may I ask?"

"Dr. Branch, you are well respected here, and —" He heard a sigh. "Aren't you friends with Dr. Daily? I mean, we're not trying to pry, but no one else seems to know her."

Eli knew that a call from Credentialing was a serious matter. Any question raised about a physician's credentials or reputation could damage or even end a career.

"Who made a call about her?"

"It was the Medical Examiner's office in Little Rock, her previous place of employment. Seems there was an incident. It could compromise her position here."

"Isn't it a little late for that? What happened?"

Eli heard the shuffle of papers. "She had an altercation with her former chairman of pathology."

"An altercation?"

"It seems that she —" and then Felicia stopped reading the report and addressed him directly. "Dr. Branch, I'm sure that you will keep this information strictly confidential."

The caller had aroused his curiosity now. "Sure, strictly confidential. Did you say Medical Examiner's office?"

"Yes, she worked there for three years, 2002 to 2005, after finishing her pathology residency at the University of Arkansas."

"There must be some explanation," Eli said. "Meg — I mean — Dr. Daily is very professional and accomplished in her field." But as he said this, Eli knew that his words weren't convincing. In fact, they were hiding his own doubt.

"She was called to examine a body," Felicia continued, "middle of the night, supposedly a high-profile case. But she couldn't find someone to stay with her daughter, so she refused to go in."

With the abruptness of a slammed door, Eli realized just how little he knew about Dr. Meg Daily. He tried to remain focused on the line of inquiry. "Surely she didn't get fired for that, refusing to abandon her child?"

"According to this call, she struck Dr. Richard Sizemore on August fourth, two thousand five."

"Struck?"

"She beat him in the face with both fists. Fractured his zyg . . ." Felicia stopped as she struggled with the terminology.

"Zygomatic arch," Eli said completing the name of the facial bone that formed the outside rim of the eye socket, a structure that could be broken only by a forceful blow.

"Yes, that's it," Felicia confirmed.

Were talking about the same Meg? Both fists?

"Listen," Eli said, "I've known her only a few days. What am I supposed to say?"

Something was missing. Why had she suddenly arrived at Gates Memorial? No history, no acquaintances. A bright, attractive pathologist stuck in the dungeon doing autopsies?

Maybe there was some truth to this.

Eli pictured Meg when he first met her, how she sat at the microscope, the smell of her hair. He didn't want to believe any of it.

"I hope you have confirmed the source," Eli said, in Meg's defense now. "Maybe someone's a little ticked off they lost a good pathologist."

Then Eli remembered an interesting detail that Fisher had told him about the Credentialing Committee. About its current chairman. Dr. James Korinsky.

"You're right, Dr. Branch, we don't want to jump to any conclusions," Felicia said. "This caller could be completely wrong. But we're concerned, to say the least."

During the next eleven miles to the home, Eli tried to shake the image of Meg pummeling her older, male chairman of pathology. He fantasized doing the same to Fisher. Tie him to that mahogany desk and beat him about the face.

As he neared his brother's residence, his vengeful thoughts turned to growing up with Henry. His father always locked the older boy in the laundry room whenever Eli's friends came over. They had good times together, but certain ugly events dominated Eli's memory, especially of his own birthday parties.

His father would cut a chunk of birthday cake, give it to Henry in the laundry room, then lock the door. Eli could not remember a time when his father had actually held or embraced his brother. Instead, Eli pictured Elizer Branch carrying Henry away, to rid the setting of his older son, the affected child who would never amount to anything but a continual source of embarrassment.

It was at his ninth birthday party, while Eli was passing out pieces of cake, that he overheard his mother talking with one of her best friends.

"Look at Eli, he's precious," the friend had said. "Remember when you talked about stopping the pregnancy because you were afraid of another Henry?"

His mother answered quietly, in a whisper. "Yeah, that would have been a terrible mistake."

At the time, Eli didn't understand. Now, he could never forget.

Eli's Bronco passed a shirtless teenage boy, a red bandana around his neck, struggling to push a mower up an incline. At the top of the grassy hillside stood a small white church. The last time he and his family had entered a place of worship was in Memphis at the Episcopal church on Madison Avenue. He was seven years old, Henry ten. When the minister asked for an offering, their mother opened her coin purse and removed two dollar bills, one for each boy.

They were told to hold the bill and place it in the collection plate as it passed. Eli folded his dollar, held it between his legs, and watched the gold-colored plate pass from one row to the next. Henry smelled his dollar, raised it above his head, and stretched it tight with both hands. The dollar ripped in half, and Henry let out a shrill laugh.

As their mother searched for another dollar, Henry continued to fidget and make noise. Eli saw the anger building in his father's face, and he tried to make Henry stop laughing. When the collection plate started down their pew, Henry yelled "eeeeee" and leaned forward so fast that he hit his head on the pew in front of them. Eli could still see, as though yesterday, his father smashing the torn piece of dollar over Henry's mouth and holding it there like a piece of tape.

The usher approached from behind, leaned over, and whispered, "We are a God-filled people, please remove this boy." Henry was silent as his father snatched him up and carried him from the building, pieces of the dollar bill falling to the floor. At the altar, the preacher put on a fake smile and said into the microphone, "God help his soul."

Eli stayed behind in the pew with his mother, too scared to leave, not even to help his own brother. Afterward, he wished he had never placed his dollar in the gold plate. And he vowed never to enter a church again.

During the decade of Henry's occupancy at Green Hills State Home,

Eli visited at least twice a year. The sheets on Henry's bed were always twisted with bits of leaves and dirt smudged at the foot. Patches of mildew suggested months between linen changes. Eli parked his truck on the hot gravel of the parking lot. There were no trees for shade. Certainly no green hills.

The reception desk was unoccupied, but Eli knew the drill and signed his name on the register. *Like anyone cares who comes or goes. As long as the check arrives.* Cost was the only thing keeping him from moving Henry to another facility. He'd already checked the few in the region that would even accept his brother.

Eli went directly to the familiar room. Henry was not there, but his roommate was curled up in bed, the sheet over his head. Eli watched for movement as though the other boy was a patient to see on morning rounds. After several seconds, Eli became alarmed. But a slow inspiratory rise of the sheet, followed by an expiratory fall, reassured him.

Attached to the foot of the bed, a small rectangular nameplate was pasted to a board with a peel-off adhesive back, the kind of tag a child name searches for on a revolving display at a roadside convenience mart. Green, generic letters spelled JIMMY.

Eli wondered where Henry might be as he examined his brother's room. Henry's grayish bed covers were peeled back and wrinkled. Eli couldn't bear to look any closer. A small black-and-white television was tuned to a Braves game. The Pirates were winning, five to four. At least the sound was turned down to a tolerable level. It was usually blaring.

The nightstand between the two beds held a box of Kleenex and a grape soda can crushed in the middle. It had been bent so both ends touched. Eli opened the door of the stand to see a stack of three magazines. On top was a *Ladies Home Journal*, then a graphic comic book written in Japanese. *How depressing.* On the bottom, a motorcycle magazine was turned facedown. Eli smiled when he turned it over. A halter-topped girl in tight jean shorts straddled a chrome-plated hog. *They must be hiding this one.*

He opened the bathroom door and was hit with an odor that made him cover his mouth. The toilet bowl was full to the brim, with brown water and feces that floated and churned. Eli closed the door and went to complain at the front desk, still unoccupied. He saw a female attendant down the hall, but she darted into a room as he approached.

If Henry wasn't in his room watching television, he could usually be found in a wheelchair outside at the rear of the complex. Henry didn't need the wheelchair, his legs worked fine, but it seemed that almost everyone else had one, so why not him?

At the back of the building, a concrete deck held a row of six industrial-sized garbage cans. The stifling smell of rotting food hovered in a cloud. A group of pine trees provided shade to only that part of the deck. The other end was used as a plaza for smoking. Henry was sitting in a wheelchair, back to him, a cigarette burned close to the filter dangling from his right hand. He was wearing a tattered John Deere cap with the green bill curved down and frayed at the rim. To Eli, the cap represented one of the few bonds that remained between them. He had given it to Henry on his birthday shortly before Henry entered the home. Since then he had not seen his brother without it.

Three other wheel-chaired occupants sat facing a square, paved basketball court with only one goal. Two younger male attendants were shooting baskets and horsing around. Neither Henry nor any of the others spoke a word. They all smoked and watched the players as if it were a professional game.

Eli walked to Henry's side, bent down by his wheelchair, and placed a hand on his right shoulder.

"Hey, buddy."

Henry looked at Eli, then quickly back at the game. No one else responded.

But as Henry brought the cigarette to his lips, Eli saw a brief smile vanish to a pucker. A long drag seemed to satisfy him immensely. Henry dropped the butt at his feet and fished a pack from the front pocket of his shirt. Eli noticed a yellowing of his fingers and wondered if he were chain-smoking now. His straight brown hair was cut in an unimaginative bowl and his sideburns were long, not stylishly so, but continued with a slant toward his chin in fuzzy curls. Henry's ears and neck were sunburned, as if all he did was smoke in the sun on a concrete deck, watching the trees or an occasional game of basketball.

Eli did not expect Henry to speak to him. Since the day ten years ago that their mother had not come home from the hospital, his brother hadn't spoken a word.

CHAPTER SEVENTEEN

Henry pulled another cigarette from the pack and took it to his lips with the grace and ease of a cardshark dealing a hand. But then his movements became awkward. Slowly, with ratcheting jerks, he extended his hand toward his brother. Eli looked at the pack, then at Henry, who blinked both eyes and nodded.

During the movement, Henry had popped a cigarette out so that the butt projected unevenly. Eli pulled the cigarette from the pack and heard the strike and crackling burn of a match. Henry held the match as Eli took two quick puffs, orange embers glowing at the end of the cigarette. Except for the occasional celebratory cigar, Eli hadn't smoked since college and he found the smell of burning tobacco and pine trees invigorating.

Henry blew out a long stream of smoke and Eli felt a quiver of the wheelchair, a few seismic shocks before the quake. That's when Henry began to shake. The wheelchair bucked violently. All culminated a few seconds later as Henry, with eyes closed as if to maximize the pressure and intensity, erupted with a forceful "eeeeeeee" that lasted through a full breath.

Eli put his hand on Henry's shoulder and he relaxed in the chair. The others continued smoking without so much as turning their heads toward Henry. Eli figured they had been around his brother long enough to know it was something Henry had to do, this release of pressure, a calming of the spirit.

Eli knew that in his brother's convoluted, cross-wired world, this was Henry, in his excitement, saying, "Brother, it's damn good to see you."

The serenity of the moment was interrupted by the sound of footsteps. Eli turned to see a black male attendant approaching. He wore the odd combination of short white jacket and blue warm-up pants.

"You here to get Henry?" he said as though expecting Eli's visit.

"To get him?" Eli questioned in return.

"Yeah, you know, take him to his appointment."

"I don't know what you're referring to. Appointment?"

The attendant looked at the cigarette in Eli's hand. He realized the mistake and took a few steps back. "I'm sorry. You looked like one of them doctors come get him every month." The attendant turned and left.

The image of the device on the X-ray flashed in Eli's mind, followed by a disordered, dream-like sequence of Henry being carted off to "appointments."

"Where do they take you, Henry?" Eli knew his question would not be replied to. But he also knew that the home was required to keep detailed records of any time an occupant went off the property. "Come on, Henry. We're going to find out."

The wheelchair rolled forward.

"No," Eli said and he cupped his hand behind Henry's shoulder and pulled him forward. "You can walk."

Slowly, Henry stood but remained bent at the waist. He grimaced and pressed on his left groin.

"What is it?" Eli asked.

Henry eased back into the wheelchair, letting his bottom hit the seat hard before he sucked in another breath of smoke. This time, the others watched as Henry was rolled inside the building. Eli pushed fast and Henry responded with deep humming noises, like a truck climbing a hill.

In the room, Eli pulled the thin curtain between the twin beds and

Jimmy, whose head was out from the covers, was staring at the wall. He helped his brother to a sitting position on the bed. Gradually, Henry extended his left leg, then reclined hard against the pillow with a forceful expiration. Eli removed the John Deere cap and set it on the bedside table. Henry quickly retrieved it and put it on again.

Other than wrestling as kids and sleeping in the same bed, he had not had physical contact with his brother. He'd never examined him as a doctor. Touching Henry's body seemed off limits somehow. Although Eli had longed for a more intimate relationship with his older brother, that relationship seemed out of reach.

However, no matter what it took, Eli could not leave without knowing the source of Henry's pain. Of all the patients Eli had examined, this exam would seem the most awkward. He peeled back the waist of his brother's pants and Henry grabbed his hands.

"Yes, Henry. Got to."

Eli unzipped Henry's jeans and pulled them down enough to see a bruise across his left groin, a dark blue bull's-eye fading to peripheral rims of yellow. In the center, just below the inguinal ligament, he discovered puncture marks. The deepest wound was closed with two silk sutures as though a large-bore catheter had been inserted and removed.

What the hell?

Eli covered Henry with a corner of the wrinkled sheet and went straight to the central office. A young woman with a metal ring piercing one eyebrow sat at the desk with a cup of coffee, reading a magazine. The director's assistant. She stood as Eli abruptly entered the office door.

Eli tried to remain calm while inquiring about the marks on Henry's leg. The woman tried to explain that Henry had been ill.

"He doesn't look sick," Eli said. "Why haven't I been told about these doctor visits?"

She rolled the magazine tight in her hands and used it to point at a stack of papers on the desk. "I'm sorry, but we have your signature to release him for every appointment."

Eli stayed with Henry for the rest of the afternoon, trying to make sense of why his brother needed monthly appointments with a doctor. But the paperwork trail was either absent or bewildering, and no one seemed to have an answer. Eli had examined "his" signatures closely. It was the best forgery job he had ever seen. Finally, he gave up and left for Memphis.

In the parking lot of Green Hills State Home, his cell phone rang again. This time it was a familiar voice, proving that the hospital operator would give his private number to anyone — even violent mothers.

"Hi Meg."

"I've got some new data on the Gaston case. Got a minute?"

The word "case" struck Eli with different meaning now, straight from Meg's stint with the ME's office, as if the two of them were part of a crime investigation unit. He unlocked his Bronco and let the July heat inside exchange itself with the heat outside.

"Sure, what is it?"

"Where are you?"

"I had to see my brother. I'm just now leaving."

"How is he?"

"He's fine at the moment."

"At the moment?" Meg asked.

"There's something wrong here," Eli said, looking back at the unkempt facility. "I'll tell you later. What do you have?"

"Remember those cells I showed you? Around the holes in the aorta?"

"Yeah, the funny-looking ones?"

Her hesitation heightened his curiosity.

"They're not supposed to be there."

With his next question, Eli realized that all of his responses must sound cretin-like. "Where are they supposed to be?"

"I haven't figured that out yet, but I did some analysis on your funny-looking cells. Ever heard of matrix metalloproteinases?"

"MMPs?" Eli said immediately. Now he was in familiar territory.

Eli's entire research effort at Vanderbilt had focused on matrix metalloproteinases or MMPs. He studied how breast cancer cells secrete the specialized enzyme to acquire invasiveness and metastasize to organs like the liver and lungs. He often wondered if the reason he had chosen the field of breast cancer research was the result of his mother's death from the disease.

"Yeah, I've heard of them," he said, reveling in his chance to play dumb a while longer before blowing her away.

"These cells are little MMP factories. They're loaded with the stuff."

Eli searched his mental files. Most of his knowledge of MMPs centered on the deleterious effects of the enzyme when cancer cells were overzealous secretors. But then a file popped up on MMPs and aortic aneurysms. One of the enzymes had been implicated in weakening the aortic wall, thereby allowing an aneurysm to form.

"Let me guess. MMP-nine."

"The PCR is still cooking," Meg said, deflating Eli's chance to shine. "But if it is number nine, you'll be one lucky son of a —" Meg stopped to laugh uncharacteristically, "anatomy professor."

"Oh, you're proud of that one, aren't you?"

"I have my moments."

Eli sighed. "Okay, so the cells make MMPs, probably just a reaction to the endograft." *Always the skeptic.*

"I don't think so. We're talking supraphysiologic levels. I mean, the enzyme ate holes in this guy's aorta, for crying out loud. Basically killed him."

Eli knew that MMP-nine could be activated in the laboratory and that investigators were studying how the enzyme contributed to the development of aortic aneurysms, how it degraded the aortic wall until it ballooned out in a weakened state. But the body could not produce enough of the enzyme, under normal conditions, to blow out an aorta.

"Meg, I appreciate your effort in his case, especially since I knew Gaston." As he said this, Eli thought of the call from the Credentialing Office and Meg's supposed employment history. "But you should focus on your job. I'd hate for there to be problems."

"Look Eli, his death bugs the hell out of me. Something's not right. I just can't prove it — yet."

Now she was talking like a medical examiner. Trying to prove things.

"One more thing and I'll hang up," Meg said. "There's another body here in the morgue waiting for autopsy. Death certificate says aortic rupture."

She waited, but Eli said nothing.

"I checked out his X-rays from the file room, an abdominal film."

"Don't tell me, the same kind of graft?" Eli waited through a silent drumroll.

"You got it. See a pattern here? Better stop by when you get back to town."

CHAPTER EIGHTEEN

The limousine arrived at exactly seven o'clock. Eli watched from the front window of his house as it pulled up slowly to the curb. It was the standard length, not outrageously long, and business black. RBI in the familiar gold letters was stamped on the first passenger door. The driver got out, lit a cigarette, and leaned against the vehicle, facing Eli's front door.

When he had called RBI to arrange the meeting, Eli first gave his laboratory address. But he changed it to his home when he considered that Fisher might witness the limousine pick up. *Why call attention to myself when I'm already in trouble?*

When he saw the auspicious limo complete with driver in a black suit and obligatory cap, Eli thought maybe this was just the attention he needed on the medical campus. Then he would get some respect. *Who does that new guy, Branch, think he is?*

Eli wished that he had told Meg about his absence from the medical center. She would wonder, later this morning, why he wasn't coming to see the body she had called about. But at this point, he didn't want anyone, not even Meg, to know that RBI had requested his visit.

"Dr. Branch?" the driver asked, crushing the cigarette butt with his foot.

They shook hands briefly. Eli wasn't sure if shaking the hand of your chauffeur was the proper thing to do but it seemed natural. He stepped into the limo, and his driver shut the door behind him. At his right hand, a steaming cup of coffee waited with a hot silver carafe next to it. Eli balanced a tiny pitcher of cream as the limo pulled away from the curb. He started to compliment the service when a solid black window rose behind the driver, isolating Eli in the back. *Not much for conversation I guess.* Mozart started abruptly and what Eli thought was a black window flashed on as a plasma video screen. The flipping RBI logo appeared and the classical piece became louder.

The video was a sleek segment about the wealth of the company and how much RBI contributed to the health of society. It came off as superficial and self-congratulatory. Eli figured he was just one of many special guests riding in this limo who had to watch the instructional video, like a preparatory infomercial.

Why am I doing this? What do they want with me?

He watched the Memphis Pyramid as they passed it, a near-blinding spark of sun reflecting off the point. He had heard of physicians leaving their practice to become scientific directors of biopharmaceutical companies. But young surgeons were not usually on the short-list. Soon after the video ended, the plasma screen descended and cigarette smoke poured out.

"Dr. Branch," the driver said, looking into the rearview mirror. "I got a call from RBI. Mr. Stone was scheduled to arrive from D.C. on his early morning flight." The matter-of-fact tone suggested this was a frequent occurrence. "But his plane's a few minutes late. They have arranged a tour of the facility for you until he arrives." The driver looked again in the mirror as if to confirm that the information had been received.

"Okay. Thank you."

His flight? Eli envisioned a Lear jet with RBI stamped on the wing. This was the first Eli was hearing of any agenda for his day. He had assumed that he would meet with Stone, but the tour was apparently a change in plans. *How long will this take?* Eli thought of Meg and the body-in-waiting.

"Excuse me," Eli said when the black window began to close again. But it shut before he could ask any questions. Limited, one-way communication. It seemed to be the trend.

The limo gained speed on the Hernando-Desoto Bridge, and Eli looked back at the line of buildings and shops along Riverside Drive. Freight trucks were backed up to the loading docks and an owner was opening his store for early-morning patrons.

Below the bridge, the river appeared as a mass of shifting land, rippled brown water moving toward the Gulf like a nation itself. To the north, Eli could see the hazy border of Sand Dollar Reef surrounded by mist that rose from the water, soon to be scorched by a July sun. A barge trudged toward a channel that led around the side of the island.

Sand Dollar Reef was an eleven-acre, vine-infested mound of mud that somehow held its ground and forced the largest river in North America to part its waters around the jagged shore. The isolated land mass sat in the middle of the river between Arkansas and Tennessee, just north of the Hernando Desoto bridge carrying Interstate 40 west. It was not a reef, nor was a sand dollar ever found in the mud. RBI had poured an excessive amount of money into clearing the land, reinforcing the river bank, and replacing all but a concealing perimeter of trees with concrete.

The piece of land had often been associated with misfortune. Eli remembered the five o'clock news stories from his years as a medical student; a barge run aground into its boggy banks or a homicide victim's body found weeks after buzzards had eaten the eyes. In earlier years, the island served as a site of prison camps for some of the Mid-South's most hardened criminals.

In downtown bars and along Beale Street, a popular specialty drink was the Sand Dollar Slew, so named because the mixture of coffee, Kahlua, and Jack Daniel's, when topped with a rim of whipped cream, looked like foam on muddy water. There was even a song that celebrated the life of the island's only known inhabitant. More fraternity chant than song, the tune was most appreciated after several drinks.

Eli began to recite it to himself, like a poem, in nervous repetition. When he thought about the words, he realized the song was appreciated only very late at night, after many, many rounds.

> Sand Dollar Jennie lives out on the Reef.
> Smells like a slew but she sure can screw.

Go Jennie, Go Jennie.
Screw, Screw, Screw.

The limo traveled into West Memphis, Arkansas, a land of factories, trucking companies, and greyhound racetracks. Eli felt a nauseous twinge of the unknown, as though he were leaving home.

They crossed the narrow bridge to the island and turned onto a concrete drive. A line of willow trees seemed to obscure the view rather than provide scenic relief. A guardhouse was positioned in the center of the road with gates blocking vehicles coming or going. A uniformed guard stepped out of the house and motioned for the limo to stop. He was a large man, with bulky shoulders and overdeveloped forearms, like a professional wrestler. When the driver opened the passenger door, Eli noticed a holstered pistol at the guard's side.

"We need to step out here for a few minutes," the driver said.

Eli complied, as though he had a choice, and was escorted into the guardhouse.

"Just a formality required by RBI security," the driver assured him.

Eli didn't feel reassured.

The guard remained silent and motioned for Eli to remove his shoes, then led him through what appeared to be a metal detector, like at an airport. Eli's shoes were examined and given back to him.

Through the window, Eli could see his driver who leaned against the limo, smoking as usual. With the guard's hand firmly against his back, Eli was shoved toward a table and told, by way of a grunt, to sit in the chair. Eli wondered if he spoke English, or even spoke at all.

Before him on the table sat a black box the size of a small microwave oven. From the box, a view piece projected forward, much like the View-Master toy used by children to see Disney characters. Again, with a nudge to his back, Eli was made to bend forward until his face met the plastic piece. He wasn't feeling much like an invited quest.

A completely dark field was suddenly illuminated by beams of light that passed over both eyes in a flash. Another grunt indicated that he was finished with this part of the examination.

When Eli stood, his vision was blurry and bright, as though his pupils had been dilated. As he rubbed his eyes with balled fists, Eli felt the guard's hands squeeze his armpits and slide down his waist and across his crotch.

"Hey," Eli yelled and pushed the man's arm away. But the guard was already down to feeling Eli's knees and patting his ankles. Eli stepped back and felt dizzy. The guard grunted a little louder and longer and pointed to the door. This time, his mouth was open, and Eli noticed the man's unusually large tongue, swollen in a thick peninsula of muscle.

RBI may be a top biotech company. But they need a lesson or two in public relations.

The driver helped Eli into the limo. "They call him Tongue," he said. "He looks scary, but he's fairly harmless." Then with a low whisper, "He ain't all there."

They pulled away from the guardhouse, and as the glass divider was closing, the driver's cheery voice said, "Now, doctor, you're ready for the tour."

CHAPTER NINETEEN

Regency Biotech International stood alone like a concrete fortress on a desolate island. Four massive antebellum-style columns created a magnificent entrance, with oversized magnolia trees planted in a semicircle. Rising four stories, square concrete sections with small, sparsely spaced windows fanned out on either side of the entry. Eli realized the company's intention with façade. Visitors would be so impressed by the charming Old-South entrance that they wouldn't notice the concentration camp bunkers.

The limo pulled a hard turn along the circular drive, which surrounded a waterfall that splashed over the three-letter logo carved deep in a piece of granite. The driver escorted Eli to the impressive front entry.

"Have a good visit, Dr. Branch." He tipped his cap and retreated in a brisk escape to the limo.

Eli stood before double glass doors that appeared twenty feet tall. Humidity rolling off the river saturated the air like the inside of a greenhouse. Reaching to his back pocket but not finding a handkerchief, he wiped beads of sweat from his forehead and slung them to the ground.

He reached for the handle and briefly caught his reflection in the glass. His black suit was at least fourteen years old. He had bought it at James Davis, a top-notch Memphis clothier, for the specific purpose of medical school interviews during his final year at Ole Miss. With a little care and scarce use, the suit had held up well. But the jacket was tight across his shoulders now and the pants hem showed a little too much sock.

As he tugged at the knot of his blue-and-red-striped Rebel tie, his focus converged through the glass on the face of a young woman sitting behind the reception desk. She was smiling, probably having enjoyed watching him primp. The doors opened toward him with a mechanical hum and a blast of cool air.

"Dr. Branch?" The receptionist stood to greet him.

Sleeveless black spandex clung to her like skin and erupted in a tight collar around her neck.

"I'm Lisa."

Eli took her hand in a professional manner and gazed into brilliant, fake-blue eyes. He was certain to keep his vision well above the nice-to-meet-you nipples that tested the integrity of him and her blouse.

"Did you get the message about Mr. Stone?"

Eli acted interested in the vaulted ceiling and a chandelier that reflected squares of light on the wall like a disco ball.

"He should be arriving any moment now," Lisa said, tapping her watchless wrist.

Large ceiling fans circulated the cool air, and drops of sweat fixed themselves to Eli's hairline as if frozen. "That's fine," he said, looking around the foyer. "Is there a restroom?"

"Sure, follow me."

Lisa stepped from behind the desk and led him into a narrow corridor. Her pink chiffon skirt bounced and jiggled as if suspended on springs.

"Here you go."

Eli opened the door and released the breath he had been unaware of holding. The room smelled of cologne. Approaching a thick marble lavatory, he grabbed a wad of paper towels, held them under a gold-plated faucet, and applied them to his face.

The voice behind him erupted like the crank of a chainsaw.

"Sticky out there, ain't it?"

Eli swung around to find an old man sitting on a stool, white towel folded across his arm. The man hopped off his perch, limped toward Eli, and presented the towel.

"Thank you, sir," Eli said, still rattled. *Attendants in the bathroom of fancy restaurants are one thing, but at a corporation?*

"Staying a while, are you?"

Eli noticed the gentle sweep of a security camera at the corner of the ceiling. "No, just visiting," he said.

The man ripped into a series of gnawing laughs. "Just visiting? Humph. My son, nobody just visits this place." His eyes darted toward the foyer. "Why would you ever want to leave?"

The man smiled, sparkling white teeth forming a brilliant centerpiece within his black face. His eyes continued to jerk and dart in a twisting glare as though in the dawn of a seizure.

"Okay, Prine, that's enough," Lisa yelled just outside the door.

He winked at Eli. "She's my little girl. Yes sirree."

When Eli approached the urinal, the bathroom attendant began to hum "The Stars and Stripes Forever." He used the towel to whip-pop the air for the cymbal parts. With this commotion and Lisa listening from the hallway, Eli couldn't start a stream, even with two cups of coffee in him. He turned to leave.

"Hold on there, son." Prine took a squirt bottle of cologne from the counter and delivered a halo of mist around Eli's head. "It's her favorite."

As Eli entered the hallway, his eyes were not only dilated but also stinging from the cologne. Lisa was waiting with a twig of blonde hair twisted around a finger and pulled toward her mouth. "Come," she said, dangling her hand in front of her. "We have just enough time to visit one of the laboratories before Mr. Stone arrives."

RBI was divided into three sections, each with a presidential name: East Wing, West Wing, and the Oval Terrace. The East Wing housed all the research laboratories, and the West Wing contained the business and administrative offices. At least this is what Lisa told him as they headed toward the East Wing. She walked fast and Eli followed close behind her. Despite his blurry vision, he tried to focus on the facility instead of a posterior view of chiffon.

Eli asked about the Oval Terrace. Lisa shrugged, pinching her spandex top even tighter. "I don't know," she said. "You need a special code to go back there."

Lisa inserted a card into a reader on the wall and they entered the East Wing. The doors swung forward and Eli had to step back to avoid being hit. Before them stretched a long, sterile corridor bright with fluorescent lights. All the doors along the hall were closed. As he passed each one, Eli looked through narrow-paned windows reinforced with steel mesh. The laboratories looked pristine, glassware arranged neatly on bench tops as if for a movie set. Not once did he see a person in a lab.

At the end of the hall, Lisa peeked through a pane of glass and said, "Good, she's here."

To enter the lab, she inserted her card and removed it quickly. She allowed Eli to enter first. The room looked the same as the other labs except it was somewhat smaller, and the glassware and equipment appeared to be in use rather than for show. By now his blurry vision had cleared.

"She" was sitting at a desk with her back to him, one leg tucked beneath her, a position that hiked her shirt up in the back to reveal a perfect line of vertebral bulges, which carried his vision down to the edge of a black pair of tight, nylon slacks. Just visible above a dipping waistline were two purple lace straps that hung off scrumptious hips and disappeared below. Either the woman didn't know he was there or she was putting on a good show. Eli turned to his tour hostess, but Lisa was gone.

When Eli turned back, the woman was moving, tilting to one side to release her captive leg, pants stretched tight, just enough tension on the purple thong straps to indent her skin.

It was one of those moments again, like the first time he watched Meg Daily at the microscope. But now Meg seemed indistinct, his memory lacking detail. The moment drew longer, then too long. Eli cleared his throat and said, "You have a very nice . . . laboratory." Eli could see now that she was writing and her pen continued to move as though finishing a sentence. Then she pushed back the chair and stood, nearly six feet tall with shoulder-length straight blonde hair. The bottom half of her navel was showing, a crest surrounded by a sea of tanned flesh. She spoke with a foreign accent, Scandinavian. He would further define it to be Swedish after her voice swirled down and vaulted off twin Alpine peaks.

"Hello, Dr. Branch."

The way she said his name, and the dragging out of the *l*'s in hello, made Eli imagine her tongue curled and fluttering along the roof of her mouth.

"My name is Tsarina," she said and extended her hand.

Her eyes were sharp, aqua blue, and indented like a cat's. She held her mouth open just enough for Eli to see the tip of her tongue pressed playfully against her teeth.

"It's so very nice to meet you," Eli said. He noticed a firm grip and an engorged vein that ran the length of her forearm.

She stood in silence and seemed comfortable with it.

Eli's mind raced. *What's next? Stand here and talk about protein chemistry?*

"Let me show you what I'm working on," she said, eventually.

Yeah, show me.

He followed her to the desk. A blueprint-sized scroll of paper held an algorithm sketched in longhand. At the top right-hand corner was the RBI logo and a bold, computer-generated title in the center:

DIVISION OF STEM CELL TECHNOLOGY

Tsarina reached for a gold-plated pen that had rolled to the edge of the desk. When she touched it, however, the pen fell to the floor and rolled under the table.

She knelt on both knees reaching to get the pen, shirt practically up to her neck, the purple straps pulled taut in a magnificent V, a formation of geese in search of warmth.

"Well, I see you found us."

Eli turned to Harvey Stone standing in the doorway. He was dressed in an elegant blended, dark blue suit.

"Sorry I'm late. Had a patch of fog over the Potomac that held us back." He extended his hand to Eli and they shook.

Tsarina was back at the desk straightening her papers.

"I hope you've had a chance to see what we're made of," Stone said, with pride.

Eli nodded. "And then some."

"I was about to show him our plans for the Stem Cell Division," Tsarina said.

Stone put his hand on her shoulder. "We want to be the world's leader in stem cell therapy," he said. "And we're fortunate to have a world-renowned scientist, Dr. Anatolia, leading the effort."

Tsarina smiled. "Thank you, Harvey."

"I'll take Dr. Branch to my office." When he turned away, he let his hand caress her shoulder. "Swing by later and show me the latest from the stem cell meeting in St. Martin."

Eli caught Stone's wink at the end of his invitation.

CHAPTER TWENTY

The cleaning woman found the body at 7:15 A.M. as she was emptying the trash from the laboratory of Eli Branch, M.D. She answered a battery of questions from the police in broken English while she crossed herself and snatched at her rosary beads. Juanita Huerta, age forty-three, had worked in the building for seven years, cleaning the hospital labs, at minimum wage, to support her family of five. She answered these questions for a full hour after she had unlocked the door to the doctor's incubator room. It was an hour of complete hysteria.

With difficulty, the police managed to piece together the sequence of events. When she entered the lab, Juanita emptied the trash receptacles and checked an empty can in Eli's office. The final part of her routine was the incubator room, for which she had a key. Her main job was to remove the thick red plastic bags marked BIOHAZARD. She would gather the bags in a knot at the top, with various pipettes and culture dishes leaking pink liquid media inside.

The door to the incubator room was always closed, a requirement of Infection Control, which conducted semiannual inspections to ensure that specifications were maintained to code. Inside, laminar flow under negative pressure prevented bacteria and viral particles from entering the building's general air circulation.

The two large cell culture hoods glowed fluorescent green from ultraviolet rays that reflected off the surface of stainless steel. A sliding glass frame could be lowered to shield the face and allow only the arms of laboratory personnel to enter the sterilized chamber, like hands selecting vegetables under the glass at a salad bar. Juanita knew not to touch the switches and buttons that controlled this specialized environment. She needed to touch only one light switch, go in quickly, grab the biohazard containers, and leave.

At 7:15 this morning, when she turned on the fluorescent lights, she entered as usual and bent over to collect the bags. That's when she noticed that the incubator door was ajar. Then she saw the pool of coagulated blood on the floor.

The body was stuffed into the culture chamber with the head twisted inward and an arm pinned under the sliding glass. Blood was smeared across the inside glass, grotesquely painted with frantic fingertips before it seeped under the glass and dripped on the floor. Legs were folded back over the head, causing the dress to collect around a pantyless waist.

Juanita did not scream. She dropped the bags of laboratory waste, culture dishes spilling across the floor. She stared at the mangled body, her hands shaking violently, and she crossed herself over and over. Then she fled.

CHAPTER TWENTY-ONE

RBI
9:00 A.M.

"Have a seat, Dr. Branch."

Eli entered the office of RBI's CEO. Twice this week he had been asked to sit in a hot seat. The first time, in his chairman's office, he was all but fired. This time had to be better.

Mallard ducks were mounted on each of the dark-paneled walls. A ten-point buck projected above Stone's desk. Eli expected to find elk, or even a prize kill from an African safari, but all the game were local.

"You're a busy man," Stone began. "I'm busy too, so let's get straight to the point, shall we?"

"I'm all ears," Eli replied. After the security guard ordeal, he decided to remain quiet and offer information only if it proved to his benefit.

To begin his pitch, Stone leaned forward in his chair, arms on his desk and fingers interlaced.

"We lost our chief medical officer a few days ago. Bernard Lankford. He was visiting our new stem cell clinic in the Caribbean. Heart attack. Tragic."

Eli nodded.

"He was a good man. Devoted husband. He and his wife, Fran, had a brand new grandchild, their first. Never saw her. Now I hear the child is very sick. What a terrible time this has been for Fran."

Eli nodded again.

Stone continued. "Bernie had been with me for almost twenty years. We were poised to lead the world in stem cell therapy."

Eli remained silent. He was bursting with a single question. *So what do you want from me?*

Before Eli could ask it, Stone told him. "We want you to be our new chief medical officer."

Eli clenched the muscles in his jaw. But he felt a smile trying to burst free.

"I'm a surgeon," he answered. "Blood-and-guts stuff. You know that, don't you?"

Without looking at any notes, Stone recited Eli's credentials. University of Mississippi, the comparative anatomy fellowship abroad, Alpha Omega Alpha in medical school, Vanderbilt surgical training.

Eli felt like someone being introduced as a frequent public speaker.

"And I talked with your mentor at Vandy, Dr. Dezillion. She said you had one of the most brilliant and intuitive scientific minds she had ever seen."

Eli basked in this compliment. Dr. Dezillion was an international leader in the field and known to be on the short list for the Nobel Prize.

"The board of directors has met. We reviewed several outstanding candidates. A unanimous decision says you're our man."

Eli's mind filled with the possibilities. Flights to New York in the company's Lear. No more Fisher. No crazy lab technician. Tsarina!

And the salary had to be better than his job in academia.

Had to be.

Stone continued the sell. "We need to boost the image of our company, both locally and abroad. You would bring a fresh perspective to RBI, a young, successful surgeon well known in the community."

Eli thought of many meanings of the word successful. His job in the Department of Surgery was in jeopardy. His lab was full of stolen equipment. Almost every penny he earned went to caring for his brother.

Stone leaned back in his chair. Since Eli hadn't said a word, the CEO continued to drive.

"We know exactly what you make. Consider it doubled."

As Eli was calculating the numbers, his beeper went off. Eli had not yet memorized many numbers at the medical center. He knew the OR, the ER. But he immediately recognized the number of Dr. Fisher's office.

"You have a future here, Eli," Stone continued. He could see that Eli was distracted now by the call. He reached in his desk drawer and brought out a small envelope. "And I happen to have two season tickets at Ole Miss, fifty-yard line. Know any Rebel fans?"

Eli held his beeper in front of him but stared at the glossy tickets that Stone had displayed in the shape of a V.

Then his beeper went off again.

It was Fisher's office followed by three numbers that made Eli rise to his feet.

*911

"I need to get this call," Eli said.

Stone had already turned his phone around to face Eli.

"Where the hell are you?" Fisher yelled into the receiver.

Eli carefully considered his answer. "I had to go downtown a minute."

"Get your ass back here, now." Fisher yelled even louder, his voice shaking with anger. "There's police all over your lab. Yellow tape damn near everywhere."

"What do you mean?" Eli said to the steady hum of a dial tone.

Stolen equipment could get me a felony charge. How many years is that?

Eli hung up. "I have to go."

Stone stood and offered Eli his hand. "Think about this, Eli." He pointed to the phone. "Fisher off your back. Permanently."

Stone made a call, ordering the limo to the entrance, then followed Eli into the hall. "One more thing," he said, "we'll move your brother out of that hellhole. You won't have to worry about him anymore."

CHAPTER TWENTY-TWO

Six police cars were parked at the front entrance. Their haphazard arrangement highlighted the urgency of the situation. One officer stood behind the open door of a patrol car and talked into a handheld radio, all the while staring up at a line of second-story windows. He was intense, focused, as if negotiating the release of a hostage.

From his seat in the limousine, Eli was amazed at the scene.

All these police cars to recover some stolen lab equipment? Must be an unusually slow crime day in Memphis.

In addition to the half-dozen police cars, an imposing red truck from the Memphis Fire Department was parked dead center at the entrance to the North building. Next to it sat an ambulance with its back doors open.

An ambulance?

Two firemen placed rescue equipment back into storage bins in their truck. They appeared calm, if not disappointed, with the whole thing.

All heads turned when the black limo pulled to a stop. Eli was thankful for the anonymity provided by the darkened window. He waited for his door to be opened since he could not find an inside handle. A mob of people stood outside as if forced from the building by a fire alarm.

"Here we go," the driver said with an apprehensive shrug. "Good luck to you."

A limo ride to my crime scene. What next?

The crowd parted as Eli approached. Custodians, administrative assistants, and a group of Asian lab techs huddled in a group. Eli recognized three guys from the Finance Department. In ties and white shirts with sleeves rolled up, they were taking advantage of the diversion to smoke.

"Isn't that Branch?" one of them said.

At least one person Eli was glad not to see.

Vera.

She would have been raising all kinds of hell.

Pig cop communists.

Then he realized the probable reason she wasn't there. Already cuffed and down at the station.

With all the commotion, Eli almost missed noticing one other response vehicle. WRUP's media van was parked behind the fire truck, a pole transmitter reaching thirty feet in the air. From the crowd, a handheld microphone was thrust in his face.

"Are you Dr. Eli Branch?"

The female reporter gave a thumbs-up toward the station's vehicle. She was a distractingly gorgeous black woman in a yellow sleeveless blouse that hugged her neck in a plunging V nipped by shoulder-length black hair, an outer strip of blonde framing deep caramel skin. She brushed a hand through her hair to achieve the perfect look.

"We're live at Mid-South Medical Center with Dr. Eli Branch." Camera lights swung to his face, their heat adding insult to a sultry morning.

This was not Eli's first television interview. He had been on CNN in a segment about cancer research and the innovative work at Vanderbilt with MMPs. The interview had been shot locally at the VUStar studios in a very controlled setting. He'd even had a bit of rouge brushed on his cheeks.

"Cancer cells release an enzyme called matrix metalloproteinase that cuts an escape route through normal tissue and allows them to metastasize," he had said.

It was the only line of his entire interview that was aired, but Eli thought it was a damn good one. So did *USA Today*, which carried the story and used the escape route part of his quote for the title.

Before the interview, Eli had been coached on how to stay on story, to pick a single take-home point and emphasize it. Here it comes, Eli thought, looking straight into the bright light. No amount of rouge could help him this time, because he had no idea how much of the theft to admit to.

"Dr. Branch," she said with an expression of forced concern. "Within the past hour, a dead body was found in your laboratory. Did you know the victim?"

In the limo, Eli had prepared a statement for his chairman to explain the stolen items. *I'm sure there's just some misunderstanding. We'll work it out.* When he saw the press, he decided to use the same statement. But this information caught him off guard.

"Excuse me. A body?"

What are you talking about?

"Yes, did you know the victim?"

Eli could not respond. No amount of coaching could have prepared him for this.

Another police car arrived with both sirens and lights going full blast. The camera swung around to catch the live action, and Eli used the distraction to escape. He sprinted toward the entrance to the North Research Building. He could feel the bright camera lights on his back and heard the reporter close the story with, "There is a lot of confusion about what appears to be a homicide on the campus of Mid-South Medical. We'll keep you updated. Reporting live, this is Shontay Williams."

Eli entered through the automatic double doors.

"I wish someone would update *me*," he muttered in the stairwell, then took two-at-a-time steps to his second-floor lab.

At the top of the stairwell, rather than hurdle the strip of yellow tape that blocked the hall, he ducked under it. The hallway was packed with people: police, firemen, and personnel from neighboring labs being interviewed.

The associate vice chancellor of health affairs was there, and at her side the hospital chief of staff. They're trying to save face, Eli thought. Wearing a dark business suit, he hoped he could pass as another administrator.

But none of these sights gut-clenched him more than seeing Karl Fisher giving a statement to the police. His chairman was probably wishing he had never heard the name Eli Branch. Eli pushed his way through the congested hall and made it into his lab without Fisher seeing him. The first thing he noticed was the incubator room cordoned off with yellow crime-scene tape. Two armed policemen stood at each side of the door frame. They stepped forward as Eli approached.

"I'm Branch," he said, looking beyond them at a young man in a white coat dusting the glass of the cell culture hood. "This is my lab."

"ID, please." The second officer spoke into a microphone attached to his lapel and almost immediately two more policemen were standing behind Eli.

For the interview at RBI, Eli had not taken his medical center photo badge, a face shot that showed him smiling, a starched white coat barely visible. He thought the photo looked much too friendly. From his wallet, Eli removed his driver's license and a business card that introduced him as an assistant professor of surgery.

One of the officers took the card, glanced at his partner, then at Eli. "Wait here."

Over the strips of yellow tape, Eli had an unobstructed view into the incubator room now. The young man in the white coat was snapping pictures from just outside the culture hood. Inside the chamber, he could see what looked like a tangled mass of human body. Eli clasped his hands behind his neck and leaned his head back, eyes closed, as if this would make it all go away.

What the hell is going on?

"Dr. Branch?"

Eli turned to see a short, heavyset man, mid-fifties, who looked like he'd just come back from a trip to Hawaii. He wore a short-sleeved shirt adorned with red chili peppers.

Instead of extending a hand, the man removed a notepad and pen from his front pocket, to which a clip-on Memphis Police Department badge was attached. He introduced himself as Detective Lipsky.

"Need to ask you some questions," he said, inserting a series of *r*'s into *r*-less words. He pressed his pen against the pad as though the task of writing might pose a challenge.

Eli started with a set of his own. "Why are all these people in my lab?"

Lipsky looked at his pad, unsure of which one of them voiced the question.

Eli continued. "I walk in with police everywhere and yellow tape and —"

"Okay, slow down." Lipsky's eyes shifted both ways without his head moving. "I'll bring you up to speed," he said and sucked some spit through his front teeth. "Then I'll ask the questions, damn it."

Lipsky referred to his pad. "Call came in at 7:23 A.M. One of the custodial staff. A Mexican lady, hysterical." The detective looked up at Eli. "You know, ayee, ayee, ayee, that whole bit."

Eli did not know. He was fixated on the crime-scene technician. With tweezers, he was delicately removing fibers from a piece of the victim's clothing. As he thought it, the word struck him.

Victim?

In my lab!

"Anyway," Lipsky continued, "when the crew arrived, some of your lab neighbors were here to help, bless their dumb-ass hearts. Prints all over the scene, the whole thing screwed to hell."

"Who is it?" Eli demanded. "Just tell me who the body is."

Lipsky hesitated a second, as though searching his database for the proper procedure. "We have an idea. But this is your turf. You need to ID."

Lipsky placed his hand in the small of Eli's back and nudged him toward the line of yellow tape. "Hey, Basetti," he yelled to the chap in the white coat that reached bare knees above a pair of ankle-high black sneakers.

Basetti looked to be in his early twenties. He sealed a plastic evidence bag with gloved hands as if forensic investigation was a summer job he picked up during college.

"You 'bout finished?" Lipsky looked back at Eli and winked. "Got the scientist dude out here. Can he ID now?"

"Sure. Send him in."

Lipsky peeled back the tape and Eli went straight to the culture hood. He reached for the glass to raise it, but Basetti stopped him.

"If you're going to touch, you need these." He handed Eli a pair of gloves.

CHAPTER TWENTY-THREE

Eli snapped on the latex and thought of Meg. If the body was taken to her autopsy suite, he'd have another chance for a postmortem tango. It was a strange, twisted thought, but at this point, Eli needed a glimmer of hope.

Together, Eli and Basetti raised the glass, and Lipsky watched them from behind. An arm fell forward and released the thin-boned form of a woman's hand. The head was turned inward, with matted, dirty curls of hair the only thing visible. Gradually, as though turning the base of an antique urn, Basetti twisted the head to face them.

She appeared comfortable in death, the hard lines of her face smooth, internal voices finally lifted, the burden of this life, gone.

"You know her?" Lipsky asked with the compassion of a pickax.

A flood of thoughts raced through Eli's mind. The stolen equipment, the racial slurs ingrained in her vocabulary. She may not have been a saint. But she didn't deserve to die. Not like this.

"Yeah, I know her," Eli said with a thick voice. "Her name's Vera Tuck. She was my lab technician. At least for a day or so."

"From the degree of rigor, we think she's been dead three to four hours," Basetti volunteered.

Lipsky did some quick ciphering. "Puts the death at, say—" he studied his watch, "six A.M." He backed up to the door, putting a little distance between them. "Hey Doc, just curious, what was your schedule like early this morning?"

Eli turned to face him.

"What do you mean, my schedule?"

"I mean, where were you this morning around six o'clock?"

Eli realized that this line of questioning was usually reserved for murder suspects. *And I am one of them?*

"At six o'clock, I was at home."

"Where might home be?" Lipsky was finally getting to make use of his little notepad.

"Harbor Town."

Lipsky nodded in approval. "Nice." After a few moments for deep thought, he asked, "So do you normally hang out there until nine or so and then cruise into work in a long black limo?"

Eli was fast losing his patience with this little chili pepper detective. "Look, I'm a surgeon and I also have a research program. I'm a surgeon-scientist."

"And this is what surgi-sciences wear?" Lipsky struggled to pronounce the term. "Tailor-made suits and limo rides. Damn, Basetti, we're in the wrong profession."

They both strained out a few laughs.

Eli looked back at Vera's body.

Why would someone want to kill her? And why cram her into such a small space?

"I met her two days ago. This is only the second time I've seen her."

"Other than at six o'clock this morning, you mean?"

The detective was proud of that one. His notepad shook as he said it.

Lipsky's presence in the doorway was making Eli claustrophobic. He pointed a finger at the detective and said, "Get out of the way; this is ridiculous."

Eli tried to pass but, the officers on guard stepped up to block the door. "Hold on there, Dr. Jekyll," Lipsky said. "Got some more questions for you."

Eli let out a pent-up breath and stepped back.

"How would you describe your relationship with the victim," Lipsky stopped to check his pad, "Vera Tuck?"

"Relationship?"

"Yeah, you two get along okay?"

"Like I said, I hardly knew her." Eli looked back at the woman's face, bluish-gray, globes of her eyes just visible through a squint. "Yes, we got along fine."

"Look doc, these are standard questions I ask at every homicide."

"Homicide?"

"You don't think she climbed in there and offed herself, do you?"

"I don't know. She was definitely peculiar. Had pressured speech, sentences running together. Manic-depressive like."

Lipsky focused on his notepad.

Eli imagined one of those fat kindergarten pencils fitting perfectly in his hand.

"Go on," he said.

"She pushed around this shopping cart and was convinced that religious groups were after her, Baptists, Jews. I don't know."

Lipsky glanced at Basetti who was replacing his tools in a white plastic container. It looked like a fishing tackle box. "Sounds like a real nut wad."

Eli wondered if Lipsky wrote nut wad in his notes as if it was a psychiatric diagnosis.

"Look doc, you seem to know her better than anyone." Lipsky flipped a few pages back. "This is all we got — Vera Tuck, age fifty-one, no address, no family, no nothing." He looked up at Eli. "Anything else you can remember?"

"Yeah, there is. She kept saying Rich Bitch Ink, over and over."

Lipsky looked up. "Come again?"

"I don't know." Eli shrugged and said it again. "Rich Bitch Ink."

Lipsky wrote it down. "Nut wad," he said drawing out the "nut" with an escalating pitch like he was calling pigs.

Standing on tiptoes, Eli scanned the main lab and tried to locate Fisher. The chief was standing in the corner, of all places, fuming. He gave Eli a look that bored right through him.

The more this drags out, the deeper I'll fall, Eli thought. *And I'm dragging the Department of Surgery down with me.*

"How much longer?" Eli asked Lipsky. "I want these people out of my lab."

"One last question," Lipsky said, followed by five seconds of silence just for the effect. He checked the facts in his notes once again. "You were at home, in Harbor Town, you say, until when?"

"Seven o'clock."

"And after that? Between seven and nine?"

"I had a meeting," Eli said. "Downtown."

"Downtown where?" Lipsky mimicked a child's voice, as though they were playing a game.

Eli glanced in the direction of Fisher, but he was gone. "At a company, Regency Biotech."

The detective looked surprised. "Out on the Reef? At RBI?"

"Yeah."

Lipsky shook his head. "Doc, I'd be careful whose bed you lie in."

Eli dismissed this peculiar line from Lipsky. A lot of people assumed that doctors took handouts from pharmaceutical companies.

"So that's whose limo," Basetti added. Lipsky nodded in agreement.

Eli was growing tired of this dog and pony show.

Lipsky winked at Basetti and motioned to his tray of tools, as if this next part had been choreographed as well.

Basetti removed a plastic bag and held it in front of Eli's face. "Do you know what this is?"

Within the bag was a 60-mm culture dish, standard supply in all molecular-based laboratories. The liquid media had leaked out and looked like pink lemonade poured in a baggie. Eli could see a thin, opaque layer on the bottom of the dish. He knew exactly where the dish had come from and reached out to grab it.

Basetti pulled it back quickly.

"Finders keepers."

"That's very important to my lab," Eli said, pointing to the cells floating in a nonsterile baggie. "Why did you take them out of the incubator?"

"Hold on there, Jekyll," Lipsky said. "Go ahead, tell him, Basetti."

Basetti motioned to the culture hood. He tugged on Vera's elbow until her hand flopped into view, a balled, white-knuckled fist, even in death.

"See this hand?" he asked Eli. "Had to pry that little dish from it. She was holding it so tight that she cracked the top of the glass." Basetti turned the bag so that Eli could see the star-shaped crack.

Immediately, Eli took two steps toward the incubator and opened it before Basetti could stop him. All the other plates of cells were gone.

"I need those cells," Eli said as he pointed at what was now evidence in a murder investigation.

"Yeah," Lipsky sneered. "I bet you do."

The week before he finished his surgical residency at Vanderbilt, Eli met with his mentor, Dr. Dezillion, to outline his plans to become a principal investigator of his own laboratory. His only hope for success was to take the MMP cells with him and continue the line of cancer research.

Even though Eli had performed all the work in establishing the cell line, the cells remained the intellectual and physical property of the Dezillion lab. Eli asked for permission to study the cells and promised to keep her involved in his findings, a scientific collaboration that could be beneficial to them both. Dr. Dezillion agreed and even gave Eli a going away party in her Belle Meade home.

Rather than carry the cells to Memphis in his car and risk damage or infection, Eli had them transported in a special biohazard package by express courier to the laboratory of Dr. Benjamin Plank. Ben was a classmate from medical school who had stayed on as faculty at the University of the Mid-South to start his own laboratory.

Ben had kept the cells in his lab and followed the culture protocols that Eli had sent him. The day Eli received the key to his lab, they transferred ten plates of cells into Eli's incubator. The incubator in which only one of the ten plates now remained. And that plate was upside down in a Baggie held by a college kid in shorts and sneakers.

"You've got to put them back in the incubator," Eli told them. "The cells will die."

"What are you talking about, cells?"

"You know, cells. That make up the human body."

Lipsky pointed at Vera's corpse. "Her body?"

Eli rolled his eyes. A discussion with Lipsky on cellular biology would go nowhere, fast.

"No, not her body. Anybody's body."

"Anybody's body?"

Eli was certain this was the most absurd conversation he had ever been a part of. During his senior year at Ole Miss, after he had been accepted to medical school and was just riding out the year, Eli visited public elementary schools in Oxford. He talked to the kids about science and biology, stimulating their interest in the health-related professions. Eli looked at Lipsky, trying to write on his notepad. The third graders had caught on faster.

"Now, about those body cells —"

Eli stopped him in mid-sentence. "I told you, damn it. Someone has stolen the cells."

Lipsky glanced at Basetti. "Dr. Hyde seems to be more upset about his precious cells than the sardine-stuffed dead woman that just happens to be ten feet from his office!" As Lipsky finished the sentence, he was all but shouting. But both of them were distracted by a thick hand that reached past Lipsky and came to rest on Eli's shoulder.

"Dr. Branch."

Fisher.

Perfect timing.

"I need to talk with my colleague, gentleman," Fisher said, addressing Lipsky and Basetti. "If you'll excuse us."

Fisher's presence was dominating. Bull shoulders rolled forward, ready to charge. Lipsky had probably had enough anyway.

"Okay, Doc, we'll be back in touch." He flipped his right hand forward in some made-up high-society gesture. "You fine sirs have a nice day."

Awkwardly, Eli tried to follow Fisher, but he had to squeeze by the detective in the doorway. Lipsky leaned forward to Eli's ear. "Don't leave town for a few days. Hear me, doc?"

As if finding his only employee murdered in his lab were not enough, with the Memphis police force and media now on his trail, the thought of Karl Fisher on the attack was unbearable.

Of all the mornings to sneak across town for a job interview, I had to choose this one.

He followed Fisher through the crowded laboratory into the hallway. Most of the employees had returned to their respective labs. Fisher turned to face Eli, a bull ready to charge.

"Where the hell were you?"

Fisher would have checked the OR schedule to see if Eli had an operation scheduled. His clinic patients had been canceled. There was only one other place he should have been.

In his lab.

Eli could not think of an adequate excuse, and Fisher did not give him a chance to come up with one.

"A little heads up for you, Branch." His face was bright red and swollen, saliva pooled in the corner of his mouth. He thrust a fat finger in Eli's face and it popped him on the end of the nose. "I don't like it when the police interrupt my morning coffee!"

He was shaking mad, a pent-up cauldron that had boiled over while he waited for Eli to be questioned.

"Do you understand?"

Through the doorway, he waved his finger at the crime-scene investigation, as though giving a decree. "Now, clear this shit out. Hear me?"

Eli looked back at the lab with the police procedures still in full swing. *I'll just say shoo and maybe they'll all run away.*

Fisher was already walking toward the elevator. Without looking back, he said, "I expect you in my office before the end of the day."

CHAPTER TWENTY-FOUR

When Eli arrived, the body had been left waiting almost twenty-four hours. After Meg's description on the phone, he was unsure if "a pattern in the deaths" was what he wanted to find. He entered the autopsy suite and was relieved when the doors closed behind him. Over the course of the morning, he had been offered a lucrative position in a leading biotech firm, then questioned as a murder suspect. Eli was glad to see Ms. Conch sitting behind her desk, a wide grin beneath horn-rimmed glasses.

"Look what the cat dragged in."

"Nice to see you too, Ms. Conch."

"What's going on over there in your lab?" She tilted her head and looked at him sideways, completely entertained. "They say it's some kind of sex ring-murder tryst."

The comment caught Eli off guard and he let out a much needed laugh. If there was one thing he could deny, unequivocally, it was proximity to sexual relations of any kind.

"I hate to disappoint you, but it's not quite that interesting."

"Don't hold out on me now," she said. "Gets sort of dead down here, you know?" She started to laugh at her pun, but it came out in a jiggle-bounced burp. "Excuse me," she said, the back of her hand placed against her lips like a debutante.

"Dr. Daily called me," Eli said and pointed his way out of the conversation.

"I know. Go on back."

Eli walked past an empty body cart and Ms. Conch's desk at a more cautious distance than usual. *I've got to find another way into this place.*

"Call me if anything juicy happens."

Eli gave her an odd look.

"You know," she said with a wink, "over in your lab."

Meg was deep into the procedure, both hands beneath the lungs as she made the final cut of her thoracic evisceration.

"Sorry I'm late," Eli said. "Got held up in my lab."

Either Meg was unaware of what had happened, or she chose not to bring it up. Eli was glad not to talk about it.

"What did you find?" he asked.

Meg continued the dissection. "This poor fellow was found under an overpass. Probably heat exhaustion." She pointed with a pair of Mayo scissors. "Your guy is over there."

On a gurney against the wall, a white sheet was draped over another hefty lump of body. Eli peeled back the sheet to reveal an older male. The breastplate had been replaced but the abdominal incision remained open.

"Recognize him?"

Eli hadn't really looked at the face. "No, should I?"

"Name's Lankford," Meg said. "Supposedly, he was a scientist at RBI."

"Bernie Lankford," Eli said in a whisper.

"What?"

Eli stared at the man he was being hired to replace. "I thought he died on a trip, Caribbean somewhere."

Meg was weighing the heart and lungs. "St. Martin. There on business. Embryonic stem cell meeting."

He must have been in charge of the stem cell division, before Tsarina, Eli thought. "So how did he end up here?"

"They didn't want the body there. Got a call from a Dr. Francisco, ER physician. Said there was something odd about his death, like he suspected foul play. Begged me to take the body, so here he is."

"And?"

Meg snapped off her gloves and faced Eli. "Like your friend Gaston. Aneurysm repaired with same kind of graft. Identical."

"An RBI endovascular graft?"

"Yes. And the aorta was blown out around it."

Eli looked again at the body. "I have a feeling there's more."

Meg went to the microscope. "Oh yeah." She focused the scope and turned on the arrow. "Most of the cells are endothelial, as you might expect, ingrowth of vascular cells trying to coat the new lumen." She rotated the knobs again for a more precise location. "Here they are."

Eli recognized the cells immediately. Their cuboidal shape, dense granules in the cytoplasm, and the way they rounded up when in contact with a neighboring cell. The same cells he had worked two years to produce and had brought with him to Memphis. He looked at Meg as if she had the answer. "How did those cells get there?"

"I was hoping you could tell me," she said, back at the microscope again. After locating the spot, she motioned for him. "There's a third population of cells this time."

Intermixed with the MMP cells were smaller, bizarre-looking cells. They weren't endothelial cells from the native aorta, but the same dense, packed granules were present.

"What are they?" Eli asked.

"You're not going to believe me."

Eli looked up from the microscope.

"They're embryonic stem cells."

He examined the cells again as though he might recognize them with another look.

"I stained them for embryonic markers. They're all positive."

"But how? How could they get here?"

"The same way the MMP cells got here, I guess."

"And how's that?" Eli asked.

Meg walked over to the white board above her desk and removed a blue marker.

"First we had your friend." She wrote the name Gaston. "We found MMP-producing cells in his ruptured aorta." She drew an arrow down and wrote MMP cells. "Now this fellow." She put Lankford's name at the top of the board, parallel to Gaston. "Death from the same cause, ruptured aorta." She drew a line down to MMP. "Same cells but now mixed in with embryonic stem cells." She wrote ESC as an abbreviation.

"Bizarre," Eli said.

"Dr. Francisco gave me some more information. At the time, it didn't make sense."

"What?"

Meg removed a piece of paper from her desk. "Lankford's wife said that her husband had his graft checked the morning he died."

"Checked?"

"Some kind of interventional radiology procedure, under fluoroscopy."

Eli thought about the natural history of endovascular grafts. A significant number required a catheter-based intervention to correct an abnormal placement or migration.

Meg continued. "Mrs. Lankford said the procedure was done by the same surgeon that placed his aortic graft, a Dr. . . ." She hesitated as she searched her notes for the name. "Korinsky."

Eli shot her a look.

"You know him?" Meg asked.

"Yeah, I know him." Eli looked at the diagram on the board. "You think these cells could have been introduced during Korinsky's procedure?"

Meg hunched her shoulders, pulling her scrub shirt tight against her chest. "You got a better idea?"

Eli looked again through the microscope. "The endothelial cells, are they endogenous or exogenous?

"What do you mean?"

"The cells don't look incorporated like normal ingrowth cells. They're scattered in patches."

Meg bumped Eli out of the way with her hip. "Okay, I'll give it to you — patches." She faced Eli again. "What would be the purpose of injecting endothelial cells?"

"To speed up the engrafting process."

Meg looked at him with both eyebrows raised.

"Consider this," Eli said. "There are hundreds and hundreds of people walking around with these aortic grafts. What if you were the manufacturer and all of a sudden they started to blow?"

"You'd do anything to stop it."

Meg went back to the board and drew a straight line between Gaston's name and Lankford's. She put a question mark below the line. "There has to be a connection."

Eli stood in front of the board and studied the diagram. He took the marker from Meg and wrote, on top of the line in capital letters: RBI.

Korinsky had just returned to his office when his secretary informed him, "A Mr. Harvey Stone called. Said it was urgent."

He took the sticky note with the phone number on it and sat at his desk. He had finished a busy day in the Gates Memorial Endovascular Clinic and needed to dictate his procedure notes. Each of the clinic patients had had an AortaFix graft placed within the past three months. Two of the company's devices had already failed, both with fatal results. For Korinsky, there was plenty of incentive to protect RBI's AortaFix device. The money that he was paid for using it in his patients made his academic salary seem like servant's pay. Frantically, Korinsky was trying to salvage the grafts that might be in jeopardy.

He performed the procedures under X-ray guidance, snaking the catheter through an artery in the left groin and up to the site of the aortic vascular graft. When the tip lay within the AortaFix device, Korinksy injected endothelial cells through the catheter, the same cells that form the natural lining of the human aorta. But these cells had been engineered at RBI, by Tsarina, to attach to the device, thereby sealing it in place to prevent graft migration and device failure. If it worked, the procedure would be the latest advance in endoluminal therapy, making Korinsky the top endovascular surgeon in the country. And when RBI obtained the patent and marketed the technique, the financial windfall would be staggering.

He stared at the note, fully aware that a call from Stone was more pressing than any medical dictation. Korinsky dialed the number, connecting after the first ring.

"I said to rock his world a bit, not kill his lab tech."

"Afternoon to you too, Harvey. Now, what the hell are you talking about?"

"Don't play dumb with me, Korinsky. That was a stupid move. We don't need the police on our ass."

"Either you tell me or I'm hanging up."

"At Branch's lab this morning." Stone hesitated. "The woman — murdered."

Korinsky remained silent. From the endovascular clinic, he had heard the sirens earlier that morning, had seen police cars outside Medical Center North, but he hadn't known it was a crime scene.

Stone was catching onto this fact. "You had nothing to do with it?"

"No, I swear."

"Who else is after Branch then?"

Korinsky thought a moment. "I don't know, but this could be good for us. Another reason for our nosy surgeon to leave the medical center and quit snooping around the autopsy room."

CHAPTER TWENTY-FIVE

Eli sat in a straight-backed chair and faced his chairman for the second time in three days. Fisher wasted no time.

"I've been chairman for over a decade."

Eli could feel the lecture coming.

"I have built the careers of more young surgeons than I care to remember. You were selected to be the next, Branch. Remember, I am the one who determines your future."

He gave that familiar hesitation, a father disappointed in his son.

"It's really not too hard. You show up, do some cases, take care of patients, and publish some research."

Fisher said this as if he was the manager of a fast-food joint instructing a new hire on how to slap a burger together.

"I run a department of over two hundred employees. All of them want more space, more time, more money."

He hesitated before the punch line.

"And you're more of a pain in the ass than all of them put together."

Eli had to admit, it was a very effective line.

"Why is that, Branch? Can you tell me why that is?"

He thought a moment but had no explanation. The case with Korinsky, Vera's death in his lab. A few weeks ago he was the hot new recruit. Now he was the subject of a criminal investigation and the lead story on the local news.

"I don't really know."

"Where were you this morning? You weren't in the OR, you don't have a clinic anymore. The only place you need to be is in your lab."

Eli knew it was time to shoot straight. Fisher probably already knew anyway.

"I was downtown."

"Downtown? While I was talking to police and trying to cover your ass, you were downtown?"

As Eli thought of his next response, his beeper went off and he quickly silenced it without looking at the number.

Fisher continued in a sarcastic romp. "A little sightseeing? Beale Street? Hey, I hear Graceland's real pretty this time of year. You should check it out."

"Not really downtown," Eli admitted. "I was invited to visit a company."

"What company?"

"RBI."

At this, Fisher stood and turned to face the bookcase behind him.

Eli's beeper screeched again and he checked the number. It was the emergency room. With everything else, he had forgotten that he was on trauma call starting at five o'clock. He checked his watch. *5:01. Of course.*

"Dr. Fisher, it's the ER."

"Sure, go ahead and answer it. I'm just here for you. I've nothing else to do."

Eli punched the number into his cell phone and walked to the back of the office, as far as he could get from the heat radiating off Fisher.

"Dr. Branch, Department of Surgery," he said with an artificial layer of authority, "returning a page."

It was Landers.

"Dr. Branch, your chief resident wanted me to call you."

"Sure, what we got?"

"Young male in motorcycle crash. No helmet. Sounds bad."

"How far out?"

"Five minutes, maybe less."

"All right, get the team ready. I'll be there."

Eli closed his phone. He did not sit down.

From the shelf, Fisher picked up a crystal globe the size of a softball and slowly turned it in his hands. He continued as though he hadn't heard a thing. "RBI, huh. In cahoots with the drug companies, are we?"

"No sir. Just thought there was room for collaboration." Eli was making this up. He knew of Fisher's disdain for the pharmaceutical industry and the conflict of interest it could create for an academic department.

"Our labs aren't good enough for you?"

"I'm not sure I have a lab anymore."

At this, Fisher swung around and pitched the globe toward Eli. He caught it just before it hit the floor.

"What you don't have anymore is a job," he screamed. "Finish the week and you're gone."

CHAPTER TWENTY-SIX

The word "bad" grossly underestimated the extent of injuries. Sixteen-year-old male, high speed into a bridge abutment. Witnesses said he flipped airborne and skidded twenty yards on the pavement.

No helmet.

The patient was intubated at the scene and transported by helicopter from an exchange off I-55 near the Mississippi border. When Eli arrived in the trauma bay, the surgery residents were lifting the boy off the stretcher. A dozen people filled the trauma room, including the paramedics who were still giving report.

"The guy did nothing when we got there. A few agonal breaths, didn't move a thing."

Dr. Susan Morris, the chief surgical resident, stood at the head of the table in a yellow protective gown, looking like most of the team, eyes above masks protected by plastic shields. Susan's tall, athletic build gave a commanding presence in the trauma room. A good chief could direct the resuscitation without much help from an attending surgeon.

Eli took a position at the foot of the table, a foreman to oversee the work. He tried to prepare himself mentally for the role. As an academic surgeon, he needed to switch quickly from the scientific method, with perfect controls and experimental groups, to complex management of critically ill patients, always taking time to teach students and residents. This time, Eli had to make the necessary adjustment in the shadow of a murder in which he was suspect, and in a hospital from which he had been fired.

At the head of the table, Susan jammed a Yankaur sucker into the boy's blood-filled mouth and the suction tubing gurgled. Trauma resuscitations were brief but intense events during which multiple procedures occurred simultaneously. Needles and even scalpels were often wielded by inexperienced team members. The risk of needle sticks and blood exposure to medical personnel was high. And patients with penetrating injuries, especially gunshots and stabbings, were often those who carried infectious blood, such as drug users and gang members.

Eli gave an affirmative nod to Landers, who held a syringe with a large-bore needle for femoral artery puncture. *Just don't stick yourself again.* Eli watched as Landers submerged the syringe into the patient's groin with immediate return of pulsatile flow into the chamber.

"Tube's in place," the chief resident confirmed as she withdrew the laryngeal blade. She flicked a penlight across each pupil. "Fixed and dilated."

The respiratory therapist rhythmically squeezed air into the patient's lungs.

"Hyperventilate with forty breaths per minute," Susan told the therapist.

Eli hoped that Susan Morris represented the quality of all the residents in the program. She appeared in command of the situation.

Eighteen-gauge IVs were placed in both arms and heated fluid was infused under pressure. A digital clock on the wall recorded elapsed time since arrival.

Two minutes forty-five seconds.

A male nurse slid trauma shears up the leg of the boy's jeans and through the crotch and easily separated the zipper. The sheers could cut a quarter in half. One snip later, the underwear was off and a stench filled the room.

"No rectal tone," the third-year resident announced as he withdrew a gloved finger smeared with stool.

Everyone in the room knew that this was a bad sign; loss of sphincter tone was indicative of neurologic devastation.

"His belly blew up like a toad in route," the head paramedic said, continuing his report. A Foley catheter was threaded into his penis and returned bloody urine.

The boy was tall and slender, maybe 140 pounds. His left collarbone was broken and trying to poke through the skin at the base of the protective C-collar around his neck. An oozing raw swath across his chest looked as if it had been buffed with a sander. But below his ribs, his abdomen jutted out like a plump watermelon.

"And it's not air," Susan said as she percussed the abdomen with a dull thump by tapping her fingers along the distended surface.

The trauma nurse knocked the stethoscope from her ears and ripped open the Velcro blood pressure cuff.

"Pressure's sixty-five."

"Ringer's Lactate wide open," Susan said. "Two liters almost in."

Eli looked at the charge nurse, held up two fingers, and mouthed "O negative."

The patient had telltale signs of hypotensive shock, both low blood pressure and rapid heart rate. His pulse was 148, an expected compensatory response in a healthy youngster who could sustain a supraphysiologic heart rate to make up for a vastly diminished blood volume.

Eli felt Landers brush against his coat.

The teachable moment.

"Why is he in shock, Landers?"

"Blood loss, sir," Landers said immediately. "Hypotensive shock."

"Good," Eli said. "Where is his blood loss?"

Landers pointed to the boy's abdomen. "It's in his belly, Dr. Branch."

Eli knew that in minutes they would be in the patient's abdomen through an emergent laparotomy. Likely a fractured spleen. Maybe his liver. The only way to maintain his blood pressure until they were in the OR would be by replacing lost blood with universal donor O negative. They could not afford waiting for results from the type and cross testing and would have to risk transfusing nontype-specific blood.

Even if they could repair his abdominal injuries, the extent of brain damage would determine the patient's outcome, what function he could hope for, if his life would be confined to a bed. A head CT scan was needed to assess for intracranial blood, but the boy was too unstable and would likely bleed out in the scanner before he ever got to the OR.

Susan pushed a portable ultrasound machine to the gurney as a nurse squirted blobs of lubricating gel into the patient's navel. As Susan moved the probe over the upper abdomen, she called out the results from snowy shadows on the screen.

"Blood all around his liver and spleen," she said so the entire room could hear.

Eli was watching his chief resident. If Susan didn't make the call to go to the OR, he would have to tell her. They made eye contact and Susan raised her index finger and pointed at the ceiling. Eli nodded.

"Okay people, we're taking him up to the OR. Pack it up. Respiratory, you bag him on the way. Landers, go get an elevator."

For a brief moment nobody moved, as if they were trying to assimilate the chaos before them. This young man had sustained life-threatening injuries. If he made it, would he have any brain function, any quality of life? It didn't take long on a trauma service to witness one of these tragedies. A young person is injured, survives, gets a tracheostomy and feeding tube, only to be transferred from the hospital to a rehab facility for weeks, months, maybe forever.

Above these concerns grew the unnerving sense that comes with namelessness. Who was this boy? Where was his family?

The chief resident sensed the immobility. "We've got to move, people."

Eli grabbed the elbow of the charge nurse as she rushed by. "Check his pants."

She picked up the crumpled pair of jeans from the corner and removed a thin black wallet. A couple of credit cards, a hundred dollar bill and five twenties, and a driver's license. The nurse glanced at the boy's face, then back at the license before handing it to Eli. The handsome, boyish face on the license could not be recognized in the blood-speckled rash of scrapes and cuts, lips swollen and blue.

With eyes flashing alarm the nurse said, "Do you know who this is?"

Eli read off the name. "Scott Tynes?" Then he found the date of birth. "He's sixteen."

Everyone in the room stopped and looked at Eli.

One of the paramedics had lingered at the door to watch the resuscitation.

"Yeah, this is Roger Tynes son," he said, as though he had known all along. "Damn, thought you knew that."

"As in Tynes Freight and Air?" another nurse asked.

The paramedic motioned through the glass doors to the loading ramp. "Why do you think the TV crew is swarming?"

Out in the circular drive, a cameraman focused on a reporter holding a microphone to her face. The trauma team clung to the stretcher like pallbearers, as they rushed Scott Tynes out of the trauma room in a sprint toward the OR elevators.

As Eli followed, he looked out the glass doors at the reporter and recognized her immediately.

"Here we go again," Eli said under his breath.

"Take two."

CHAPTER TWENTY-SEVEN

The boy lay naked on the operating room table, arms extended to his side at right angles, as though crucified. Lubricant had been applied to his eyes and they were taped shut. Hidden beneath the tape was the most telling prognostic sign — pupils fixed and dilated.

The circulating nurse painted his abdomen with deep brown swipes of Betadine, which turned yellow as it dried and desiccated bacteria on the skin. Intravenous lines pumped fluid and blood into veins at the inside bend of both elbows. The anesthesiologist stood poised at the left wrist inserting a radial artery catheter to monitor continually intraoperative blood pressure. Two nurses were stacking units of blood in a cooler, calling out identification numbers as they worked.

A breathing tube projected from Tynes's mouth secured with wide swaths of tape that pulled against the boy's denuded, swollen cheeks. Overhead monitors beeped rapidly. A yellow tube sprouted from his penis and drained red urine into a bag hanging below the table.

Eli watched a single number, the systolic blood pressure, transduced in real time from the arterial line — sixty-four, then sixty-one, down to fifty-seven.

The third and fourth units of blood had been transfused. But Eli knew that this blood would circulate through the heart only once before spilling out of damaged organs into the free space of Scott Tynes's abdomen.

Already gowned and gloved, Eli stood with folded hands and lowered his head for a moment, eyes closed. Even in the most emergent situation, he made time for this plea, however brief. Then he looked at Landers, who was watching him across the table.

Eli remembered his first surgical role model when he was an intern. The older man was so skilled in his craft that his movements appeared effortless. He would take charge of a room just by entering it. Yet, he brought a gentle bedside presence to each of his patients. Eli knew that Landers was looking to him for that modeling, whether he wanted to provide it or not. It was a responsibility that Eli found both empowering and intimidating.

"Okay, that's enough," Eli said to the nurse who methodically, and by protocol, painted the cleansing Betadine solution, strip by strip. "Towels."

In concert, Eli and Susan draped off the operative field with square blue towels leaving only the protuberant, blood-filled abdomen before them. The anesthesiologist had dropped the table to the lowest level, and yet Tynes's abdomen ballooned up to the level of Eli's chest.

"Ten blade," Eli instructed, and the scrub nurse presented the scalpel to Eli, handle first.

To everyone's surprise, Eli motioned for the scalpel to go to Landers. "Cut him."

With eyes wide, Landers looked at Eli and hesitated as though to give him time to reconsider. "That old man's blood tests are back," he said, referring to Gaston.

Eli couldn't ignore this, although the timing was awful. "And?"

"He was HIV-positive."

Eli tried to hide his surprise. "I'm sorry, Landers. Have you started the pills?"

"Yeah, triple therapy."

Eli nodded and placed one finger on Tynes's sternum, another on the boy's pubis. He looked at Landers. "Can you do this?"

Landers took the knife.

"Into the deep sub-Q," Eli instructed the intern. "From here to here."

Landers placed the scalpel against the skin just below the breastbone and cut a straight line with a gentle curve around the belly button. Rather than spurting bright red, the subcutaneous bleeders oozed a dark mixture of deoxygenated blood. Landers handed the knife back to the scrub nurse.

As soon as the scalpel was out of his hands, Susan nudged him toward the foot of the table. "Don't get carried away, big guy. You're holding a retractor from here out."

Imagining a compressed abdominal clot that had kept the boy from bleeding to death, Eli told the anesthesiologist, "I suspect he has some degree of tamponade. When we release the dam, he'll bottom out."

As he said this, Susan incised the tough fascial lining that held the pressurized abdominal contents. The thin peritoneal lining bulged with a purple dome and then erupted, blowing partially congealed blood up and over the sides of the abdomen like oil from a newly tapped well.

The scrub nurse was ready with a large basin and Eli and Susan used cupped hands and lap pads to evacuate the blood. In the center, fresh arterial blood mixed and swirled with darker heme to form a deeply toned mosaic.

"Get me some more blood!" the anesthesiologist yelled.

Eli glanced at the monitor. The pressure of fifty-seven had been replaced with a big, red zero.

"Pack him," Eli said.

One by one, Eli and Susan submerged thick absorbent towels into the abdomen like a load of clothes into a washing machine.

"Damage control," Eli said, referring to a series of maneuvers to control bleeding by packing towels around the lacerated organs, resuscitating the patient in the ICU, and returning to the OR twenty-four to forty-eight hours later to remove the packs and repair the injuries.

A good plan if the patient survives the first few hours.

After packing the cavity with towels, many of which had to be replaced as they floated out on hemorrhagic waves, Eli and Susan pressed hard against the abdominal wall as if packing overstuffed luggage, paradoxically recreating the tamponade they had so effectively released.

It worked. At least temporarily. Scott Tynes's blood pressure increased to fifty-one. Still life-threateningly low, but at least his heart had started pumping again.

"Let me catch up," the anesthesiologist demanded as he hung another unit of blood along with components to replace diluted clotting factors.

Eli looked at Susan. Both were breathing hard as if they had held their breath for the last five minutes.

"You know his brain is squash," Susan said. She was referring to her neuro exam when the patient arrived. On the Glascow coma score, any number less than eight predicted a negligible chance at recovery. "He had no eye opening, no verbal response, but he withdrew to pain," she said. "That makes his Glascow a six."

It was tempting to become fatalistic in this situation, saving a body only to support a devastated brain. But even the best set of predictors could be wrong. *Especially in this sixteen-year-old with a full life ahead.* It was times like this that Eli had to believe that hovering above their tired, blood-stained hands, an infinite force held the destiny of Scott Tynes. And it was Eli's responsibility to keep the team moving toward that destiny, whatever it might be.

"We're going to take out his spleen, pack his liver, and get him to the ICU," Eli told Susan. "You with me?"

To pull off an operative feat like this, Eli needed unflappable cooperation from the entire team. He conversed briefly with the anesthesiologist about the plan, then glanced at Landers. It was during a very similar life-or-death trauma case that Eli had decided, as a medical student, to become a surgeon.

Landers looked scared but excited.

"This is what it's all about," Eli said.

With a quick nod, Landers confirmed his allegiance.

Susan said, "Let's do it."

The next seven minutes was a combination of surgical finesse and brute force. The spleen lay in the left upper abdomen like a cracked sponge submerged in a tub. The splenic artery pumped blood into the organ and it spouted like a broken water main. Recalling the anatomy from hundreds of cases before, Eli navigated into the left upper quadrant as though on automatic pilot, blind hands moving in a crimson sea.

Eli found the spleen's vascular inflow and clamped across both artery and vein. Susan pulled out two large chunks of pulverized spleen and dropped them into a metal basin that Landers held for this purpose. But the space previously occupied by the spleen now filled with blood that spilled from the cracked liver.

The anesthesiologist looked over the drapes. "I've given nineteen units of packed cells and his pressure's barely holding."

They had replaced practically the boy's entire blood volume. Eli pointed to the cut edge of Tynes's skin and subcutaneous tissue. Small vessels that would normally have constricted with clot were open and oozing freely.

"Give him platelets and fresh frozen plasma," Eli told the anesthesiologist. "And start packing him for the ICU."

Eli placed his hand over the smooth surface of the liver, but then, as though slipping from the edge of a cliff, his hand plunged into the center of the right hepatic lobe through a crack that had split the organ in half. It would be impossible to repair the laceration and, unlike the spleen, the liver was essential to life.

They placed sponge packs into the cracked organ, counting each one that would be removed in reverse order two days later. The first dozen pads were as effective as Kleenex to mop up a flooded basement. But the second dozen began to compress the open venous channels, and a modicum of hemorrhagic control was achieved.

"Excuse me, Dr. Branch," the circulating nurse said, interrupting the closure. "There's a phone call for you."

"Take a message, please. I can't talk now."

They continued to close Scott Tynes's abdomen, pulling the abdominal wall over loops of swollen bowel. Eli forgot the phone call.

"Dr. Branch?"

Eli could sense the hesitation in her voice.

"You won't believe who's on the phone."

A bad time for another interruption.

"Who? Who is it?"

"A reporter from Channel Four news. She wants to know the condition of Mr. Tynes."

The phone lines to each operating room were private, to be used only by operating room personnel for the care of patients. If someone asked the hospital operator for the OR, they would be questioned for identity, then forwarded to the front desk. Even a call from family or friends would not make it into the operating room unless there was an emergency. Certainly, never a call from the press.

"You're kidding." Eli said.

The nurse shook her head and blocked the receiver with her hand. "It's Shontay Williams, from Channel Four. Says she knows you?"

"This is way out of line," Eli blurted. "I've not even had the chance to tell this boy's family." Eli thrust his hand down as if he was hanging up the phone. "Just hang up. Do it."

The nurse hesitated and pointed to the phone.

"But it's . . ."

"Hold this." Eli handed the needle driver to Landers. With a bloody glove, he grabbed the receiver from the nurse, and slammed it on the hook.

CHAPTER TWENTY-EIGHT

The Mid-South Forensics Laboratory occupied an abandoned warehouse on the north end of Third Street. From outside, it looked like a concrete fortress, with steel bars reinforcing the windows and doors. But what it lacked in outward charm was more than compensated for by an elaborate diagnostic facility on its second and third floors. In an effort to combat the region's surplus of violent crimes, a tristate commission from Mississippi, Arkansas, and Tennessee appropriated generous funds to acquire state-of-the-art forensic equipment and technology from DNA testing to entomologic analysis and ballistics. At the completion of the spending spree, Mid-South was way over budget. No funds were left to support the laboratory personnel. After the lab director resigned, only one person was left behind to handle all the work.

Basetti pushed back in a reclining office chair and stared at his new title: Interim Director of Forensic Investigation. He didn't care that it was written on a wide piece of bandage tape and stuck to his coat. He still thought it was cooler than hell.

Since he was the lab's only occupant, he was free to choose both the musical selection and the lighting. Nine Inch Nails tested the capacity of two desk PC speakers, and eerie light from a black lamp reflected off police tape strung from the ceiling like an orb spider's web.

But tonight, there was work to do in the form of a single plate of cultured cells that Basetti had removed from the facility's incubator and placed on the bench top. He had already analyzed what little trace evidence was found at the Branch Laboratory crime scene, as it was now officially called. A sample of foreign DNA found on Vera Tuck's body was being amplified by PCR, with the final results still a day or two away. These were all standard procedural skills that the interim director had acquired during a summer lab internship at the medical school. A year later, while obtaining his degree in forensic science, he learned how to apply these skills to actual criminal investigation.

But what the hell am I supposed to do with a dish of human cells? Basetti wondered.

The cells had been obtained as the primary evidence at the crime scene, pried from the hand of the victim exactly nine hours earlier. Now it was up to Basetti to figure out why they were worth killing for.

He slid the cells under the microscope. At 10X view, the cuboidal cells formed a monolayer, all snuggled together in colonies. "Well, how cute," Basetti said. To magnify the view, he changed the lens to 40X. But he flipped the wrong switch and activated the fluorescence microscope.

"Whoa!" A green glow emanated from the dish. He focused on individual cells, each shape sharply outlined by a flash of fluorescent green pigment.

At the top of the staircase, Detective Frank Lipsky rattled the door of the second-floor laboratory. Loud music pulsed through the wood as if from a freshman dorm. Lipsky removed a ring of keys from his pocket, selected the one he thought would work, and entered the lab.

He stopped to let his eyes adjust to the darkness. Basetti was seated at the microscope, his back to him. Lipsky tiptoed around the central desk, past a set of upright freezers.

"What you looking at?"

The desk, the scope, and Basetti's body shook with deep riveting jolts. The interim director had half-climbed onto the table when he turned around.

"Damn, can't you knock?"

"I could've come in on a bulldozer and you would've never heard it. Turn that shit down."

Basetti reached for the speaker. "I swear, trying to get some work done and you pull something like this."

Lipsky raised himself up and sat on the bench. "Figured I'd find your nose in some girly magazine."

Basetti gave him a disgusted look and pointed to his taped-on name tag.

"Oh, I forgot, Mr. Forensic Directorship," Lipsky mocked. "You're so above that now."

Basetti was back at the scope, his full attention on the cells.

Lipksy admired the yellow tape streamers along the ceiling. "Like what you've done with the place, Martha."

The technician-turned-director remained silent.

"Can you at least turn on some lights? This place creeps me out."

"Take a look at these cells first," Basetti said.

"Cells?"

"What we took off that old lady in the doc's lab."

Lispky bent over the scope. He misjudged the distance and banged his nose on the view piece. After a series of expletives, he said, "Are they frog cells?"

"What?"

"I said, are they frog cells?"

"What the hell are you talking about?"

"They're green, aren't they?" Lipsky said proudly. "I cut open a frog or two in science class myself."

Basetti shook his head. "I bet you then dipped them in batter and fried 'em up."

"Matter of fact I did, asshole."

Basetti stared at him. "Stick to firearms, will you. This is my territory."

The detective formed his hand like a gun and pointed at Basetti's crotch. "You going to tell me about that green puke or not?"

Basetti turned on the desk lamp and faced Lipsky. "It's called green fluorescent protein, or GFP. Scientists insert the gene into cells and then the cells make the protein. It's a method to track cellular movement within the body. You don't know it's there unless you use a fluorescent microscope or a lamp, like this." He picked up an instrument that resembled a large magnifying glass. It flickered on and the green color illuminated again when Basetti held the lamp over the dish.

Lipsky seemed to be taking it all in.

"Maybe," Basetti continued, "just maybe, some of this spilled on whoever killed Vera Tuck."

Lipsky looked uncharacteristically serious. "You know, we had a guy just like you in high school," he said. "Wore these thick glasses with a band of white tape in the middle. Poor kid got so many wedgies, he just stopped wearing underpants."

"Screw you."

Lipsky took the fluorescent lamp from Basetti. "So this'll be easy," he said as he waved it across Basetti like an airport metal detector. "I'll just take this light here," his voice becoming louder, "and shine it on every Tom, Dick, and Larry in a hundred-mile radius."

"Look. I came up with the clue. The rest is up to you." Basetti tapped on Lipsky's chest and said, "That's why your badge says Detective."

CHAPTER TWENTY-NINE

The Tynes family huddled in a small room reserved for private discussions between family and surgeon. Good news could be delivered.
We got all the tumor out.
The heart bypass was successful.
Expect a full recovery.
Not today.
There must have been at least ten people in the room, all holding one another. Eli took a quick survey through the glass door before they noticed his approach. Four teenagers sat cross-legged on the floor. Three adults were standing to the side of a couch, in the center of which sat the mother and father, who faced each other in embrace. The mother's head was bowed and rested on the man's shoulder.

In surgical residency, Eli had been singled out for his communication skills. He was asked to teach the third-year surgical clerkship students how to establish a doctor-patient relationship, one that would last beyond the acute illness. Eli found it hard to impart a coherent methodology. Relationships could not be reduced to a number of steps to follow. For him, the relationship with patients and their families started with a basic level of trust, one founded on the tenet that as their physician, he would do everything in his power to heal and relieve suffering. Often, this foundation was formed upon the subtle revelation that Eli, the doctor, was also a son, a brother, a friend, and had carried similar fears, experienced great sorrow, but still maintained at least a glimmer of hope for the future. But no level of training or savvy communication skills could prepare him for a room filled with family about to hear devastating news of their loved one.

Once before, as a third-year resident on trauma surgery, it had been his responsibility to inform whoever was waiting of the death of a gang member who had been dropped off outside the ER, riddled with bullets. When the young man died on the operating table at two A.M., Eli stood in a pool of blood, exhausted and bewildered at the senseless loss of young life. He entered the conference room, similar to the one before him now, and told those waiting that he was sorry, that the boy had died.

They did all they could do.

But on hearing of the boy's death, his "friends" barricaded the door and demanded, with wailed threats and bashing against the wall, that Eli bring him back to life. Eli had gone in alone, unaware of the danger. He was held hostage for a full five minutes, pleading that no one could have done anything more, and hoping that no weapons had escaped the metal detectors downstairs. The hospital police eventually arrived, knocked down the door, and escorted the gang members from the building.

Standing now, just outside the door, Eli quickly outlined how he would deliver the news. Laying some crepe, they called it in residency, preparing the family of a critically ill patient for what was inevitable. He would allude to the possibility of head injury, but assure them that confirming tests were yet to be done. This would warn them without removing all hope.

The family was watching him now, their eyes pulling at him to enter the room and tell them everything was going to be fine. Although Eli knew this would be a totally different scene from that with the gang members, for a moment he though it might be worse.

Roger Tynes stood and extended his hand. He was middle-aged, with a deep-bored tan, a blue blazer over a white golf shirt. There was no excessive jewelry or fancy watch. Eli was impressed that the man felt no need to display overtly his Fortune 500 wealth. Scott's mother remained seated and partially hidden behind a tissue, her face blotched with red.

"Hello, everyone. I'm Dr. Branch."

"How's Scott?" one of the teenage boys blurted out. He had his arms crossed and his chest puffed out.

Roger Tynes held up his hand toward his younger son and said, calmly, "Let the doctor tell us, Mark."

Now it was all Eli. He wished he had asked the hospital chaplain to accompany him for support. But before Eli could speak, a soft trembling voice asked, "Is my son alive?" Mr. Tynes resumed his seat beside his wife and held her.

"Yes, ma'am, Scott is alive."

There was a shifting of the room, as though a valve had been opened to release an explosive pressure. Mrs. Tynes's expression did not change, however. Her gaze remained fixed on Eli.

"But he's in critical condition."

"What do you mean, critical condition?" Mark blurted.

"He has internal injuries to his spleen and liver. We just finished surgery to control the bleeding."

"So you stopped it. He's going to be okay?"

Eli nodded to Mark but tried to direct his comments to Scott's parents.

"We removed his spleen, but his liver was injured so badly that we had to pack towels around it and take him to the intensive care unit." As he said this, Eli realized that his choice of words — packs, towels — was confusing to them. But Scott's mother could see past this and voiced the most important point.

"Scott wasn't wearing a helmet, was he?"

"No," Eli said. "We're very concerned about a head injury. I'm sorry to tell you, but it could be very serious."

Eli's beeper went off and shattered the morbid silence. It was the ICU. Almost certainly, Scott Tynes was crashing.

Roger Tynes stood again. He took Eli's hand with both of his own. "We have every faith in you, Dr. Branch. Scott's a very special boy. We know that you will take good care of him."

Upon hearing those words, Eli knew that his laying of crepe had been ineffective. He also knew that Roger Tynes expected him to be the physician in constant communication with the family.

Here I am. I've lost my job but still had to take one more night of trauma call, the very night that the son of one of the wealthiest men in Memphis would have a near-fatal accident. Eli thought of the multiple reoperations Scott Tynes would require if he lived — a tracheostomy, weeks of intensive care, possibly months. *How can I say to Roger Tynes, Oh yeah, I won't be taking care of your son after tonight.*

It was Scott's mother who drove the final nail.

"God bless you, doctor."

Eli held his beeper and said, "I have to go now." But as he turned, another question was asked. This time from one of the teenaged girls. She was crying.

"How is Marisa?"

Eli searched the faces of the other family members. "I'm sorry, who?"

Mark answered for her.

"Scott's girlfriend. She was riding on the back."

From the scene of the accident on I-55, twenty minutes after the BK-117 twin-engine helicopter had departed with Scott Tynes, an ambulance pulled away and entered the interstate, traveling five miles per hour under the speed limit.

No lights, no siren.

In the back, a sheet covered the body and face of a young woman. She carried no identification, too young for a driver's license. She had been found in the rubble of the construction site by a state trooper as he collected parts of the broken motorcycle. The first responders on the scene saw no indication of a passenger on the motorcycle. The trooper determined that she was thrown twenty yards on the other side of the concrete divider.

Dead at the scene.

At the same moment Scott Tynes was being whisked away to the operating room, the second ambulance backed up to the emergency entrance of Gates Memorial. The paramedics chose to transport the girl to the same hospital, where a determination of her injuries might facilitate the treatment of the surviving victim. Also to facilitate identification of the deceased.

The body of Marisa Svengoli was wheeled into the trauma bay, where a resident and ER attending confirmed that she was dead. The nurse removed her jean shorts and sleeveless blouse, which was tied in a knot above her navel. She was wearing no shoes. The resident completed a brief examination of her injuries.

A deep vertical gash along the back of her skull was embedded in thick blonde hair. Her neck had been broken upon impact. But what the doctor found remarkable was the absence of visible injuries to her body, especially given the ejection and impact among the metal implements and concrete at the interstate's construction site.

The nurse estimated her age as between fifteen and seventeen years. She was a tall girl with magnificent features. On her right hip, just below the curve of her back, was a beautifully crafted, pink butterfly tattoo.

The absence of bodily injuries made the resident uncomfortable about continuing with the physical examination of the teenaged girl. He decided to stop, and they rolled the girl on her side and stuffed a body bag beneath her. Although it was not medically necessary, the nurse held traction on her neck to prevent further twisting and grinding of the vertebra. It just seemed like the right thing to do. They zipped the bag closed and parked her body in an isolated room to await transport to the morgue.

CHAPTER THIRTY

No sooner had Eli reached the Surgical ICU than his beeper went off again. This time, it was the ER. He quickly located neurosurgeon Thomas Champ, the physician who had mercifully paged him away from the Tynes family. The CT of Scott's head had been completed and showed exactly what they all feared.

Diffuse axonal injury with severe swelling.

An ominous sign.

Dr. Champ had paged Eli to tell him that an intracranial monitoring device was needed to relieve pressure on the boy's brain. The procedure was already underway as Eli arrived. Scott's scalp was shaved and painted yellow with Betadine, and Champ was screwing the bolt into his head.

"It doesn't look good," the neurosurgeon called from beneath his mask amid a medley of electronic beeps, buzzes, and hums. "All we can do is keep his intracranial pressure low and hope for the best."

"Thanks for coming so quickly," Eli said. He thought of the days and weeks ahead for Scott Tynes. A few patients in his condition would live, the majority wouldn't. Those who did make it required prolonged rehabilitation and would exist in a vegetative state, dependent on a feeding tube for life. And in less than twenty-four hours, Eli would no longer be a member of Gates Memorial medical staff. He would not even have hospital privileges that would allow him to take care of his patient.

Eli took this opportunity to make a request.

"Dr. Champ, I'm off to the ER again. Would you mind updating his family?"

The neurosurgeon looked up from his procedure. "What do they know?"

"I told them about his intra-abdominal injuries and that we're concerned about his head."

"Concerned puts it mildly." Champ calibrated a monitor that showed life-threatening intracranial hypertension. "Sure, I'll talk with them. They should get prepared for a final visit."

The remaining portion of Eli's call proved one of the busiest trauma nights of the summer. Not the usual knife-and-gun-club stuff. More in the dark and twisted category of domestic violence.

At midnight, an ambulance brought a woman shot in the abdomen with a nail gun. She had poured out her husband's last bottle of beer. Eli and Susan rushed her immediately to the OR.

Two hours later, they were asked to see a man with a wooden dowel crammed up his rectum. A carpenter had discovered the man in bed with his wife and decided to use some of his woodwork to take care of the problem. The patient survived, albeit with a colostomy.

The woman shot by the nail gun didn't fare as well. The nail pierced and lodged in her aorta. She arrived in stable condition, the nail plugging the hole like a thumb in a dike. During the fluid resuscitation in the ER, the woman's blood pressure shot up, the nail dislodged, and she promptly coded. In the elevator on the way to the operating room, she exsanguinated through the aortic hole and never regained a pulse.

At the end of his night on call, Eli walked through the empty surgery lounge, an orange-yellow burst of sun showing through the only window. There would be no more consults, no stat pages to the ER. He would finish morning rounds and try to salvage the day ahead.

In the intensive care unit, he found that Scott's vital signs had stabilized. His intracranial pressure remained elevated, but the diuretic medication had drawn fluid off and the numbers were slowly coming down. But the question of brain death remained.

Eli pulled Scott's covers down to expose his chest. One of the main predictors of brain stem activity was response to pain. As a medical student, Eli cringed when the pain reflex was demonstrated. As he reached down and grabbed the boy's nipple, Eli felt impending remorse. But he had to know. He pinched the nipple hard and twisted in a clockwise direction. From the depth of his coma, Scott reflexively pulled both arms inward to the pain and Eli released the plug of skin.

"I'm sorry, buddy," Eli said as he replaced the warm covers around Scott's neck. "I had to do it."

The lobby of Gates Memorial Hospital served as the waiting room for family and friends of those in surgery. A coffee stand provided hot beverages and Danish pastries. The morning newspaper was used as a distraction to the invasive events occurring on the third floor.

At seven o'clock, Eli walked through the lobby. Every available chair was occupied, arranged in semicircular units of family and friends. Behind the information desk, a couch served as a makeshift bed for a couple that couldn't have been over eighteen. A group of four adults huddled in one corner of the room, their eyes red from lack of sleep.

Eli's own sleep amounted to less than an hour. He eyed an empty couch against a wall. *How easy it would be to just crash here.* He was almost to the exit when he slowed his pace for a young woman in front of him. She wore a bandana on her head and her mouth was covered with a surgical mask tied at the base of her hairless skull. It was easy for Eli to substitute a similar image of his mother, sick from the chemotherapy in her last weeks of life.

The woman held onto the IV pole and pushed it with difficulty, its wheels getting hung up on the carpeted floor. When she turned toward the hospital chapel, Eli quickly walked around her. As a pair of nearby doors opened automatically for him, he looked back at the woman and saw her struggling to enter the place of worship. She held the door with one arm and yanked on the IV pole with the other. With calm persistence, she tried to lift the pole, heavy with two full bags of fluid and a pain pump attached. Eli stopped, reached around her to hold the door, and hoisted her pole over the threshold. Metal blinds covering the glass of the door shifted and announced their entrance.

Eli had not noticed the chapel before, an unadvertised room with a single door off the rear of the lobby. Inside, four short pews on each side of a center aisle faced a wooden cross that rose from the floor. The small sanctuary was half-full with fewer than ten people.

"Please come in, we've yet to start."

Eli looked up. A priest in a purple robe that appeared too small for his bulky frame extended both arms to his impromptu congregation.

The woman cleared the doorway and sat at the closest end of a pew. Eli, still holding the IV pole, placed it beside her.

"Thank you," she said, her voice weak and muffled behind the mask.

Eli had the feeling that someone was looking at him. He turned and saw Regina Tynes in the back pew across the aisle. Her hair was pulled back and secured with a barrette. She looked like a worried mother who had not slept the night, but her face seemed to ease when she saw Dr. Eli Branch enter the chapel. She nodded with a slight but graceful smile. She appreciates that her son's surgeon would seek a place of spiritual refuge, Eli thought.

"Welcome all," the priest called again.

As the door shut, Eli felt smothered. At once, he was back in church again, thirty years ago, with his parents and Henry. Everything was there, the pews, the candles, and a priest waiting to reprimand and embarrass them all.

Despite the eyes of Regina Tynes and the congregation upon him, Eli scrambled out the door, a set of shifting metal blinds declaring his escape.

CHAPTER THIRTY-ONE

NORTH RESEARCH BUILDING
FRIDAY MORNING
7:24 A.M.

The yellow tape had been removed from around his laboratory, and the police and reporters were gone. Early morning was usually a time to be productive with research grants and manuscripts to prepare before the constant interruptions of the beeper. Eli just wanted to get to his office, sit at his desk in silence, and try to make sense of the last few days.

As he approached the lab, he saw that his mail had been dropped in a pile outside the door. Usually, the administrative assistant for the labs sorted the letters from the journals in designated racks inside his office. He scooped up the mail with one hand and inserted his key in the door.

But only halfway.

He tried it again but the grooves ground against the new mechanism.

Then he knew. He was being shut out.

What will be next? My house?

He tried one last time, twisting hard, and his key broke off in the lock.

Eli stopped his truck at the gate of the medical center's parking garage. He waved a white plastic card across the invisible beam, eased off the brake, and pulled forward. But the gate remained closed.

Another swipe.

Nothing.

A Land Rover pulled up to the opposite gate to enter the garage.

Eli rubbed the card, back and forth against the black surface as if he were sanding furniture. The silver LR3 idled with the gate open. Eli looked at the driver.

Dr. Karl Fisher.

Well, this is awkward. Surely he'll give me his card and let me out.

But Fisher just revved his engine, pulled forward, and disappeared into the concrete maze. Eli waited a few minutes until the next employee arrived, who was nice enough to let him out of the garage.

The morning was gray and overcast, and a bank of fog pushed low against the river like a cloud. Eli drove slowly along Riverside Drive, his mind as thick and muddled as the water itself. He stopped for the light at Jefferson Street. Not a car in sight. *If only it could stay like this, deserted and lonely, like the morning after nuclear devastation or maybe, Armageddon.*

Just before the final operative case of the long night, Eli had a chance to lie down for an hour. But his mind buzzed as though on a double-shot caffeine high. He sweated into the sheets one minute, shook with feverish chills the next. He never had difficulty with sleep before. In medical school and residency, he could fall asleep instantly, a blessing for postcall nights, a curse for lectures and conferences.

I could just keep driving, he thought. He could take Interstate 55 down to Batesville and on to Oxford, maybe cut over to the Natchez Trace, or get lost in some small town along the river where they don't watch the news, and don't give a damn. Take a labor job, hire out and drive a tractor sunup to sundown in rich delta land, and ride out of the field in the back of a truck across acres and acres of cotton, sharing a cigarette with men too tired to talk, but counting dollars and change for a quart at the package store ahead. He could feel the openness of the land and the desolation, the gratifying ache in his muscles and —

Eli woke abruptly to a horn blaring as a car passed to his right and shifted to the lane in front of him. He looked up at the light where he'd come to a stop.

Green. Back to yellow.

Eli pressed the accelerator with an overcompensated stomp and gripped the steering wheel with both hands. Forty-five seconds of precious sleep. He caught a fleeting whiff of smoke from the shared cigarette in his dream.

Eli was halfway across the Hernando DeSoto Bridge before he felt his grip on the steering wheel slacken. He had been driving in a dream-like state, staring straight ahead, fantasizing about what he could do to Fisher and Korinsky. He pictured the slews and bottoms in North Mississippi, miles and miles from nowhere. Eli had hunted there during duck season while at Ole Miss. He had felt the stark isolation of the frozen channels and lakes. How long would it take? Months? Years? before the bodies of the two men were found.

The tranquility of first light on a flooded cotton field overcame his homicidal thoughts. At Ole Miss, four o'clock on Saturday mornings in the winter, he would leave the fraternity house with hunting buddies Charles Jackson and Frank Ames. They would take Highway 278 over to Sardis Lake where Frank's uncle leased a duck blind in a flooded corner of land they called Buzzard Slew. It would be pitch-dark as they drove out to the lease, tires of the four-wheel drive cutting ruts in frozen mud, stars overhead, crisp air in the mid-twenty-degree range.

How easy we could do that then. Keg parties the night before. A few times they didn't even go to bed.

Dressed in full camouflage and toting their guns in cases, they would ease down the stairs of the Phi Delt house so as not to awaken their brothers. They would pass by the den, littered with cups of spilt beer and couch cushions thrown on the floor for those who couldn't quite make it up the stairs. They would crack the front door, line up as a trio, and bring their duck calls into position. They would take one final moment to relish the complete silence and anticipate the shattering soon to come. With their calls poised, Eli would mouth "one, two, three"—

"QUUUAAACK."

"QUACK, QUACK, Quack, Quack, Quack."

"QUUUAAACK."

"QUACK, QUACK, Quack, Quack, Quack."

At full blow, three unified duck calls could pull a formation of mallards from a thousand feet. Still, it took a couple of rounds before the house came fully alive. A chorus would start from the bedrooms upstairs.

"Shut up, you crazy bastards."

"Go to hell. Go straight to hell."

The three of them would retreat to an idling truck in the parking lot, laughing at the smack of beer cans thrown against the wall. The brothers of Phi Delta Theta grew to hate those early Saturday mornings of winter. And a legacy was born.

From the bridge, Eli watched the muddy water pass slowly below him like a huge, even-tempered monster. The river had always had a calming effect on him. In medical school, before the big block of do-or-die biochem and anatomy tests, he would jog down Jefferson Street until he saw the reflection of evening sun off the water. He would sprint across Riverside Drive to a park bench on a grassy hill along the bank. The minutia and detail of oxidative metabolism, the precise point of insertion of every muscle along the pelvic bone, all of it took on a certain insignificance, a much-needed perspective, when he considered the vastness of water that moved every day past this little spot of the world.

As his truck entered West Memphis, Arkansas, Eli remembered a woman on a Riverside park bench who had sat not thirty feet from him one clear afternoon in the middle of May. She was dressed too warmly in a green overcoat and plastic rain hood. From a sack of bread ends, she methodically pinched off little pieces and delivered them, one by one, to the faithful pigeons that gathered at her feet. Isolated in the immense pleasure of her task, she never looked at Eli. After the last bread crumb was thrown, the birds still pecking and strutting in the patch of grass, she sat a while in a blank stare, as if her only enjoyment in this life had ended. Then, with no fanfare, she pushed the cellophane bag into her coat pocket and drifted away.

Eli turned onto the tree-lined RBI drive and coveted the simplicity of the woman's selfless act.

At the guardhouse, Eli stayed in his Bronco as Tongue pressed a handheld iris scanner against his face. A single wave of light confirmed his identification, and the gate opened before him. To Eli's surprise, Tongue spoke.

Pointing to a row of parked cars, he said, "You can park right of the building." He formed his words as if his tongue were competing with a mouthful of potatoes. "Your spot's the third one down."

Eli thanked him and pulled away.

My spot?

Past the fountain he slowed at a line of parked cars, discrete signs identifying each spot. The first was occupied by Harvey Stone's silver BMW. Next was a racing green Jaguar that belonged to A. Zaboyan, according to the sign. The next parking space was empty, so Eli eased the Bronco in place. To his amazement, the sign read: E. Branch, M.D.

He leaned forward with both arms draped across the steering wheel and stared at his name. He thought of the old saying, when one door closes, another opens. He looked at the immaculately detailed cars to his right, then at the patch of rust that grew on the center of his hood. Eli shook his head and laughed.

He entered the marbled foyer and was disappointed to find that Lisa was not at the reception desk. He had envisioned her popping up from the desk to greet him, maybe in a classy blue blazer hugging a pink halter top.

"Good morning." A thin woman, fiftyish, her thick grey hair pulled up in a bun, stood at the desk holding a clipboard. She wore hoop earrings the diameter of a dinner plate.

"Any trouble with your parking, Dr. Branch?"

Eli was surprised that she knew his name, but his expectations were being surpassed now on a frequent basis. He thought of the parking privileges that had been revoked at the medical center.

"No, no problems at all."

"Good," she said. "Can I show you to your office?"

As she nodded her head, Eli watched the big rings sway and tug at eroded earlobes. *How long before they cut all the way through?*

"Office?"

"Right this way," she said and stepped from behind the booth.

"That's okay," Eli said, preferring to find it himself. "Remind me again."

She pointed at the elevator. "To the second floor and down the hall, last door on the right."

He recalled the second floor layout of the East Wing. Tsarina's lab was down the hall on the left.

How convenient.

"Thank you," Eli said.

Adjacent to the elevator was the restroom where he had met Prine. Eli wondered if the old man was in there waiting for visitors. He pushed open the door, but the room was vacant. There were no cheap fragrances, no breath mints on the counter. And Prine's stool was gone.

He walked past the elevator and took the single flight of stairs. On the second floor, the hall was empty and the doors to all the laboratories remained locked.

All except one.

A plaque on the door signified the new occupant.

ELI BRANCH, M.D.
CHIEF MEDICAL OFFICER

Eli closed the door behind him. The office was completely furnished. A solid mahogany desk held a brass lamp. He knew the deep leather chair reclined in multiple positions, because he tried it. But what attracted his attention was a long rectangular photograph framed high on the wall behind his chair. Vaught-Hemingway Stadium at dusk, lights illuminating sixty thousand fans as the Rebels took the field. Below the picture was the date: October 9, 1996.

Eli felt the muscles around his jaw loosen. This photo wasn't of just any game. It was a picture of the night game when Eli received the IMHOTEP award, given to the student with the highest potential for success in the medical profession.

His father had been there for the award presentation, which took place at halftime on the fifty-yard line. Eli had insisted that Henry also be a part of the evening, so he had driven his brother down from the State Home. They arrived just before kickoff. But during the second quarter, Elizer Branch insisted that Henry not take the field with them nor be in any of the photographs. The evening was a bittersweet memory then, just as it was now.

Highest potential for success. Humph. Considering the events of the last few days, his professors should have been more selective in their choice. Centered on his desk so he would be sure to find it, a glossy brochure advertised Coates Island Home and Resort. The cover showed a large, beautiful building surrounded by oak trees. In the front courtyard two young men sat on a bench next to a duck pond. Behind them, an attendant in a short white coat pushed a wheelchair. Inside the brochure, he found page after page of amenities: tennis courts, horseback riding, trails through the woods for long walks, and a swimming pool with a curved slide.

A paradise for your disabled loved one — A home away from home.

The brochure described the private rooms and meal service. The building was locked down each night at nine P.M. Security and safety was assured. Eli imagined his brother living there. Henry would love the open space, the woods. As Eli thumbed through the brochure, there was a knock on his door.

Three slow evenly spaced knocks.

Tsarina!

Eli considered the circumstances.

It was early, very few if any employees had arrived. They would be alone in his new office.

More knocks on the door, this time in a playful string. The door handle rattled with a couple of twists, but the door had locked behind him.

She knows I'm in here. She's just going to come in and start the whole thing. Right here. Right now. On the floor.

Eli thought about her legs, sculpted, with an ankle bracelet on the left one. He had always liked those ankle bracelets, he realized now. He readjusted his pants and buttoned his white coat below his waist. His hand shook as he opened the door.

CHAPTER THIRTY-TWO

Tsarina had transformed into a short, elderly black man.

Prine.

"Big man done got him an office," he said with a knowing smile. "See, I told you no one ever leaves this place."

Eli's breathing slowed and he smiled as his fantasy quickly dissolved.

"Hello, sir," Eli said and extended his hand.

"Sir? I ain't no sir."

Prine grabbed Eli's wrist, turned his hand palm up, and slapped him five.

"I'm Prinobius Calloway. Mailman, trash collector, airport attendant."

He did a little three-step tap dance.

"You can call me Prine."

Eli laughed at the entertaining performance. Prine wore a formal black jacket and a starched white shirt with the collar high on his neck. His black shoes had lost their shine and the pants were frayed at the hem, like a rented tuxedo from thirty years ago. Eli bet he wore it every day.

Prine shifted through letters in the bottom of his mail cart. "Let's see here." He turned and looked at Eli's name on the door. "Branch."

He stopped and said the name again.

"Branch?"

He stared at Eli as though trying to place him. "Branch — like at the medical school?"

Eli was surprised at the question. "Yes, my father."

At this, Prine looked down the hall, both ways, as though assuring himself that no one was within earshot. Just as he took a step toward Eli and leaned forward, a door down the hall closed with a slam.

Startled, Prine backed out of the office and pushed his mail cart down the corridor, hobbling as though his right leg were shorter than his left. Eli stuck his head out the door and watched the old man reach inside the flap of his mail cart, remove a small bottle, and take a long swig.

The telephone rang in Eli's office. He located the phone in a drawer and sat down behind his desk.

"Branch speaking."

A confident and proud voice greeted him. "Good morning."

Eli had expected the call.

"Good morning, Mr. Stone."

"Harvey, please. How's the office?"

Eli looked behind him at his alma mater lit up at night. "It's fabulous."

"Great. Why don't you come to my office and we'll chat."

Eli wondered when he would be given a job description. *What the hell am I supposed to do here?*

"Sure. And Harvey?"

"Yeah."

"How did you know about that night at Ole Miss?"

There was a short hesitation. "Just a lucky guess."

The door to Stone's office was open just enough for Eli to hear voices. Stone's and a female's. With his hand on the knob, he delayed a moment.

"Need to lay low on device marketing a while," Stone said. "Ramp up the vaccine line, regain some credibility."

The next voice was unmistakably seductive.

"What would you like for me to do?"

"We need a patient for the stem cell procedure. That would make big news. Put us back on top."

After a pause Eli heard movement coming toward him. He tapped on the door just before Stone opened it.

"Eli, come in."

Tsarina's back was to him, bare legs crossed with a calf muscle bulging like a hen's breast. She recrossed her legs, scissor-like, with cinematic speed. Stone motioned for Eli to sit in the chair next to her so they would both face his desk.

"Hello again," Tsarina said, rocking her foot in a quick tapping motion.

"Welcome," Stone said and leaned forward on his desk with folded hands. "I hope you found things satisfactory this morning." He repeated this formality for Tsarina's sake.

"My parking space could be two spaces closer," Eli said, also for Tsarina's benefit. She must have liked it, foot shaking like a puppy's tail.

"Gives you something to work for, now doesn't it."

"So it does," Eli agreed.

Stone leaned back in his chair. "Let me give you a vision." His voice took on a prophetic quality. "We need an image boost. Some of this press lately," he pursed his lips, "not good."

"Yeah," Eli agreed. "I've experienced some of that myself."

Stone didn't acknowledge this.

Surely he's heard about the murder?

"RBI built its name on vaccine development," he continued. "Third World, children, the whole bit. Admirable, right?"

"Sure." *What else could he say?*

"Problem is," he pursed his lips again, "vaccines don't pay shit."

Eli thought of the flu vaccine, a dime a dozen, all the problems with production. "I can imagine."

Tsarina was fidgeting in her seat. She had removed a cigarette from a tiny purse in her lap and held it between two fingers. As though anticipating this, Stone leaned over and flicked a gold-plated lighter. Eli felt as if he were watching a scene from a 1940s movie.

"Medical devices — they're our bottom line. Keeps the company afloat." A grin spread slowly across Stone's face. "More than afloat."

This made Tsarina's foot tap again and she took a deep drag.

"Unfortunately, we've had a few mishaps. Untimely mishaps. You with me?"

Eli pictured Gaston's blood-drained body lying on the operating table. "Yes, I'm with you."

"The future, my friend, is stem cells." Stone looked at Tsarina. "And we're all over it. In a few days, we'll be front page news, the envy of every biotech firm in the nation." Stone leaned forward again. "But these deaths are putting a damper on the party."

"I have a feeling this is where I come in."

"You're sharp, Branch, you know that."

"So they tell me."

For the next fifteen minutes, Stone laid out a plan of immaculate detail and perfectly timed publicity. The resurgence of RBI into the biotech stratosphere hung on the visit of one Sister Frances D'Aquila.

Stone had met Sister Frances in 1993 on one of his yearly trips to Maseru, in the African country of Lesotho. At the time, GlobeVac was supplying the majority of vaccines to the small country on the north-west border of South Africa. In what turned out to be a very effective publicity campaign, Stone and his team took a series of photographs of the nun holding a vaccine-filled syringe and injecting a toddler balanced on her knee. The images were picked up by CNN and broadcast in an exclusive report on Third-World vaccination. Fortuitously positioned in the background of each photo was the GlobeVac logo.

Sister Frances D'Aquila held the dying, AIDS-stricken child close to her heart. According to the spin, for her the disease carried no connotation of blame or fault but rather an overwhelming need to care for each patient, one at a time. This impromptu relationship seemed to benefit both Stone and Sister Frances. GlobeVac's stock saw a steady increase, and humanitarian aid flowed into the poverty-stricken villages of the sister's beloved country.

Stone handed Eli a recent photo of the sister. She was sitting cross-legged on the grass outside a small village. Behind her, a beautiful mountain range towered over her and the dying infant cradled in her arms. In the background, and slightly off focus, was a Land Rover with the letters RBI painted on the side.

Stone continued his story about the unusual joint venture between

Sister Frances, his pharmaceutical company, and their yearly vaccine campaign. The sister understood the importance of the company's support to her mission and she began to cater to the photographers, using the media attention to advance her worthy cause. For the past five years, Harvey Stone had hinted to her about a visit to the United States. "You're practically a celebrity there," he told her. But she had always declined.

Until now.

She came to realize that while millions lay waiting to die, one child at a time was not enough. So in a totally unexpected offer, she agreed to travel to the United States and give one woman's plea for help. For RBI, her visit could not have come at a better time. The company planned to take full advantage of Sister Frances's altruism.

"Her itinerary is set," Stone told Eli. "She'll arrive in Memphis, early morning, and come straight here. A brief press conference will be held outside the front entrance. I want you there at her side, Eli, in a white coat. Say a few words about this being a historic visit, smile for the cameras, and then she's off to D.C. on the jet for an appearance on *Meet the Press*."

"*Meet the Press*?"

"Oh yeah, we're cooking now," Stone said proudly. "You'll escort her in the company Lear. The publicity for RBI will be unparalleled."

"I've had some rather negative exposure in the press myself."

"Eli, that's nothing for our publicity department. They can turn that around and make you look like a saint."

Sisters, saints. This was spiraling into quite the multifarious event.

"When does her visit take place?"

Harvey Stone glanced at Tsarina. "Sister Frances arrives early Sunday morning."

Eli walked in a dream-like state back to his new office through the sparkling laboratory facility. He tried to fit the pieces together.

RBI was planning a publicity stunt. That's what it was, for all practical purposes. Stone was exploiting the credibility of Sister D'Aquila, her years of servitude to the poor and suffering, to justify to the public the use of embryonic stem cell therapy before federal legislation allowed it. And Eli would be the front man for RBI, to add medical credibility to the whole scheme.

As he sat behind his desk, Eli noticed that one drawer was ajar and the corner of a letter stuck out. Eli removed the envelope, which was embossed with the RBI logo and address. The seal had been torn. Inside was a small piece of paper folded in half.

Prine's handwriting, he assumed, was shaky but readable.

And the message disturbingly simple:

They're hurting Henry.

CHAPTER THIRTY-THREE

RBI
EAST WING
BIO SECURITY LAB #3

The cells lined up in a neat little row, one after the other, like school children waiting for recess. They clung together in a cluster, safety in numbers. Other cells, a few, remained apart, isolated, each wanting to fuse with an identical sister cell, yet unable to move. All of the cells had one thing in common — naïveté. Yet each cell was full of life, wanting to express in full scream exactly who it was meant to be.

Their home was warm and dark, precisely controlled at thirty-eight degrees Celsius. The cells spread out evenly on a playground of plastic and bathed in a wondrous straw-colored potion abundant with nutrients, balanced to perfection, much like the amniotic bath from which they were suctioned a few weeks before.

"Hello, my darlings."

Tsarina stood before an open incubator and spoke to a single petri dish that lay on the metal rack.

"How was your sleep? I prayed that you were warm."

Carefully, with both hands, she removed the dish and sat in a rocking chair in the corner of the laboratory. She cradled the dish, rocking ever so gently, the line of fluid steady in a mother's calm lullaby.

"Bring the cells, Tsarina." James Korinsky was seated behind the microscope as he motioned to her. "Stop being foolish."

She eyed him with the jealousy of an estranged parent, but she followed his demand nonetheless. Just before the cells reached the hands of her former lover, Tsarina leaned over with the grace and intention of a goodnight kiss, pressing her lips to the plastic top.

"Mama loves you."

Korinsky reached for the plate. "Tsarina! If these cells get infected, that's it. What's left of our child will be gone. You don't want that, do you?"

During the transfer, in Korinsky's agitation, the plate tilted to one side and a stream of warm liquid media ran down the side of the dish and dripped on the floor.

"See!" he yelled now. "Look what you've done." He slid the plate beneath the microscope lens and moved the platform until a blurred mass of cells was visible through the liquid layer. He focused the scope until the ragged borders coalesced into sharp, clear membranes. Each cell resembled a tiny fried egg, the edge of the white bordering the next cell, the nucleus a central round yolk.

Korinsky was distracted by escalating sobs coming from Tsarina, who stood next to him. Without moving his head, he glanced sideways at her, then back at the cells.

"Have you prepared the endothelial cells? I have three new grafts that need to be coated. All scheduled for this afternoon."

Tsarina turned her back toward him.

"Okay, I'm sorry." Korinsky said as he put his hand on her hip and caressed it.

Tsarina walked away, letting his hand drop.

Korinsky stood abruptly and the stool rolled backward and banged into the wall.

"I've got to have those cells, Tsarina. You know that. Something's wrong with the aortic grafts. They're not engrafting like they should. Any more deaths and we could be finished."

Tsarina didn't budge. *All you care about is your surgery and your money,* she thought.

Korinsky kept berating her. "If device production shuts down, you can forget your precious stem cell therapy."

Tsarina slapped the door of the incubator. "I've got your damn cells." She opened it and removed a T-60 flask. She held it up to the fluorescent light before setting it down on the bench top. "That should be more than enough."

Tsarina watched as Korinsky concealed the flask of cells in a leather briefcase. She would never forgive him for what he had done to her.

To their child.

It was more than three months ago when Korinsky told her, over and over, that as a surgeon, he could perform the procedure as well as any obstetrician. Tsarina eventually gave in, climbing on the table and lying there with her legs spread while he prepared the instruments.

The sounds continued to haunt her, the horrid sucking, fluid gushing into the wall canister as though a clogged pipe had burst free, the clog ripped into a million cells, never to rejoin. And then more scraping, dull spoons against the rind.

Why had she listened to him? Why did *she* have to be responsible for keeping *his* family together? *His* wife, *his* children?

In the end, it was her guilt that made her go through with it, the guilt he placed on her that having the child would destroy his marriage, his family, and — as Tsarina knew was most important to him — his career. Now, all that remained was her guilt.

They had met six months earlier at Bernie Lankford's house. The senior RBI scientist was building the Division of Stem Cell Therapy. Dr. Tsarina Anatolia was the newest recruit, having finished a prestigious stem cell biology fellowship in Sweden, followed by a position as research scientist at the International Stem Cell Consortium in Singapore.

Their affair started late that night, fast and furious, in her room at the Peabody Hotel. Korinsky didn't tell her he was married until three months later, when he used that information to force her into the abortion.

After the procedure, Korinsky left her there, cold and shaking in the sterile procedure room at RBI, with the additional duty of disposing of the evidence. She cried as she cleaned herself. After throwing away the bloodied sheets, she looked in the canister — at what was left of what would have become her baby.

During the week after her home pregnancy test, Tsarina had decided that she was having a girl. She began to talk to her daughter, singing to her at bedtime. Alone in the procedure room and longing to have her daughter back, Tsarina was sickened by the thought of embryonic stem cells used as therapy. Tsarina realized the contradiction this created in her position as director of stem cell therapy. To her surprise, she laughed, amazed at the newfound power this directorship afforded her. She exhaled a defining laugh and removed the canister, cradling it as she limped back to her lab. The cells would live as they were for a few more minutes, and if she kept them warm in culture fluid, they could live indefinitely.

In her laboratory, Tsarina felt sharp, stabbing pains deep in her pelvis. She limped into the incubator room and sat down on a metal stool. The endometrial tissue had settled to the bottom of the canister, leaving thin bloody fluid on top. Using a long pipette, she aspirated a sample from just above the tissue layer and placed a drop on a microscope slide.

"There," she whispered, looking through the scope at a group of embryonic cells floating across the glass surface, her focal vision obscured by a welling of tears. "I'm so sorry, sweetheart." The pain hit again and Tsarina felt dizzy, the room spinning. "Mama will take care of you," she said, closing her eyes. In the sterile room, with ravaged bits of what she was sure was her daughter floating across a microscopic field, she thought again of this sacrificed life. Her only hope in facing the tragedy was to realize the incredible position she was in. She controlled the fate of the embryonic stem cells stored in the incubator beside her, with their hyped-up promise of curing human disease and the unforeseen complications that could arise from their unmitigated power. Tsarina knew that the treatment protocols planned by RBI would require the sacrifice of many more human embryos — just like her daughter. Finally, her nausea and dizziness passed and out of despair came clarity.

Under the sterile culture hood, Tsarina distributed the cells from the canister into individual flasks. Later, she would separate the embryonic cells from their somatic counterparts and place them on a layer of feeder cells, a surrogate for her womb. She realized then why she had been given her position in charge of stem cell development. At first skeptical about the move to the United States, and then to Memphis, Tsarina came to believe that divine providence had placed her in this powerful role. Though her relationship with Korinsky had turned into a nightmare, her purpose at RBI was evident.

Tsarina knew that RBI had all the pieces in place to make human embryonic stem cell therapy a reality: near unlimited financial support from venture capitalists, a deep infrastructure of scientists, and the trust of the community and of the world, a result of RBI's generous vaccine distribution. Only one additional ingredient was essential for the stem cell program's success — a renegade doctor like Korinsky, whose greed would drive him into unauthorized human experimentation.

In spite of her pain, Tsarina developed a plan. Each of RBI's scientific divisions, from the public relations of vaccine production to the highly profitable biomedical device core, was poised to support the mission of stem cell therapy. Tsarina had seen the profit margin reports. The funding of RBI's stem cell mission rested on the success of the AortaFix device. *If it fails, RBI fails. If RBI fails, hundreds of unborn babies, like my daughter, will be saved. I will be the mother to all these precious embryonic lives,* Tsarina vowed to herself. She looked at the embryonic cells floating in warm culture fluid and made them a promise. "You will live forever."

Now, as she watched Korinsky leave the lab with the flasks of cells, Tsarina removed a notebook from her desk and recorded an entry for the third batch of the metalloproteinase-producing cells she had given him. She laughed at the thought of Korinsky trying to prevent another rupture of an aortic device by coating the grafts with those destructive cells.

The deaths will come quickly now.

CHAPTER THIRTY-FOUR

Eli held the note with both hands and tried to read beyond those three words.

They're hurting Henry.

They? Who?

And how are they hurting my brother? He thought of the fresh puncture marks on Henry's leg.

Doctor visits each month?

His beeper went off. *They changed the locks on my office, canceled my parking, but no one would ever deactivate this annoying beeper.* Eli sighed with each successive irritating blast.

You can run, but you can't hide.

As soon as he looked at the number on the display panel he answered Meg's call.

"Vera Tuck?" she asked.

"Hi Meg."

Eli heard her searching through papers. He imagined her in the autopsy suite typing the findings into the computer, or leaning forward at the microscope in tight scrubs, just as he had seen her the first time. It seemed so long ago, yet it had only been four days.

"You could've told me. We don't always get the latest gossip down here in the dungeon."

"How did you find out?"

"Her body's right in front of me, all twisted up like a pretzel."

Eli imagined the position of Vera's body as it was removed from the incubator, rigor locking it in place.

"These deaths, Eli, they're not a coincidence. I'm sure of it."

He looked again at the note in his hand. "Yes, I know."

"Are you okay? You sound different."

"I'm okay, I think."

There was silence on both ends before Meg asked, "Anything I should know before I slice her?"

Eli wished the whole Vera thing would just go away. But he knew that clues from her autopsy could potentially prove who killed her.

"I want to be there for it." He thought about how long it would take to drive — and find a parking place. "Give me half an hour."

CHAPTER THIRTY-FIVE

Meg had the body prepared on the autopsy table. An assortment of tools and instruments were set out in the order they would be used. Scalpel to make the V cut, rib cutters, Metzenbaum scissors, Stryker saw for the skull, and basins for each individual organ.

Vera's body was completely uncovered. Eli thought this unnecessary before the procedure had even begun. *I don't care if she did hate everybody; a sheet should cover her at least, in deference to basic human dignity.*

Although her face was gaunt and wrinkled, her body was surprisingly fit: full muscular legs and a scaphoid abdomen sloping to a tiny waist.

"This her?" Meg asked as she left her office and entered the room.

Eli stepped closer. "'Fraid so." He focused on her left groin. Three puncture wounds just lateral to dark tufts of pubic hair. They were in the anatomic site used for femoral catheterization. Identical to the wounds that Eli found on Henry.

"I noticed those too. Fairly recent, don't you think?"

Eli didn't answer.

Meg handed him a pair of gloves. "Here, put these on. I've got more to show you."

She lifted Vera's hand and pressed the skin away from a long, chipped fingernail. "Vera neglected her nails or the police overlooked this one."

Eli leaned over for a closer look. "Ouch."

"Yeah," Meg said. "Whoever killed her left the scene missing plugs of their skin."

"That should be incriminating evidence."

"I'm sure the crime-scene investigators collected a sample," Meg said. "There is epidermis under every fingernail." She removed a hand-held fluorescent lamp from the table and flipped off the overhead lights. The room was completely dark until the lamp flickered on. Eli watched the light move toward Vera's face. Meg's gloved finger pried the jaw open. A green fluorescent glow emanated from the dead woman's mouth.

"What in the world?" Eli asked.

"I was hoping you could tell me."

Eli moved closer and saw that the glow separated into tiny green specks. They were everywhere: on her teeth, her tongue, and down the back of her throat.

With the room still dark, Meg pulled him over to the microscope. "Take a look."

Eli recognized the source of the green color immediately. "It's green fluorescent protein." He could feel Meg beside him, the sweet smell of her hair stronger in the darkness. "I always transfect GFP into my cells, to track their movement."

Meg flipped on the overhead lights. "Do you usually feed them to your lab tech?"

Eli looked again at Vera. Her mouth was still partially open to reveal a swollen tongue. "I knew she was crazy, but —"

"But not crazy enough to eat cells from a culture dish?"

Eli tried to imagine the minutes before her death. If someone was trying to steal the cells, Vera would have definitely tried to stop them.

Even if she had to eat them.

Meg interrupted the crime scene re-creation. "Why didn't you tell me?"

"Tell you what?"

"That you put GFP in the cells? That they would light up like fire-flies?"

Eli knew where she was going with this. They could have searched for the green protein in the aortic grafts.

"The specimens from Gaston and Lankford?"

Meg wore her one-step-ahead-of-you smile. "Like a St. Patrick's Day parade."

One of Vera's ridiculous outbursts rang in his head.

Rich Bitch Ink.

This was her only phrase that carried no religious or racial connotation. And she had said it only in the presence of Stone.

Rich Bitch Inc.

RBI

"And I'll tell you what else," Meg said.

"What?"

"We're starting to receive calls from medical examiners in the region. Jackson, Tennessee and Tupelo. Each reported a death from aortic rupture."

Meg waited for Eli to respond.

He said nothing

"And a local hospital out in Cordova had two similar deaths, just last night."

The voice of Ms. Conch gurgled over the intercom. "Dr. Daily? A Detective Lipsky from the police department called."

Meg looked at Eli and pressed the button on the intercom. "What did he want?"

"He wanted to know if a Dr. Eli Branch had been here."

Eli pointed at Vera's body. "Lipsky's the one conducting the investigation."

Ms. Conch crackled back in. "When I didn't answer him, he said he was coming over and hung up."

"Look, Meg, I need to talk to you some more." Eli quickly headed to the door. "I think we're onto something big, whether we want to be or not."

"I've got an hour before my next autopsy. Want me to come to your office?"

My office? If she only knew.

"No, I need to lie low away from the medical center for a while. Let's meet later tonight," Eli said, trying to think of a place off campus, somewhere no one would expect.

"Do you know Automatic Slim's?"

"Automatic whose?" Meg asked.

"It's called Automatic Slim's Tonga Club. Downtown on Second. Got an Asian-Caribbean thing going on."

"Sounds like a sexy place for a mother and her young child. We don't get out much."

Eli had forgotten about Margaret. His silence indicated this to Meg.

"Don't worry, I'll get a sitter," she said. "There's a nursing student who lives on my street who can stay with Margaret. What time?"

"I need to visit an old friend first. Is nine o'clock too late?"

"That's okay. See you then."

Eli turned to leave, but Meg stopped him.

"I don't know why, but I feel compelled to tell you."

"What?"

"Be careful."

CHAPTER THIRTY-SIX

The back entrance of Anatomy Hall was hardly ever used anymore. Until the late seventies, bodies for dissection had been transported in and out through the back of the building, a discreet method that could not be observed by those walking between other academic buildings. Now there was a side entrance through which bodies were transported, concealed in wooden boxes indistinguishable from other supplies.

Ragged blades of Johnson grass hung over a cobblestone walkway and ivy climbed the brick wall. A strange combination, Eli thought, the horticultural symbol of academia and a weed that could snuff out the most fertile crops in the delta. He was dressed in scrubs and carried only a penlight and a set of keys in his pocket. Long seed stems brushed his leg as he approached.

Anatomy Hall was virtually unoccupied during the months of June and July, after the first-year medical students went home for the summer. The place would remain this way, visited only by cleaning and maintenance personnel, until mid-August, when the hall would become alive again with nervous medical students, anxious to meet the dead body with whom they would spend the next six months.

Eli had not entered the building since returning to Memphis. It had been almost ten years since he walked among the portraits of anatomy professors, the oldest — Dr. Latimer Stemfield, first chair of the department — dating back to 1904. There was something daunting about the building now, this place where young Eli had spent most of his summer days, enthralled with the mysteries of life and death. To be twelve and watch the hands of young men and women explore the depths of the human body was a unique experience, a privilege off-limits to anyone but surgeons, morticians, and the criminally insane. But along with the fascination of it all, he was not shielded from the harshness, the gradual loss of compassion that Eli, though young, had recognized happening to almost every student after they'd spent hours picking away at fascial layers, uncovering strands of muscle, memorizing each point of insertion and origin on tiny nubbins of bone.

It was tradition at the University of the Mid-South that each cadaver be given a name by the group of four students assigned to that table. Eli's favorite time in the hall was to walk among the tables and listen as a student from each group read a brief description of the person who died and how. The most common scenario was that of a patient in his or her seventies or eighties who died of cancer or heart disease. Eli was comforted when the cause of death was that broad, ill-defined category, old age.

Then there were patients whose deaths disturbed Eli, kept him awake at night; a fifty-two-year-old vagrant found in a diabetic coma, a thirty-year-old homeless woman with extreme hypothermia discovered on New Year's Eve. How had they given consent to donate their bodies to medical science? None of these individuals, he was sure, had a driver's license or a signed donor card. They didn't even own a wallet. Were their bodies used by the school because no one claimed them? No grieving family members to make funeral plans? So they were carted to the hall with a tag on their toe.

Other troubling images kept the young boy awake in his bed: a middle-aged woman with Down syndrome, a prisoner on death row, the teenage girl in a car accident. Eli had heard the sexual innuendoes from the male medical students as they dissected the girl's pelvis. Memories good and bad were ingrained in the history of this place.

Once, Eli had asked Gaston about these people. Unaware of ethics as a discipline, he nevertheless asked how it could be ethical to use their bodies if they had not given permission. The boy's suspicion grew when Gaston told him to mind his own business. To ask this of his father would never have occurred to Eli.

The youngest son of Elizer and Naomi Branch, Eli was considered a prodigy by everyone in Anatomy Hall. At ten years of age, he could draw the branches of the brachial plexus with three-dimensional accuracy, including spatial relationships to the subclavian artery. At twelve, one group of students let him open a skull with the circular saw. When he finished the task, he peeled back the bowl-shaped skull and handed it to a squeamish female student, to the cheers and accolades of a male-dominated class. But none of the students knew that Eli was troubled by these things.

How did I come out of those years without being psychologically crippled? Or maybe I am.

Eli approached the rear door, wood-framed with a stone arch of Gothic design. He twisted the knob, anticipating that it would be locked. From his pocket he removed a chain of keys and opened the door as if he were the janitor or night watchman. Eli had always kept a key to the hall, but didn't know why.

Until now.

He stepped into the back storage room, musty and stale, careful to watch his footing on a wet layer of slime that covered the concrete floor. He swung the beam of his penlight across wooden crates of formalin fixative stacked in the corner. The rest of the room was empty.

From this part of the building, Eli could not remember how to get to Gaston's room. He thought of the layout from the front entrance and tried to work backward. Students entered through the foyer, ignoring its marble floor and dark-paneled walls hung with anatomist's portraits. Instead, they peered at the antique display cases lining the walls that held dissection instruments from the early eighteen hundreds. As a boy, Eli's favorite relic was a human skull with a line of bone missing, a hatchet having been driven through.

Immediately off the foyer, he pictured the hallway leading to the great room, the Hall of Cadavers. The size and shape of a basketball court, it held thirty-five tables spaced ten feet apart. Each table was seven feet long with a stainless steel center and legs that could be adjusted for height. All the tables would be empty in July.

The room had as many windows as it did tables. Before the building was air-conditioned, the massive windows, placed high along the ceiling, could be opened to allow the formalin fumes to escape. It had been Eli's job to open them early each morning before the students arrived. While his father and Gaston uncovered the bodies and prepared them for dissection, Eli would remove a long wooden pole from the wall. Using the hook on the end of the pole, Eli would release the latch, find the notch in the bottom sill of each frame, and pivot the windows open. He could still hear the creak of grinding, rusty hinges that marked the beginning of each new day. Afterward, he walked the half-mile to his school to study the mundane subjects of English and math.

Late afternoons, he returned to lock the windows. They could stay open to provide ventilation, but on a wet day, if the wind blew hard enough, the rain would splash in.

The first week that ten-year-old Eli was responsible for the windows, an overnight thunderstorm awakened him. With the wind and rain beating on the window of his bedroom, Eli immediately knew he had forgotten to close the windows in Anatomy Hall. He crept out of the house and ran the near-mile to the medical campus, drenched to the skin. When he arrived, the rain and wind had subsided, with only a few flashes of lightning to give him a glimpse of the damage to the hall. The large center window on the west side had rotated into a horizontal position. That's when he heard movement in the corner of the room full of cadavers. When the next flash of lightning illuminated the chamber, he saw Gaston lying naked on top of one of the bodies. The man had braced himself on his hands and was rhythmically pushing and pulling against the body beneath him, his back arched. Abruptly, he turned his head and looked straight at Eli. The image of two bodies, their pale skin starkly lit by the last signs of the storm, remained imprinted in Eli's memory long after the room became dark again. A few seconds later, a final flash, and Gaston was gone.

Eli ran home as fast as he could. He returned the next morning with his father, saying nothing. Gaston was already there, mopping up the water that had blown in overnight. But the damage had not been caused by the rain. The wind had blown the plastic covers off three cadavers, and their open abdomens and dissected extremities had become the resting place for the leaves and twigs that the storm had torn from the maple tree outside the window. One exposed brain had bits of trash contaminating deep into its recesses.

Eli was sickened by the sight of what his forgetfulness caused. He knew his father would be furious. But before Eli received the blame, Gaston spoke up. He told Elizer Branch that he was the one who had opened the window before the storm and had forgotten to close it. Eli looked at Gaston and wondered why he was taking the blame that was his alone.

Then he knew.

Eli spent the rest of the day with those who had donated their bodies, picking out the dirt and leaves that he had allowed to defile their dignity. Nothing further of that stormy night was ever spoken.

Behind the hall, close to where Eli stood in his scrubs with his penlight, were the boiler rooms where large black pipes hissed and emitted loud eructations of steam every three minutes, even in July. This performance was preceded by a rhythmic pecking of steel against steel, as if someone were inside trying to knock free with a hammer. No matter how desensitized the anatomy students became, this sound reverberated in their ears for months after leaving the hall. In the midst of formalin and death and the noise of the boiler, Gaston had lived for over forty years.

Eli left the storage area and moved along a side corridor that led him toward the sounds of pecking and hissing. Humidity condensed on the walls and oozed to the floor, where a sheen festered, waiting for summer insects to brood and lay eggs. Everywhere the corridor was wet and unnaturally cold, as though the underworld were sending up drafts off a block of ice.

Eli followed the hallway that emptied into a room he recognized as the embalming chamber. In its center stood the familiar wooden table, the same splintered planks, weathered like a neglected deck but pickled from years of formalin seeping from overfilled veins. Of all the sights and smells of death that infused Anatomy Hall, it was this room, this table that disturbed Eli most. Maybe because it looked like an instrument of capital punishment, leather straps for ankles and wrists, as if its occupant would struggle free or be pardoned by a last-minute court decision. Eli skirted the table as though it were electrified.

Gaston's room was strategically positioned off the embalming chamber, since this room was where he spent most of his working day. A single bare lightbulb hung from a ceiling cord where it cast an irritating glare. Eli stood in the doorway of Gaston's tiny room, sadness sweeping over him like wind through a vacant house.

How could anyone live here, day after day, year after year? Every respiration a breath of formalin until mucous membranes morphed into leather. A life oddly preserved in a world of death.

The sadness he felt was not from the loss of Gaston as a friend or teacher or estranged family — whatever he was. It was the cruel reality that Eli was the only witness to the morbid pleasure the man had found in his life.

The room was the size of a mansion's walk-in closet, an exact square of maybe twenty by twenty feet. A foldout cot was pushed against the corner, low to the floor. One straight-backed chair held multiple layers of clothes folded over it. Against the wall stood a cardboard table holding a pyramid of cans — a week's worth of food. A washbasin in the corner sat on a square board. For a moment, Eli could see the old man standing there, a can held close to his mouth with the sharp lid pried open, long grey hair mingling with a cold bite of soup.

A prison cell. This is what it's like to serve in prison.

Gaston had no television or radio. Certainly no home computer. What was there to do? Yet Gaston was free to go and come as he pleased. Eli imagined the old man lurking in the hall to check on the inhabitants, an innkeeper for the dead.

Even though the room offered no toilet, Eli did not detect the smell of urine. He noticed that hooked on the cot was a plastic urinal, the handheld kind from a hospital. He remembered there was a toilet in the locker room where the med students changed into scrubs.

He must have emptied it in there.

This was all there was. *Is it possible,* Eli wondered, *for someone to live such a bare existence?* He looked along the wall and under the table for some relic of Gaston's life. Something that held together the scraps of who he was, where he came from, who he wanted to be.

The bulb cast a shadow off the edge of Gaston's cot, and spider webs beaded with dust bridged the foot-high gap off the floor. There was no other place to hide what Eli was hoping to find. He leaned down, brushed the webs away with his hand, and felt along the floor until he reached the edge of a box. Even Gaston had a few possessions to collect and pass on. As Eli pulled the box from under the cot, it scraped heavily along the cement floor.

It was a hatbox. And it was not covered with webs and dirt, so it must have been removed and opened recently. Only a thin layer of dust partially obscured the brand name. Stetson. Eli could not imagine Gaston in a cowboy hat.

He placed the box on the cot and removed the lid, the old, thin mattress sagging as he sat on it. The box was full, and on top of the stack lay a purple notebook, the kind with spiral binding that leaves ragged bits when a page is torn out. On its pages, Eli saw remarkably elegant handwriting, not at all the scribble he expected. It was a journal, each entry a page or so in length, separated by a single dateline in quotation marks.

The final entry was dated July ninth, the day Gaston died. It began:

They came for me again today at 10 o'clock, Benny the assistant, and the muscle they call Tongue. I was up and waiting for them this time, not having slept the night. Tongue grabbed me by the neck but I waved him off.

Eli remembered the feel of Tongue's hands on his legs. A chill passed through him.

After we crossed the river, they drove around back and we entered through the loading dock, as before. I climbed on the table and Benny and the nurse lingered over me. Their stares told me this was the beginning of the end. As if they cared.

The doctor did more work on the graft without a drop of local anesthesia. I watched the catheter on the screen, piercing the femoral artery and snaking through the iliac to the aorta. The tip of the catheter wiggled like a worm in the metal graft cage. Retribution for all those bodies. Now me, a living cadaver.

They brought me back to the hall and Tongue dropped me on the cot. Benny put a bottle of Percocet in my hand. Said to take as many as I wanted. I put them away and waited for the pain to hit. I want to feel completely alive for the final hours.

Eli closed the journal and placed it on the cot beside him. Eli's brief pang of compassion was quickly replaced with the details of Gaston's clinical history; diagnostician merging with criminal investigator.

Gaston was transported somewhere for a procedure, a catheterization through his groin — to his aorta.

The puncture wounds at the crease of Henry's leg.

It was all connected somehow.

The tiny holes that Meg had found.

Lankford's death.

But how did the catheterization cause the rupture? By poking holes with a needle? No, couldn't be. With the pulsating aortic pressure, the vessel would rupture immediately and Gaston would have bled out. Whatever was done was a gradual process, like a slow-release capsule. If the catheterization took place a little before noon, the rupture did not occur for another ten to twelve hours.

Eli looked back in the box, the sum of the man's possessions, a life. Beneath Gaston's journal lay a stack of newspaper clippings held together with a single paper clip. The first clipping was from the *Commercial Appeal*'s business section. Eli was surprised to see himself — a head shot as part of the article that announced his appointment as assistant professor at the medical school. He thumbed through the other articles quickly, puzzled. This was not Gaston's life but that of the Branch's. His mother's obituary, his father's, an article from the Sunday *Appeal* about Anatomy Hall, the pair of father and son anatomists. Then a headline that made Eli's stomach clinch.

REGENCY BIOTECH INTERNATIONAL RELOCATES TO MEMPHIS

Why would Gaston care about RBI?
The next article was faded and brittle. The date in the upper left corner read 1973, and the headline announced:

ANATOMY PROFESSOR'S SON UNDERGOES RISKY, LIFE-SAVING OPERATION

Eli read the article quickly, skipping to find the names. Elizer and Naomi Branch. The child's name — Henry.
He skipped to the bottom of the article.

> The expense of the operation will be covered by a start-up company, Regent Biotech, located in New York City. Dr. Branch expressed gratitude to the company for covering his son's medical bills.

Eli remembered Regent Biotech from his Internet search, the precursor to RBI. But that was 1973, surely a different company. The final sentence of the article confirmed his fear.

> Regent Biotech is trying to develop metal stent devices to be used in cardiovascular disease.

Eli was completely absorbed in his reading now, unaware of the room's glare and formalin stench. He held the brittle paper with both hands. A fine tremor began and the paper rattled.
I must have read it wrong, Eli thought. *Could my father have been involved with this company, Regent Biotech?*
The room had been quiet until Eli felt air moving under him. This was immediately followed by the escalating whine of a hydraulic lift, like an amusement park ride starting slow and gaining speed. The sound was not loud, but it was abrupt and difficult to locate. Eli felt disoriented.

Later, Eli would remember dropping the clippings. *I should have stuffed them in my pocket.* He stood, and as the room seemed to spin, he closed his eyes a moment.

When he opened his eyes, Eli could tell the noise emanated from below him. But he was confused by the fact that the building did not have another floor below the basement — not one he was aware of. He felt a draft of air pulling toward a corner of the room. Eli pushed the washbasin away and lifted the board to reveal a square hole, two feet across, as though a chunk of concrete had been excised. The high-pitched sound dropped off, the monster whip ride coming to a stop. But the noise of the machine, or whatever it was, continued to run. Eli heard a series of knocks, evenly spaced about a second apart, like gears catching in the loops of a giant chain. And then the whirring sound again and the process started over. Eli leaned over the hole and felt a slight tug, as though a vacuum pulled him down.

What the hell?

There was no flash of light or flame such as Eli expected to see. The hole beneath him was completely black. But one swipe of his penlight revealed the iron rungs of a ladder. In all the years that Eli had spent in this building, he had never known of another level or heard sounds such as these. He hesitated, but then his curiosity got the best of him. He stepped onto the ladder.

CHAPTER THIRTY-SEVEN

Meg Daily told the waitperson to give her a corner table. "Someone will be joining me. Tall, with slightly graying hair, cut short."

"Can I get you something to drink while you wait?"

"No, thank you."

The waitperson removed the wine list from her table.

"You know," Meg said. "I will have something after all. A margarita, frozen, with salt."

"Sure, and I'll keep an eye out for that Mr. Someone," he said with a swagger of his hip, as though he might snatch Eli for himself.

The restaurant was filled with dinner guests and the bar scene festive. A young crowd stood at the long polished driftwood bar with drinks in hand, continuous chatter. The décor was anything but bland. A zebra-print banquette lined the wall and each colorfully upholstered bar stool was occupied. Meg removed her cell phone from a tiny black purse that she hadn't used for years. She called the sitter to check on her daughter as the waiter brought the margarita. She wiped off the excess salt and took a sip while hearing that Margaret was fast asleep. She placed her phone on the table and took another mouthful of the frozen drink. She opened the menu and an offering of voodoo stew caught her eye as did the coconut mango shrimp. Above the rim of her glass, she noticed a young man at the bar looking at her. He turned on his orange bar stool to face his friend.

Meg savored the drink, letting the ice slide along her tongue. She tried to remember the last time she had a margarita but the memory was erased by the rush of a cold headache. Meg closed her eyes and put her head in her hands. When the sensation passed and she raised her head, the man at the bar was smiling at her. She looked away and fidgeted with her purse. But through her peripheral vision, she knew he was walking toward her. She saw that her blouse had shifted off her shoulder and her bra strap was showing. It was too late to fix it.

"Are you okay?"

His V-neck sweater had short sleeves that revealed rippled biceps. He looked as if he had just left the gym. And he was young, very young, college age or just beyond.

"Yes, I'm fine, thank you."

"If you don't like that drink, I'll buy you another one."

Meg laughed and then covered her mouth.

This cute young hunk just gave me a line.

Meg looked over at his friend as though maybe this was a bet or a dare. "You're kidding, right?"

"No, I'm very serious." He offered his hand. "My name's Jake."

During the brief handshake, Meg felt bits of salt stuck to her fingers. Jake motioned to the empty chair at her table.

"Thank you, really, but I'm meeting someone."

He backed up and said, "If you change your mind, I'm right over there."

Meg winked at him as he returned to the bar. She glanced at her watch.

At least I think I'm meeting someone.

At the opposite end of the bar, away from Meg, a man opened a copy of the *New York Times*. He was older than the bar patrons around him and dressed in black slacks, a black, long-sleeved shirt, and fancy dress shoes. He stroked his goatee methodically, pretending to read the paper, as he closely watched Dr. Meg Daily.

CHAPTER THIRTY-EIGHT

Eli held to the ladder and searched blindly for the floor with his foot. The only sound now was that of water dripping, not the pat-pat cadence of a faucet, but the spew of a leak through cracks in the wall. When he felt an uneven gravel surface beneath him, Eli stepped off the ladder. He turned to face a dark room, degrees cooler than the upper level and with the pervasive smell of an electrical fire, snuffed out.

Before he turned on the penlight, he took a few steps forward until the crest of his right hip met the solid edge of a table. The faint light from above revealed the splintered surface of thick wood, more workbench than desk, pushed against the wall. He could see a lamp on the table and felt for the switch before he realized it didn't have one. Conveniently located at the base was a pile of stick matches. He struck one against the lamp base and let the flame locate the kerosene-saturated wick. Eli smiled at the ease and proficiency with which he lit the antiquated lamp. He was equally surprised by the warm light cast across the room, shadows dancing with each flicker.

Directly behind him was the ledge of a trough cut into the concrete floor. Like an underground subway in quarter scale, the four-foot-deep channel traveled into a tunnel and disappeared into darkness.

Next to the lamp on the table was an oversized book, its pages open and resembling a wedding register or a ledger for recording guest's at a wake. Eli pulled the lamp closer and the pages appeared as frail parchment. Only the right-hand page was inscribed in a column along the fold. Eli recognized the slant-angled cursive letters, Gaston's handiwork.

The open page contained a single name with identifiers listed on skipped lines below.

Name: Patrick Sorenson
Date: June 24, 2005
Age: 32
Cause of Death: Motor Vehicle Accident

There were two categories, both unfilled, that did not fit with the traditional processing of cadavers.

Shipped to:
Price:

Price?

Eli flipped to the next page but it was blank, so he turned back. During his early years in Anatomy Hall, Eli had witnessed certain events that he could not understand — cadavers that arrived by shipping trucks but were gone the next day, Gaston dismembering a cadaver but the body parts never being used by the medical students. Reading what was before him now, the commodity of bodies, he felt as though some of his questions were about to be answered.

Then the sound returned — an unwilling, unpredictable churn of rusty cogs against the grain, amplified by both proximity and confinement. Eli sensed motion below the ledge, confirmed by the parallel traction of chains pulling a metal cart into his peripheral view, like a subway train approaching without light or urgency to decelerate.

Instinctively, Eli stepped back and the cart came to a halt directly in front of him, its sheet-covered cargo shifting with the abrupt stop. Eli guessed the cart was seven feet long, four feet wide, and about three feet deep. Like a large metal bathtub, the cart sat within the concrete trough and had an open compartment below that was mostly hidden. Below this, the cart was secured to the heavy chains that pulled it.

The familiarity of the cart was unnerving. Staring at it, Eli could see a younger Gaston pushing a similar cart alongside the dissection table, locking it in place while he lifted a body, his strained leverage released by the bony thud of skull against steel.

The grinding noise changed to idle mode, an over and over repeated like a scratch on an old record but with a metallic click and grind, a cog stripping a gear. Eli approached the cart as though to fulfill an obligatory function: a role, he assumed, which had been filled by Gaston for many years. The machine, in its momentary delay, neither grieved for Gaston nor perceived his replacement.

Eli imagined the likely occupant of the cart, unified with other cadavers by the process of aging — tanned, wrinkled skin transformed into a leathery shell that obliterated any expression of the living person. This familiar image stayed with Eli as he pulled back the sheet from the cart. It took a moment before the deep wrinkles in his mind's eye adjusted to the smooth, perfect complexion of a young woman, nude, arms folded modestly across her chest. Eli glanced away as if to preserve her dignity. As a doctor, he was used to clinical nudity, but this seemed perverse. *But what dignity remained? Her body pulled anonymously, alone, in an underground cart? To where? To what end?*

Eli examined her skin, his curiosity overcoming any self-consciousness now. She was without blemish or the bruise of trauma, no cut or wound of entrance or exit. As he moved his light over her left hip, the beam caught a mark. He leaned closer so that the circle of light contracted onto the pink butterfly tattoo folded along the iliac crest, wings pulled back in a position of rest, or caution.

He twisted the tag on her toe into view but the name meant nothing to him.

Marisa Svengoli.

The clicking sound increased at a sickening pace and the cart lunged forward. Instinctively, so that the girl was not transported uncovered, Eli flipped the sheet over and toward her head. But the edge caught on her elbow, leaving the left breast exposed.

The concrete furrow led the cart past a stone wall that jutted at a right angle and separated the room from the tunnel beyond. He squeezed past the wall and stepped into a second room illuminated by the flicker flame inside a dome-shaped incinerator.

Was this her fate? Cremation?

But as his eyes adjusted, he saw that the cart's path led past the furnace, not through it. And there wasn't a white-hot fire required to cremate a body but rather a maintenance flame, like a pilot light in a gas heater. Eli glanced around him as if to find the true perpetrator in this morbid practical joke.

The cart moved at a steady pace toward an uncertain destination. *Was he supposed to stoke the fire and hoist the body in like a stump of wood? Is that what Gaston would do?* Even though he would never consider it, Eli was relieved when Marisa's body passed by the incinerator. He felt like her protector now, the mental pronunciation of her name imparting a sense of chivalry. The cart continued toward a dark opening, square and just large enough to allow entrance. At this pace, the cart was four, maybe five, seconds from entrance to the tunnel.

And then what? *Can I still follow it?*

He decided that not knowing was worse than the unseen. Eli stepped off the ledge and landed with his feet balanced on the cart's rear axle and both hands on the push bar, like a child freewheeling down a grocery store aisle. The cart's momentum changed to that of the ratcheted pull of a roller coaster up an incline before the breathtaking plunge. Just as the cart broke over the ledge, during that brief moment of equilibrating plateau, Eli realized that this ride would be without the benefit of a safety bar.

The plunge was hard and deep, into complete darkness with only stone walls rushing past, inches away. Eli gripped hard, his back frozen in the posture of a wind surfer. He endured the ride as the cart bucked and shuddered as if it might disintegrate. He felt the front of the cart rise and then it began to slow, pulled along a flat surface. Dim light seeped through portals spaced wide and high on the walls as the tunnel opened into a corridor. With the cart's inertia abated, the chain pull caught and it jerked forward.

The force of acceleration had pushed Marisa against the back wall of the cart so that her neck bent at a right angle, her eyes partially open and staring at him. Eli leaned over and pulled the sheet to cover her again.

He looked ahead to study their path. Only three, maybe four minutes had passed, but he was now far removed from Anatomy Hall. Water dripped from the ceiling and trickled from the tunnel walls. It filled the trough beneath them and Eli felt his shoes submerged. The trickle of water increased until miniature waterfalls seemed to sprout from the walls, and Eli sensed water rising to his ankles. There was more light now, oblique smoky columns penetrating from the left side. At a distance of thirty yards he saw a door-sized opening in the wall with stone steps leading down into the tunnel. They passed within ten feet of the opening, which was littered with newspaper as if blown in from the street above.

We must be two or three floors below street level, Eli thought. *What am I doing, anyway, riding with this woman underground? She is dead. What further harm could come to her?*

Eli could rationalize it now. Maybe this was the way that the city disposed of the dead, those unknown without family to claim them. Growing up in Memphis, he had heard about tunnels that existed beneath downtown. The newspapers reported the underground passages were a haven for the homeless and an escape route for criminals. Some believed the tunnels stretched farther than downtown. Like the Queens-Midtown tunnel in New York City under the East River, although on smaller scale, one Memphis tunnel reportedly cut below the Mississippi River the length of a mile out to an island that housed a prison camp decades ago. Eli knew now that the tunnel actually existed.

Farther down the tunnel, another faint column of light appeared along the wall. At that opening, Eli planned to jump from the cart. He would follow one of the stairwells to the street, dial 911, and inform the police. He briefly considered the story he would tell.

I entered Anatomy Hall and heard a strange noise underground. A young dead girl, her body pulled along a tunnel.

He could imagine their response.

So, Dr. Branch, you broke into a medical school building. Aren't your medical privileges suspended?

It did sound absurd, coming from the crazy doctor with the murdered lab technician. Eli decided it was best to tell no one.

They were halfway to the next doorway now. He considered how high he would have to jump to clear the cart. The water would provide resistance, his feet heavy. But still, it was only a yard or so up to the ledge. He could almost step that far. He tried to relax the muscles in his left leg, stiff with a developing hamstring cramp. Even though the cart moved at the same slow pace, the light from the opening was coming closer, twenty feet away. As he shifted to his right foot, the light diminished, as though a shade had been drawn. A shadow descended, one step at a time, and the silhouette of a man filled the opening in the wall.

Eli slid into the hidden compartment beneath the cart. He balanced on the narrow metal platform, his knees soaked by the swirling brown stew. He heard the man moving forward, his appearance perfectly timed with the cart's arrival. Through a small gap between the cart and the concrete ledge, Eli saw the man, a baseball cap pulled low to his eyes, baggy shirt over sweatpants. The man leaned forward and grasped the side of the cart. With a lateral swing, as though clearing a fence, he hoisted himself inside, landing on top of the body. The buggy rocked sideways with enough force to dislodge it from the track. Eli's knee slipped and the chain scraped his shin down to the bone. The putrid water bathed the wound and set fire to the gash. He crouched lower under the cart, staying out of sight of the man who was not more than five feet away.

What is this guy doing?

Then Eli thought that maybe this was part of the plan. Another processing site for the body to be disposed of, an underground burial to save space in the crowded city cemeteries. He's just a city employee for this glorified waste management system, the final caretaker.

The cart stabilized and Eli could hear nothing other than the grind of the chain. He planned to stay hidden and escape up the next set of steps.

Has the man removed the body? Is he still there? Eli looked behind him but there was nothing but a swirling yellow-brown wake that filled the path. Through a background of falling water, Eli heard the man speaking in a low groan.

"That's it now, precious." And then louder as though signaling ahead. "You're going to like this one, you dirty bastard."

Looking just above the lip of the cart, Eli could see the man's back humped in a grotesque bend over Marisa with the sheet pulled away. Further down the corridor, a second man appeared. He moved quickly toward the cart, rubbing the palms of his hands together as if preparing for a meal.

Eli's confusion resolved to clarity. These men were predators, the dead their prey. Eli's childhood memory of Gaston, alone with the cadaver, flashed briefly. He couldn't stop the intrusion then, but he would not let it happen again. With his footing secured on the cart's axle, Eli pulled himself above the cart and hooked the man's neck with his arm, pulling him back in a headlock that brought them eye to eye. But instead of struggling, the man yelled, "Hey, wait your turn," as though a game had started and he was in line before his partner. When his gaze on Eli came into focus, the man twisted violently and Eli strangled him so that the next sentence stopped with "what the?"

From the force of the man's pull, Eli knew the man would fight rather than try to escape. He was equal to Eli in age and build and he threw an elbow that sent a compression wave deep into Eli's right ear. Eli's head recoiled and he felt the cart shake as the man jumped from it. For a moment, Eli saw nothing.

CHAPTER THIRTY-NINE

Eli knew that he was still vulnerable to another blow, either from this man or his partner up ahead. Upon regaining his focus, however, he saw that both of them had disappeared and he could no longer gauge how far he and Marisa had traveled since the assault. The ringing in his ear distorted his equilibrium, and he held onto the cart handle, waiting for it to pass. The burning pain in his leg changed to a deep ache, and he examined the cut with his fingertip, the swirling turbid water below. The smooth hard surface of his shinbone was exposed. He opened his eyes at intervals for fear of another unwanted visitor. The openings that led to above ground were no longer present. He was relieved that he and Marisa were alone.

After what seemed like another mile in complete darkness, Eli felt the front of the cart tilt upward and they were pulled along an incline. He thought about the route they had taken since leaving Anatomy Hall. There was a sharp plunge at the beginning followed by a long route deep underground. Now they were being raised back to ground level. Eli was sure that along this track was the cart's final destination.

At the top of the incline, the tunnel widened to a mouth flooded with bright light. Eli's vision had accommodated to that of a cave dweller and he closed his eyes to adjust. His hearing seemed hyperacute as well. There were voices ahead, men's voices. They had been waiting for Marisa, no doubt.

As the cart came into full view, Eli crouched again in the bottom compartment so that he was hidden. He could hear approaching foot-steps.

From his floor-level view, it appeared that they were in a narrow concrete corridor, like the receiving dock of a warehouse. A man spoke loudly, as if into a speaker.

"The body's here. Where you want her?"

There was a crack of static in response. "Set her up on the table, Bennie. We're ready."

There was an electrical buzz and the cart came to an abrupt stop, as though a brick had been thrown at the wheels. The name Bennie struck Eli hard — from Gaston's journal. Bennie had carried Gaston to the final procedure that initiated the old man's death.

"Look boss, she's so pretty."

Eli recognized Tongue's garbled speech from the guardhouse at RBI. He could see the man's enormous boots at the rear of the cart.

"Just get her feet and quit looking. You know we're on camera," Bennie said.

Eli felt the cart shift as Marisa's body was lifted. He watched the legs of both men, shuffling under the weight of her body as they carried it through a doorway off the platform.

Eli was alone now. The cart was parked below the concrete ledge and there were no signs or any indication of where he was. He studied the cart path before him as it made a sharp U-turn and doubled back on a parallel track from where they had come. A red light began to flash, fol-lowed immediately by a loud buzz as the cart jerked forward. Just before it reached the U-turn, Eli jumped off and caught the edge of the plat-form, pulling himself up to the concrete floor. He looked behind him as the empty cart fell out of sight.

Eli followed the trail of voices down a brightly lit hallway angling sharply to the right. The floor was made of white tile that had been scrubbed hospital clean. He looked around the corner and saw that the men had stopped at the end of the passageway. They pushed a gurney in-side an elevator and the doors closed behind them.

Eli ran the full length of the hall. There was no light above the elevator to indicate which floor it was on. He entered a stairwell just to the left of the single elevator shaft and climbed one flight. He tried the door but it was locked.

The door on the next level opened into a foyer, like the lobby of an old theatre. The light in the foyer came from a single column of glass erected in the center of the crescent-shaped space. The column appeared empty but when Eli approached it, he saw a small flesh-colored object that rotated in a counterclockwise direction. It was no bigger than a marble but there was a remarkable set of eyes and the buds of little hands and feet — a human embryo.

Eli stepped around the column, following the same direction as the life form rotated. It had no attachments as if suspended by the light itself. As he circled, however, the embryo diminished, losing its distinctive features until it was barely visible as a grain of sand.

Eli reversed his circle, moving right. The embryo not only regained its original form but developed and grew fingers and toes and an arch in its back, the head tilted gently to reveal tiny ears and a wispy tuft of hair.

Eli wanted to study the illusion further, but at the far end of the foyer, the shadow of a figure distracted him and he hid behind the glass column. The glare obscured his vision but he could tell that the person was moving toward him. A door off the foyer opened, the influx of light revealing the person in the doorway to be Tsarina. She held a blanket-covered bundle in the crook of her arm. The door shut behind her.

Eli's mind raced as he tried to make sense of it. He had gone to Anatomy Hall to search Gaston's room for information that might explain his death. He wasn't prepared to find the journal that linked his brother's childhood operation to the company that had now hired him. *The operation was funded by Regent Biotech.*

And then the tunnel, the girl's body, traveling underground a mile, two miles? The systematic transport of bodies for experimentation. Bodies for sale? He was sickened by the sudden realization that his father had allowed the smuggling of cadavers to the biomedical device company.

Eli waited a full sixty seconds. He guessed he had traveled at least a mile in the tunnel. Now, with Tsarina's appearance, he knew exactly where he was. Seeing no further movement, he crossed the foyer, opened the door, and entered the Oval Terrace of RBI.

CHAPTER FORTY

Eli stood outside the top grandstand of a deep amphitheater, with semi-circular rows of chairs at least thirty feet above the center pit. All of the seats were empty. Although modernized, Eli recognized it as similar to the old surgical amphitheatres in which students peered over their seats to watch an operation being performed below.

Eli stepped inside and wedged himself between two wooden support posts where he had a clear view of the stage below. The young girl, Marisa, had been placed on the operating table. She was naked, with safety straps across her thighs. Bennie and Tongue hovered over her.

Eli heard movement to his left. He eased forward to see Tsarina in a seat next to the far wall. In her arms was an infant whom she held against her left breast. The baby was not moving. It appeared rigid, as though preserved, and Eli immediately knew that it was dead.

Tsarina positioned the frozen mouth of the child over her left nipple. She bounced the baby gently and leaned close to the banister to have an unobstructed view of the proceedings beneath her.

Eli turned away from the sight of Tsarina with the dead child and watched Tongue as he wheeled in another body. It was a young man lying on a stretcher and hooked to a ventilator. Eli recognized the boy, the soft, innocent features of his face. Just as Eli had seen Henry's roommate at Green Hills State Home, it was evident now, the body curled in a fetal position beneath the sheets.

Jimmy.

Tongue pulled the gurney while Bennie carefully rolled the anesthesia machine forward, which hissed and clicked with every breath delivered. Accompanying them were two hired hands in security guard uniforms. Each carried a holstered pistol on his belt.

Tongue and Bennie positioned Jimmy parallel to Marisa's table, only three feet between them, but with Jimmy's head adjacent to the dead girl's feet. The two men waited a moment while looking toward the door from which they had come. And then, wearing a gown and gloves but no mask, Korinsky entered.

Eli thought of the night, earlier in the week, although it seemed like months ago, when he was called in to assist Korinsky. Everything had been downhill since then. He had been chewed out by his chairman, questioned as a murder suspect, and, after being fired, was the primary surgeon to oversee the long, painful hospitalization of the son of one of the richest, most influential men in the mid-South. He wanted to blame Korinsky for it all.

Bennie exited briefly and returned with a man Eli had not seen in surgical garb before. The man had always worn a white coat stretched over broadly humped shoulders, or a business suit that made him look more like a high-ranking mobster than chairman of surgery at a major medical center.

Karl Fisher walked on stage. Korinsky and the others stood at attention. It was obvious that Fisher was in charge.

How can this be? Eli further concealed himself by sliding behind the wooden columns. *I was fired for consorting with the biopharmaceutical devil, and here is Fisher leading the whole ghoulish pack.*

"How's the boy?" Fisher asked, nodding to Jimmy, whose only sign of life was an occasional breath from the ventilator.

"He's stable," Korinsky answered.

Fisher stopped at Marisa's side and looked her over. "Damn shame."

Then, he became trance-like, eyes lingering on her body.

Bennie looked at Korinsky for direction as the awkwardness continued. Korinsky held up one finger and they all waited for Fisher to come out of it.

"His young age should make this a good run," Fisher said at last, referring to Jimmy. "Let's get started."

Bennie removed the drape from the side table to reveal a set of surgical instruments. Even from his elevated position, Eli could discern the collection. Vascular clamps, a Bookwalter retractor, all of the instruments needed for a major abdominal operation.

What the hell are they planning?

It made no sense. A dead girl and a young, institutionalized mental patient?

Fisher moved to the right side of Jimmy's table and Korinsky stood between the two tables. Since they were right-handed surgeons, they were both in position to make an incision.

Bennie handed a scalpel to Fisher and one to Korinsky. Both held their scalpels poised over the abdomen, Fisher over the young boy, Jimmy, Korinsky over Marisa.

"Okay, start the timer."

A digital clock was inset high on the wall, large red numbers displaying twelve minutes. The countdown started and it changed to eleven minutes, fifty-nine seconds.

In synchrony, each surgeon cut a long and deep abdominal incision. Old dark blood oozed from Marisa's incision, but Jimmy's entire abdominal surface was flooded with bright red spurting blood. Remarkably, Jimmy had not been anesthetized and the pain of the incision racked his body and he rose up flailing.

"Damn it, Korinsky," Fisher yelled. "He's not under."

Korinsky laid his scalpel on Marisa's abdomen and turned to help, but Jimmy grabbed Fisher's hand and yanked it violently.

"Open the gas, I can't control him." Bennie and Tongue pushed Jimmy's shoulders and slammed him against the bed. The force jerked Fisher's hand, and his scalpel sliced a hole in the anesthesia tubing. Korinsky twisted the purple cylinder to the full position and halothane gas escaped through the open conduit.

As he watched the scene deteriorate, Eli moved from between the posts and now stood out in the open. Because his natural response was to move toward the scene of a medical disaster, he ran unthinkingly down the stairs toward the stage.

The anesthesia machine emitted a loud signal to warn that a break in the circuit had occurred. A second warning signal started, this one a loud shrill that indicated a life-threatening change in ventilation. The pressure had escaped the tubing and the ventilator could no longer breathe for Jimmy. His pulse was dropping rapidly.

Eli ran down the stairs now, pointing at the anesthesia machine. "You've got to bag him, he's going to code."

Everyone froze. Korinsky stared at Eli with his mouth open.

Fisher appeared disgusted. "How did he find us?"

Korinsky pointed at Eli to alert the guards. "Stop that son of a bitch."

With hands on their guns, the guards sprinted toward Eli, who stopped at the base of the stairs. He continued to focus on Jimmy. "You're killing him."

"We all die," Fisher yelled as Jimmy writhed in an anoxic struggle. "This is no concern of yours, Branch."

Eli backpedaled up the stairs and pointed at Jimmy. "That boy lives with my brother." As he said this, Eli was struck with the thought that if they had access to Jimmy, they had access to Henry. He turned and ran up the stairs, the guards a few steps behind. When he reached the top, he could feel them on his back, about to lunge. From behind the glass column, Tsarina stepped in front of the guards and they collided. Tsarina twisted sideways but remained on her feet. The guards stopped and were shocked to see a bundled infant knocked from her arms and sliding across the floor.

Eli ran through the foyer straight for the stairwell. Tsarina's diversion had created a much-needed gap from his pursuers. He wondered why, if she was part of this travesty, she had done this for him.

In the stairwell, Eli could hear their voices behind him. Taking three steps at a time, he burst onto the loading dock.

"Yes," he said when he saw his fortunate timing. An empty body cart was seconds before the U-turn. Without slowing, Eli leapt from the platform and landed feet first in the cart. It shook wildly. He crouched low in the cart just as it made the turn.

"There he is," one of the guards shouted as they ran to the edge. The cart accelerated and began its descent into the tunnel.

Seeing both men take aim, Eli flattened himself in the cart. A two-inch layer of water in the bottom smelled like sewage. The first shot missed the cart but it made Eli plunge his face into the putrid water. The second shot was more accurate. It ripped through the side of the cart inches above Eli's head. He lifted his face out of the water and could no longer see the bright light from the receiving area. The cart descended into darkness.

CHAPTER FORTY-ONE

Detective Lipsky punched the numbers to Police Headquarters into his cell phone.

"Forensics please," he told the operator.

Since Basetti was usually the only one there, he answered the call with, "You got him."

"You won't believe where I am."

Basetti thought and hesitated a second. "Sounds like you're in the bottom of a toilet."

Lipsky looked at the sides of the cart, illuminated only by the soft glow from his cell phone. The seat of his trousers was wet and he could feel a line of water trickle down between his buttocks. "How did you know?"

"Where the hell are you, seriously?"

"Following Branch's ass."

Basetti snickered. "Sounds like you lost him."

"He broke into the Anatomy building . . . on campus," Lipsky said, still out of breath. "Let me tell you . . . that's one creepy place. Dark as hell. Pickled body parts floating in jars."

"Didn't his father work there?"

"Yeah, no wonder Branch is so screwed up. Anyway, he sneaks down in the basement. By the time I get there, he is jumping into this," Lipsky hesitates and raps his knuckle against the aluminum side, "this moving buggy."

"Buggy?"

"Yeah, and guess who he has with him?"

"Who?"

"A young girl, deader than wood."

There was silence on the line.

"Basetti?"

"Chief, what you been smoking?"

"I'm serious. Branch dragged this young naked girl down a tunnel. He's some weird cat, I'm telling you."

"Where's he now?"

"I lost him, he's up ahead in this damn tunnel somewhere."

Basetti could hear a steady churning through Lipsky's phone. "So let me get this straight. You're in a tunnel, riding a buggy, and Branch has escaped with a naked dead girl?"

"All in a day's work, my friend."

"What's that noise?"

"It's the . . . look, don't worry about it. I need you to contact Sargent Wallace, the chief of police. Every patrol car in the city needs to be looking for Branch."

"Do you have any idea where you are?" Basetti asked.

"Must have gone a mile or more down this tunnel. Who the hell knows."

Before Basetti could ask the next question, he heard gunfire through the receiver followed by a metallic thud, and the line went dead.

CHAPTER FORTY-TWO

After a long stretch of darkness, Eli saw first light from one of the stairwells. Behind him, he heard the men sloshing through water, stopping to search each cart as it went by. As their voices became louder, Eli knew they would be searching his soon. When he was aligned with the stairwell, Eli jumped from the cart.

"There," one of them shouted. Each took a shot, the bullets showering Eli with fragments of slate chipped off the wall.

Eli sprinted up the stairwell. At the top was a metal grate that pedestrians could walk over. He slid his fingers between the rungs and lifted the grate from its recess, sliding it across the pavement above. Eli pulled himself through the hole like a rat coming out of the sewer. The men were climbing the steps as Eli slid the grate back over the hole.

Cars passed on the street in front of him, and Eli knew immediately that he was downtown in the center of Mid-America Mall. He walked quickly along the sidewalk, the glare of street lights overhead. When he heard the wobble-roll of the metal grate against pavement he began to run, his shoes squishy, pant legs heavy with rank water that burned the raw flesh on his leg.

Across the street was Square Park. Up ahead, the intersection of Second Street and Madison. He was at least a mile and a half from his car in the medical center. He looked up Second. Not a cab in sight. Behind him, only one of the guards was running toward him now.

They must have split up.

A police car turned at the corner of South Main and headed straight toward him. Eli's pulse quickened and he slowed from a dead run to a brisk walk. He didn't know whether to stop the officer and ask for help or duck in between the next set of buildings. The patrol car pulled up to the curb beside him and stopped. The officer spoke into his mobile radio and studied Eli as he passed.

When Eli looked behind him, his pursuer was nowhere in sight. He took a sharp left on Monroe. The roar of Redbirds' fans erupted from AutoZone Park and its lights flooded the street.

Great night for baseball.

My season ticket seats will be empty. I could sit there the rest of the game and these buffoons would never find me.

He checked his watch. Over thirty minutes late for his meeting with Meg. Automatic Slim's was only two blocks away.

Could she possibly still be there?

Eli started running again.

It was worth a try.

CHAPTER FORTY-THREE

By the time Eli reached Union Avenue, two more police cars had passed him. The first, with lights and sirens blaring, gave him no thought as it raced toward the Greyhound Bus Terminal. The next patrol car crossed the intersection and slowed just as Eli reached Automatic Slim's Tonga Club.

From the sidewalk, Eli looked among the Friday night patrons lined up at the impressive bar. It was a young crowd meeting for drinks before heading off to the next stop. As far as Eli could tell, there were no young mothers in the crowd.

He waited for his breathing to slow and considered what he would look like to the hostess. Sweaty, his pants leg torn and bloody, wet to the knees. He heard a siren getting closer and he walked through the crowd and opened the door.

A leggy blonde in a black miniskirt greeted him.

"How many in your party?" Her eyes drifted down to his torn pants.

Eli looked beyond her at the guests. The place was pure chic. He felt like pure shit. "I'm supposed to be meeting someone."

Meg's waiter approached and studied Eli a moment. "You're Mr. Someone, aren't you?"

"Excuse me?"

"Mmm, yummy." He placed his hand on Eli's arm and turned to the corner table. "Your lady friend — adorable, short hair, very important looking?"

"Yes, that sounds like her."

"She just left," he said, slapping his hand to his hip. "I mean, she waited at that back table for a good forty-five minutes."

When the waiter turned around, Eli stepped past the waiting guests and was outside again. Across the street, a black Honda Civic pulled away from the curb. Eli cut in front of the car and Meg slammed her brakes to keep from hitting him. Eli opened the passenger-side door and hopped in.

"I assumed we were meeting *inside* the restaurant," Meg said.

"I'm sorry, got tied up."

Meg looked down at his pants. "What happened to you?"

"It's a long story. Keep driving and I'll tell you."

Meg turned onto Union and stopped at the first red light across from the Peabody Hotel. A police car stopped behind them and Eli slouched down in the seat.

Meg looked in the rearview mirror. "You've got some explaining to do, doctor."

She drove just below the speed limit and the police car passed them in the right lane.

Eli decided to skip the tunnel part for now. "I think you're right about the graft device in my brother. It was placed by this RBI, GlobeVac, whoever the hell they are." Eli took a deep breath. "They wanted to test the device in a few human subjects, to make sure they could do it, before taking it to the FDA."

"Why your brother?" The light changed to green.

"My father was involved with the company all along, supplying cadavers and body parts for their device testing. He allowed them to do the experiment on Henry because he considered my brother severely retarded. Figured no one would ask questions or even care. They made out like the operation was a life-saving procedure."

Meg wasn't buying any of it.

"So how does Gaston fit into this?" she asked.

Eli thought about her question. His father must have known about Gaston's perversion with the cadavers. He must have coerced Gaston into receiving the device in exchange for hiding the old man's criminal behavior.

Deciding to avoid that discussion, Eli said, "I'm not sure. But I've got to find Henry. I think they're still experimenting on him."

"Experimenting? What? Who's they?"

"It's RBI, Meg. Fisher. Korinsky. They're all in on it."

"I've heard excuses for being late to dinner," she said. "But this is ridiculous."

"I'll tell you all about it. Just take me to my truck at Anatomy Hall."

They turned left on Dunlap and passed a couple of students leaving the library. Otherwise, this part of the medical campus was quiet and fairly vacant for a Friday night. Down Jefferson Street, an ambulance backed up to the ER ramp. Meg turned right on Monroe toward Anatomy Hall.

"Stop," Eli said and thrust his hand in front of Meg's face.

She stomped the brakes and the tires screeched against the pavement.

"What the hell is going on, Eli?"

Eli pointed down the alley. "Look."

Two police cars had parked obliquely at the front and back of his truck. Both doors were open and the officers were leaning inside, searching Eli's Bronco.

"Back up, slowly."

Meg complied without more questions. She pulled away and drove down Union Avenue in silence. After they passed Methodist Hospital Central, she turned right on South Cleveland and pulled into an alley behind the old E. H. Crump Stadium. She left the car idling.

"I'm not driving another foot."

After he confirmed that no one had followed them, Eli said, "There's a secret wing of RBI, they keep it locked down, isolated."

Meg did not look impressed. "Go on."

"I was there tonight. They have a surgical amphitheater, turn-of-the-century style, gallery seats and all."

Meg responded to Eli's hesitation. "How romantic."

"They pull in cadavers from the Anatomy Hall for experiments."

"Okay, maybe they buy them," Meg said. "Happens all the time."

Eli decided there was no time for the tunnel explanation. He jumped right to the point. "Henry's roommate at State Home is a young man named Jimmy. They have him there."

"Have him?"

"Yes, hooked to a ventilator on a stretcher, next to this dead girl."

Meg held up both hands in surrender. "Eli, stop. Listen to what you're saying. The company you work for is stealing dead bodies and has kidnapped a young man for an experiment?"

"That's right and —"

"When is the last time you slept? Three? Four days now? You're exhausted."

Eli buried his head in his hands.

"The police back there are searching your truck because it's abandoned in a back alley." She put her hand on Eli's shoulder. "Come on, I'm taking you home."

Eli jerked away from her.

"It's Fisher and Korinsky." He was yelling now. "Some kind of synchronized abdominal operation." Eli made a slicing charade of the double incisions. "But it fell apart. The ventilator tubing cut in half."

Meg shook her head.

"I think he's dead. Jimmy. They killed him."

They faced each other, Meg in silence, a rank odor from Eli's damp pants filling the space between fogged windows.

"My mother warned me to stay away from surgeons," Meg said with a hint of a smile. "This is some date."

Eli heard voices outside the car, on his side.

"Lock the doors, Meg."

But before she had time to react, Eli's door flew open. Standing there was Bennie, Tongue next to him, pointing a gun straight at Eli.

"Get out of the car."

Eli started to move, but Meg put her hand on his thigh and squeezed hard. With a swift move to the gearshift, she put the car in reverse and slammed the accelerator.

The open passenger door clipped Bennie in the side and dragged him along the pavement. Eli kicked Bennie in the neck to knock him free. He closed the door to muffled screams.

Meg backed all the way to the street and stopped.

Tongue fired a shot that ripped through the back door.

"Go!" Eli yelled, and Meg peeled out, the Civic fishtailing away from the rapid fire of three more shots.

CHAPTER FORTY-FOUR

Basetti drove his beat-up Celica down Second Avenue at sixty miles an hour. Clamped on top was a light he had taken from Lipksy's car that he had not had a chance to use before. It flashed strobe-like to Nine Inch Nails cranking from a set of busted speakers.

Lipsky had called on his cell phone and told Basetti to come to Mid-America Mall. He was sitting on a park bench smoking a cigarette when Basseti ground his front tire into the curb.

"Wouldn't the department be proud," Lipsky said, flicking his cigarette into a drain chute and plopping low into the bucket seat.

"Got some more information for you," Basetti announced as he peeled out of the parking lot. "Branch is traveling with a woman."

"So, he's got himself a bitch, what of it?"

"Some bitch all right, her name's Meg Daily."

"The medical examiner lady?"

"Yeah, the one you talked to on the phone."

"Well, I'll be damned," Lipsky said, twisting in the seat to remove an empty can of Red Bull jammed in his back.

"I ran her through the computer."

"You did, did you? I thought they hired you to study T and A."

"It's DNA, boss."

"Whatever."

"Anyway," Basetti continued, "seems as though Miss Dr. Daily has a record."

"What did she do? Cut someone open while they were still alive?"

"No, but wouldn't that be interesting, you sick bastard. She got into a little altercation with her boss in Little Rock. Assault. Broke his face in three places."

"Umm, Kum Pow Chicken."

"Exactly," Basetti said as he stopped at a red light. "Now we're proud to have her in River City."

"Get out." Lipsky elbowed Basseti and climbed over the console. "I'm driving this piece of shit. Let's go find Bonnie and Clyde."

CHAPTER FORTY-FIVE

Meg's babysitter answered the phone from a deep sleep.

"Jessica? This is Meg. How's Margaret doing?"

The nursing student cleared her throat. "Oh, she's fine. Been asleep for at least two hours."

"Good. Listen, is there any way you could stay there tonight? All night."

After a moment's hesitation, Jessica answered. "Sure, I guess."

There had been only one other time Meg had left her daughter with a babysitter overnight. Her boss had made her stay for the murder-suicide of a politically connected couple in Little Rock. Three months later, she refused to leave her daughter again and was fired the next day.

"Just sleep in my bed, that's fine, but Margaret will need her insulin shot by seven A.M."

"The same dose as tonight?"

"Yes, the same dose. I'll have my cell phone on if you have any questions."

Jessica was fully awake now. "I guess the night has gone pretty well, huh."

Meg exited I-240 onto Jackson Avenue. Through the evening, she had waited alone at a restaurant, picked up a smelly surgeon, backed over someone with her car, and been shot at more times than she could count. She glanced at Eli, who was turned sideways so he could see out the back window. He gave her a weak I'm-so-sorry-ass smile.

Jessica waited on the line for a response. Meg rolled her eyes. "You have no idea."

Jessica didn't quite get it. "Ooh, ooh, hot."

Meg pretended not to hear that. "I really appreciate this and I'll pay you, big time."

"Just have fun."

Meg pitched her phone onto the dash.

"I'm sorry, Meg," Eli said. "Is she okay with this?"

"I guess she doesn't have a choice, now does she? I'm driving to who knows where, trying not to get killed, while we go bust your brother out of the asylum."

"It's not an asylum, Meg."

Meg pulled off the accelerator and slowed to seventy-five. "I know, I didn't mean it that way."

Eli checked behind them again. Jackson Avenue had a line of cars cruising into Raleigh. At least no one was on their tail.

He took a deep breath. "I swear I think we've lost them." Just saying those words allowed Eli to relax a bit. He removed a torn slip of paper from his wallet and punched a number into Meg's cell.

"Who are you calling?"

"Coates Island. I want to make sure Henry's still there, at least."

Coates Island is a thirty-seven acre mass of land connected to Lauderdale County by a 150-foot bridge. Originally a cotton plantation, it still contained slave quarters scattered across the island in great disrepair. In the late 1990s, Ray Dean Coates, great-grandson of plantation owner Nathaniel Cobb Coates, sold the land in a lucrative deal to developers for an upscale living community for the disabled. Stone had shown Eli the brochure, more resort than institution. It would have been a decade or more before Eli could have financed Henry's move to such a luxurious location. Stone's offer had seemed almost too good to be true.

A woman's voice answered.

"This is Dr. Eli Branch. I'm calling to check on my brother, Henry."

"It's eleven o'clock at night."

"Yes, I'm aware of that. Would someone please go make sure he's okay?"

She sighed loudly into the receiver. "Hold on."

A few seconds later, she said, "the night nurse told me your brother's fine. Asleep, just like the rest of us were."

Eli exhaled. "Thanks, sorry to bother you."

Meg pulled off Highway 19 and headed straight for the river. "I don't trust you country boys and your dirt roads."

"It's not a dirt road," Eli said. "Besides, I'd need the bed of a pickup for what you're thinking; this car's not big enough for anything."

"Maybe you just need a challenge," Meg said, her Civic kicking up plumes of white gravel dust.

She stopped the car just before the bridge. A historical marker with an engraved plaque announced the island as a historical location. The Coates's magnificent plantation home had burned near the end of the Civil War.

"I don't know about this," Meg said, before crossing the long, desolate bridge. A full moon reflected off cypress planks that appeared to dissolve into water midway down.

"This is it," Eli assured her. "There's only one way across."

"If it's so fancy, you'd think there would at least be some lights."

Across the river channel, the island rose from the water. Outlined by a perimeter of willow trees, it was now surrounded by gathering fog.

"It's almost one A.M.," Eli said, trying to be persuasive but fully aware of Meg's valid point. "Lights out."

Slowly, Meg pulled onto the bridge, testing it to make sure it was solid. The wheels caught between each plank and a clack-clack rhythm developed as they crossed to the island. Just beyond the line of willows, the island seemed to open up into an enormous space. The land had been cleared of brush and lay flat except for two massive mounds of dirt made by a bulldozer, currently parked between two cement trucks.

Eli opened the door before the car fully stopped. When Meg caught up with him, he was standing in the middle of a concrete foundation the size of a football field. There were no lights, no tennis courts, and no swimming pool with a curved slide. There was no Coates Island Home and Resort, just a group of three stone slave quarters at the far border of the foundation.

How could I have been so stupid? Eli thought.

He had not, however, relied solely on the brochure Stone had given him. He had researched the facility on a fancy Web site that offered a virtual tour of the place — spacious rooms, a game parlor with a pool table and pinball machines. It even had a lake and a place to walk in the woods. But Eli knew the mistake he had made. How could I let my brother be sent to a place I'd never even seen? He felt a mosquito bore into the side of his neck. Eli slapped it away and emptied the air from his lungs with a prolonged "Damn it."

The words echoed between the slave quarters. Meg walked up behind Eli and cupped his elbow with her hand. He moved away from her and locked his hands behind his head.

"Who did I call tonight? Who answered the phone and told me that my brother was sound asleep?"

Meg stared at him but said nothing.

Eli turned to face her.

"Stone's responsible for this." Eli walked back to the car. "He never moved my brother. The fancy brochure, all of it, just a big lie." Eli opened the driver's door and looked back at Meg. "I'm taking RBI down."

Sighted through a pair of binoculars, a hundred yards away on the top floor of the old quarters, Meg's silhouette appeared smoky-silver as she returned to the car. The sentry placed a phone call.

"They're leaving now."

CHAPTER FORTY-SIX

Lipsky sat in the booth of an all-night coffee shop filled with truckers. The police dispatcher had notified them of gunshots behind the old Crump Stadium and a car matching the description of Dr. Daily's was seen on the north loop of I-240. He and Basetti had followed in pursuit but after finding nothing, they took an exit into the town of Raleigh. Lipsky nursed his second cup of coffee and watched the carnivore across from him.

Basetti was downing an extra-large bowl of chili, into which he dumped a bag of Fritos.

"Why not just swallow a hand grenade. Be much quicker," Lipsky said, watching Basetti wash it all down and suppress a burp. He pointed to Basetti's Diet Coke. "That makes a lot of sense."

Their waitress approached and refilled Lipsky's cup, all the while talking on her cell phone. He lit a cigarette and blew smoke toward Basetti. "How about some second-hand fumes for dessert?"

Basetti pushed away from the empty bowl. "Had an English professor in college," he began and wiped his mouth on his sleeve, "said if you can't make sense of something, tell a story about it."

"Tell a story?"

"You have no idea what this guy Branch is up to, do you?" Basetti asked.

Lipsky took another long drag.

"Start from the beginning." Basetti said. "Tell me his story."

Lipsky leaned forward with his hands on the table, about to stand up. "Should I come sit in your lap first?"

"You're just scared 'cause you don't know how."

Lipsky leaned back in the seat. "Such a moron."

Basetti started the story for him. "In the beginning —"

"Branch comes back to the medical center," Lipsky began. "Home-town boy. Mr. Surgeon-save-the-world. A known commodity. Dad was a bigwig with the dead folks." Lipsky stopped.

Basetti, the facilitator, "Then?"

"He gets pissed off at his lab tech and offs her. Stuffs her into the microwave or whatever that thing was."

Basetti stared at him. "You don't believe that for one second."

"Okay, try this. Someone comes into the lab and asks to borrow a cup of sugar. She says, 'hell no you communist bitch whore,' and they stuff her in the cabinet. Like that version?"

"Yes, except the cup of sugar is a batch of cells."

"Oh yeah, I forgot, green frog cells."

"Go on," Basetti said.

"His boss, Fisher, tells him to get lost and he skips across town to work for the evil empire, otherwise known as RBI." Lipsky took another drag.

"Meanwhile, back at the ranch?"

"It's hotter than hell and maggots are eating my garbage." Lipsky shrugs. "I don't know."

"Allow me." Basetti continued the story. "Branch is doing some dead body dancing with the most pleasant Dr. Daily girl, who then comes up with a connection between the deaths." He took out a folded set of papers from his back pocket and threw them on the table.

Lipsky pulled back like it was used toilet paper.

Basetti pointed. "The autopsy reports."

"How did you —?"

"Got a friend who's an EKG tech. He copied —"

"Don't tell me," Lipsky said, studying the reports. "What's the bottom line here?"

Basetti leaned forward and whispered, "Both patients had a faulty medical device. Supposed to keep that aorta blood vessel from busting."

"So?"

"Except these —" Basetti mimicked a balloon bursting. "Poof."

"Ouch."

"Yeah, and guess where they were made?" Basetti answered his own question. "Back at the RBI ranch."

Lipsky thought about it. "And then Branch goes to work for them?"

"Or maybe," Basetti said, "he's on to them."

The waitress walked up with a full carafe. "No thank you," Lipsky said. "I'm drowning in bullshit already."

She slapped the check down and walked away.

Lipsky stood to leave. "So you're betting the farm on Sand Dollar Reef?"

Basetti followed him. "Better take your waders. Hear the water moccasins are nasty this time of year."

CHAPTER FORTY-SEVEN

"We're on a dirt road now," Eli said as he drove slowly through a thicket of trees.

"Just can't help yourself, can you?" Meg said.

Eli stopped at a barbed-wire fence strung across the road. Meg watched him in the headlights as he unhooked a wooden post and laid the fence along the side ditch.

After he got back in the car she asked, "Where the hell are we?"

Up ahead, through a grove of trees, the faint outline of a house came into view.

"This was my grandparents' place."

The car lights illuminated the front of the house. The roof sagged over a porch that stood on concrete blocks. A tree limb had fallen through one of the side windows.

"Someone lives here?"

"No, they died when I was in high school. But my father never sold the place. We used to come out here every summer."

"Both your grandparents died?"

"My grandfather had Parkinson's. When he died, so did my grandmother, two months later." Eli opened his door. "Let's try to get some rest. We'll leave at dawn."

Meg followed him. "At least we're not getting shot at."

Just off the side yard, the ground sloped up and continued into the tree line. Embedded in the side of the hill was a wooden frame with two feet of roof jutting out above it. "What a cute little door," Meg said.

"Storm cellar. Used to go down there when the tornados came."

They walked through the moonlit yard and a couple of wild chickens ran past Meg's feet. She started singing the tune to the '70's sitcom, *Green Acres*.

"Make fun if you want, but it's beautiful out here during the day. We still have horses in the back pasture."

"Who takes care of the animals?"

"Old man named Silas. Been here all his life. Just lives up the road a piece."

"A piece? You're starting to talk *really* country, you know that?"

Eli helped Meg as they stepped up on the porch, the boards creaking and moaning beneath them. He felt Meg's hand linger on his arm a moment longer than necessary.

In the corner of the porch, Eli reached up and felt along a two-by-six oak beam. He brought the key down and showed it to Meg. "At least some things never change."

Meg held the screen door while Eli inserted the key. Just inside the threshold, Eli said, "Stay right here," and he disappeared into the dark house.

Meg heard cabinet doors open, then saw a flicker of flames down the corridor. Eli returned holding a lamp that illuminated the room. It was a den of sorts, wooden floors, sparse furniture.

"I really did need my sleeping bag, huh?"

"There's a couch for you," Eli said. "I'll sleep on the floor."

He put the lantern on an end table and sat on the couch. "My leg's killing me." He peeled back his torn jeans. He imagined Meg washing and dressing the injury and wondered where that might lead. "Wish we had some gauze," he added. "This looks nasty."

Meg gave a slow shake of her head and said, "Nice try, Romeo." She sat on the couch beside him. "I don't do fresh wounds. Not the living kind, anyway. Grosses me out."

Eli lay his head on the back of the sofa.

"Ever thought about leaving it all and coming out here?" Meg asked.

"What. For good?"

"Yeah, fix the place up, buy some more land, plant cotton."

Eli sighed. "I'll admit, it's crossed my mind a few times this week."

"Show me your leg," Meg said.

Eli propped it on the coffee table.

Meg barely lifted the frayed edge of his jeans and said, "Too dark. I can't even see it." She leaned across Eli, reaching for the lamp.

Eli felt the softness of her chest pressing against his lap.

"Oh, you'll live." Meg said as she scanned across his shin and set the lamp on the table. She leaned back hard against the couch, her arm wedged against Eli's shoulder. "You thought I'd be charmed by this rustic place, didn't you? With your chickens, and your storm cellars, and candlelight." With each rise and fall of Eli's breath, Meg nestled deeper into the couch. "I'm a city girl, don't you know?"

She waited for a response.

"Eli?"

His breathing had slowed, deep and rhythmic.

"Eli," she whispered, because she knew he had fallen asleep.

Outside, she heard the rustle of leaves and a branch scrape against the window. Thunder grumbled far in the distance.

"Oh well." Meg rested against his arm. She thought of her babysitter. Jessica sure will be disappointed.

Meg had curled up, her head in Eli's lap, when a crash of thunder awakened them both. She bolted upright and Eli smelled the sweetness of her hair, like ripe peaches. A gust of wind slapped the window shutters against the wall.

"It's just a storm," Eli said and stood up. But they heard the rattle of the door handle. At the next strike of lightning, the door flew open to reveal the silhouette of a man holding a shotgun.

"What do you want," Eli shouted.

The man shined a flashlight in Eli's face.

"Eli? Is that you?"

Eli let out a breath he hadn't realized he'd been holding. "Silas, you scared us to death."

"I saw the car in the driveway. Sometimes high school kids sneak over here."

"Come in, get out of the rain." Eli said.

Silas removed his floppy leather hat, nodded, and said, "Ma'am."

Meg saw deep wrinkles in the side of his face under a gray stubble beard.

Silas turned to Eli. "Did your truck quit on you?"

"What truck?"

Silas pointed behind him. "The one back under the trees."

Eli glanced at Meg and he went to shut the front door. This time, he locked it. "Someone must have followed us out from Memphis."

"Followed you? Who?"

"I don't know," Eli lied. "But they've already taken shots at us."

This confused Silas, but before Eli could explain, the silence was broken by a wood-splintering blast through the rear of the house. Then the beam of a flashlight reflected off a hallway mirror.

"Follow me," Silas said, and he led them toward the central stairway. At the base of the stairs he opened a cubby hole and pushed Meg toward it. He handed the flashlight to Eli. "Circle back to the car and get the hell out of here."

"But you —"

"I'll keep them company," Silas said, raising his shotgun. "Go!"

Eli pulled the door behind them and turned on the flashlight. They walked down four wooden steps to a small room carved out of the dirt. The air was cool and smelled of dry, dusty earth. Crickets jumped from the rocky floor ahead of them.

Meg ducked her head and followed the light. "Where are we going?"

Eli turned toward her. "Remember that cute little door?"

CHAPTER FORTY-EIGHT

They escaped the storm cellar in a deluge of rain. A layer of muddy water covered the ground between them and the Civic, twenty yards away. Eli held to Meg's hand and pulled her across the yard. He fumbled with the keys and just as he opened the car door, three quick gunshots rang from inside the house. Meg climbed in through the driver's side, but Eli stood in the drenching rain and looked back at the house.

"Eli, don't," Meg called from inside the car. "Please, come on."

They were at the end of the driveway before Eli got the wipers on. As they passed the partially hidden Range Rover, Eli saw the letters RBI stamped on the side.

Saturday's sun was breaking the horizon as Eli turned onto Highway 51, the rapid cracks of gunfire replaying in his head. They had not spoken since leaving his grandparents' house. Meg broke the silence.

"Those shots we heard? Wasn't a shotgun, was it?"

"No, it was a handgun."

"I'm sorry, Eli."

From the console, a cell phone beeped from a low battery.

"Must be yours," Meg said. "Mine's already dead."

Eli flipped his phone open and punched in some numbers.

"Who are you calling?"

"I assume that they never moved Henry, but what if—"

"Hello," someone answered. "Green Hills State Home."

"This is Dr. Eli Branch, I need to ask about my brother, Henry."

"What about him?"

Eli hesitated but his phone beeped again, his battery dying. "How's he doing?"

There was a brief pause. "Your brother was moved out three days ago, you know that."

More silence. "Dr. Branch, are you there?"

"Yeah I'm here." When he asked the next question, he already knew the answer.

"What about Henry's roommate?"

Just before his phone went dead, he heard the woman's reply. "They moved Jimmy out at the same time."

As they approached the Memphis city limits, Meg began to worry.

What if there's been a problem and Jessica couldn't get me?

Her cell phone had been dead all night and it was time for Margaret's morning shot of insulin.

"I'm not sure where to go," Eli said.

"What?" Meg asked, drawn away from her dreadful daydream.

"The police will be watching my house, my truck's probably towed, and security is waiting for me at the hospital."

"Why don't you stay at my place, it'll be safe there."

Eli thought about Meg's tempting offer. It had been thirty-six hours since Scott Tynes's operation. His abdominal packs needed to be removed today. If no traumas were left over from last night, his operation would be scheduled as the first case.

Eli turned on a side street off Madison Avenue, stopped at the loading docks behind Gates Memorial Hospital, and got out of the car. "Go home to your daughter, Meg. I owe you one."

Meg immediately knew that something was wrong when she pulled in her driveway. Bobbie Stafford, her widowed neighbor, came running out of her house.

"Dr. Daily," she yelled, visibly upset. "They took your daughter in the ambulance, early this morning."

Meg got out of her car. "What happened? Where's Jessica?"

"She went with them in the ambulance," Bobbie said, and pointed in the direction it took, her hand shaking. "Little Margaret, I don't know."

As Meg jumped back in her car, she heard her neighbor say, "I'm so sorry. She tried to call you all night."

CHAPTER FORTY-NINE

Biohazard waste containers, stacked in columns, lined the back wall of
Gates Memorial. Eli was becoming very familiar with back entrances
and alleyways. Large rectangular troughs were filled with trash, waiting
for pick up near the loading dock. Days that reached nearly one hundred degrees had turned the liquid waste into a boiling, infectious soup
that ran out of the containers and collected on pavement in thin cus-
tard pools. The putrefied smell hung in tiny droplets compressed by the
humid air. He had read in the hospital's monthly newsletter about the
tons and tons of trash that Gates generated in the course of a day. And
here it is.

Just before he reached the loading ramp, a car accelerated in the lot
behind him. A blue Chevy Impala came to an abrupt stop a few feet
behind him. A young man in a yellow tee shirt and golf visor jumped
out of the car.

"Dr. Eli Branch?"

Eli looked up the ramp. Only thirty feet to the door.

*No way this guy can catch me. It'll be easy to lose him inside the hospital
basement.*

But he didn't appear to be a cop or a reporter.

"Please sir, I've been looking for you for more than twenty-four
hours." He handed Eli a business-sized white envelope and a clipboard

that held a signature form. A pen was stuck under the clip. "Sign for me, please," he said while waving the odor away from his nose.

"What is this?" Eli asked.

"I'm just paid to deliver it, Doc. Now if you could just sign, I'll be out of your hair."

Eli held the envelope. The paper felt thick in his hand as though woven from cloth. The address was embossed in the left upper corner:

BELOSI AND McCRUMB
ATTORNEYS AT LAW
PARK AVENUE
GERMANTOWN, TENNESSEE

"What kind of doc are you, anyway?"

Eli remained silent, distracted. A certified letter from a law firm could mean only one thing.

"You a Ph.D. researcher?" he asked again.

Eli looked at him. "No, I'm a surgeon. And I've got to see a patient, right now." Eli shoved the papers toward him, but the man held up both hands and stepped back.

"I'm not taking it back. You got to sign or they'll just keep coming after you."

"Okay, fine," Eli said as he signed the paper and pitched the clipboard back to him.

"Thanks, Doc." The man retreated to his car. Just before shutting his door, he yelled out, "Hope you got some good malpractice insurance."

Eli entered the hospital basement through swinging doors. He had managed to avoid a lawsuit throughout eight years of surgical residency. He thought about the Tynes case. He had done all he could. *Scott's brain damage had occurred well before I took him to the operating room. Roger Tynes seemed to understand that. But he wants someone to pay for his devastated son. Just what I need. What a time to get sued.*

He found a stairwell that he thought would lead to the back of the ICU. He leaned against the rail, staring at the folder and thinking of the last words of its deliverer.

If they changed the lock on my office, I'm sure they canceled my malpractice insurance as well.

It was too much to think about; with Henry missing and both the police and the RBI thugs after him, this would have to wait.

The stairwell opened adjacent to the nurse's lounge. It was shift change, so all the intensive-care nurses were in their assigned rooms giving reports. Eli walked through the empty lounge. The coffeemaker sat on a cabinet that stored paper towels and cleaning supplies. He dropped the certified letter behind two bottles of ammonia and shut the cabinet doors. Eli poured a cup of old black coffee and started toward Scott Tynes's bed.

From the nurse's desk, he saw that the boy's room was full of medical personnel. The nurses were transferring IV bags to an empty bed. Kanter, the anesthesiologist, stood at the head squeezing an Ambu bag. To Eli, this was a familiar scene; they were in the process of transferring Scott Tynes and all his intensive-care equipment to the operating room. His instinct was to go in and help with the transfer. But a lot had changed in the past forty-eight hours. He wondered if the nurses knew that he was no longer a member of the medical staff. It would take only one call to the authorities, and Eli would be shut out. He decided to meet them in the OR.

CHAPTER FIFTY

Fran Lankford held onto her daughter in the family room of the pediatric ICU. This time, Fran did not cry. She had returned from St. Martin after making arrangements to transport the body of Bernie Lankford, her husband, back to the states. Upon arriving in Memphis, she learned that RBI had already replaced her husband as chief medical officer with a young surgeon from the medical center.

She cradled her daughter's head to her chest and stared through the glass doors, watching doctors and nurses continue to care for other critically ill infants and children. Just minutes before, a doctor had entered their room, sat on the soft ottoman, and informed both mother and grandmother that the severity of the rare, infantile form of leukemia had been too much for their fragile baby. The medical staff had tried through extraordinary means to keep her alive. In the final hours, they had tried to reschedule, from Sunday morning to Saturday, the risky stem cell operation, which would be a historic first for the nation and a long shot for their child. But as the infant's body decompensated, she was no longer a candidate for the highly experimental procedure.

Fran was both angered and in a state of disbelief. Less than a week before she had lost her husband, right after he had delivered a groundbreaking presentation at the International Conference on Embryonic Stem Cell Therapy, the culmination of his life's work. Although the details of the autopsy report had not yet become available to her, she sensed that Bernie's aortic rupture was a complication that should never have occurred. Then, the comfort that her first grandchild brought dissipated with each worsening report of the pediatric specialists.

They should never have made my daughter consent to the stem cell operation. It had been a blip of false hope that now made their valley of despair much deeper.

CHAPTER FIFTY-ONE

From his hideout in the supply room, Eli watched Scott Tynes's processional pass and enter Operating Room Six. There were two IV poles to push, each loaded with bags of fluid and pumps. An orderly pulled at the foot of the bed while Kanter squeezed air into the patient's lungs. Eli noticed that Scott's face appeared twice as swollen as when he had last seen him, thirty-six hours ago. Susan Morris, the chief surgery resident, walked beside the bed, trying to untangle a wad of tubing and wires. She would be able to perform the operation, Eli thought, even if he wasn't there.

He was most glad to see his circulating nurse, Virginia. She would know if the staff had been warned about his suspension of medical privileges. Eli waited until the bed was being pulled through the doorway before he stepped from behind a rack of sterilized instruments.

"Virginia."

She turned to him and pulled down her mask.

"Eli?" she said and looked down the hall each way.

Not a good sign.

"What are you doing here?"

"My patient's going to the OR."

Virginia pulled him back into the supply room, behind a rack of suction canisters.

"Don't you know? They've told us to call the police if anyone sees you."

CHAPTER FIFTY-TWO

Sunlight filtered through magnificent stained-glass windows, a kaleidoscope of colors peppering the wooden pews. The temperature in the sanctuary was cool compared to the boiling asphalt heat. Eli appreciated the contrast between walking alongside traffic from the medical center and entering this sanctuary, with its quiet reverence. The sanctuary was the same as he remembered it all those years ago when the church staff forced Henry to leave.

The pews appeared empty, but as he moved down the center aisle he saw a man laying on his side, asleep, a stuffed garbage bag molded into a pillow. Midway toward the altar, Eli slipped into a pew. He was unsure why he was there, but when he left the medical center that morning, he was certain of his destination.

In the pulpit, a priest quietly prepared the Communion dishes. He nodded to Eli and continued in his work. The man seemed young for a clergyman, not much older than Eli. Eli thought about the difference in careers they had chosen. For the first time, Eli considered how a physician was limited in affecting life changes compared to a priest who bore daily, life-changing witness in ordinary lives. Eli focused on the flame of a candle that burned on the offertory table. He closed his eyes.

A few minutes later, Eli heard someone enter at the back of the sanctuary. He turned to see a young man in a wheelchair pushing himself down the handicapped ramp. The man stopped at the far edge of a pew and locked the chair in place.

Eli stayed a few more minutes, then stood to leave. He noticed the young man again, his head bowed in prayer. Eli thought of Henry, years ago, the torn dollar that fell to the church floor. The priest who criticized them. The reaction of his father. *How did that one event cause my entire family to turn away from the Church?*

As Eli walked the length of the pew, he removed his wallet from his back pocket. When he reached the wheelchair, Eli leaned over and placed a folded dollar bill in the man's hand, just as his mother had done with him and Henry. Eli departed the sanctuary and felt a sense of closure. But then he wondered if perhaps he had insulted the man by such a meager gift. Eli reached the narthex and looked back to see the man nod in appreciation.

Outside, Eli walked to a gas station and found a pay phone. He had left both his cell phone and his beeper in his OR locker. A phone book, without a cover, hung from a flexible wire. Eli scanned through the pages and saw numerous entries for the last name Calloway. He searched the *P*'s looking for Prine. He smiled when he found only one listing, as he expected, for the name Prinobius.

CHAPTER FIFTY-THREE

A white '65 Mustang drove down RBI Drive and stopped at the guard-house. Tongue heard the tap-tap-tap of the old motor well before it arrived and he was waiting outside the gate.

"Prine, what are you doing here on Sunday?" Tongue asked. He enunciated Sunday with a "th" and then looked through the dusty windows at an empty back seat and floorboard.

Every morning, the gate was lifted for Prine automatically and he never had to stop. But Tongue had been given instructions to be extra careful today. He even had a list of approved names on a clipboard.

"They got me cleaning up after the bigwigs take a crap," Prine said.

Tongue laughed at this but continued to look inside Prine's car.

"You going to let me through or what?"

Tongue turned the clipboard toward Prine. "See this list of names? You ain't on it."

"Is that right?" Prine said as he put the Mustang in reverse and slowly backed up. "That's fine," Prine said. "I'll call and tell them you'll be cleaning the toilets later."

"Okay, okay," Tongue yelled as he hustled back in the guardhouse and lifted the gate.

Prine waved and smiled as he drove past. He knew that Tongue would never think to look in the trunk.

•   •   •

Eli lay in a fetal position, the edge of Prine's spare tire pressing his ribs. With the smell of gasoline and exhaust filling the small compartment, he had tried to take only shallow breaths since leaving Prine's house in South Memphis where he had cleaned up and changed clothes. Through the thin, rusted-out wall of the trunk, Eli listened as Prine pulled away from the guardhouse and described the scene.

"Oh yeah, Dr. B. We got television crews all over the place."

Eli felt the car turn to the right and he arched his back away from the tire.

"I'll take you through a back door that no one ever uses. Just hold tight until I tell you."

A minute later, Prine opened the trunk and the full morning sun poured in. Eli clamored out with his eyes shut, a mole using his sense of touch.

"That's one of my biggest fears, getting locked in a trunk," Prine said, grabbing Eli's arm to steady him. "You put a lot of trust in old Prinobius."

"I didn't have much of a choice." Eli squinted to see where they were. "I need to get inside before they start the press conference."

Prine led him through an unmarked door off the back parking lot, which Eli thought would have been locked. They went down one flight of stairs to a basement hallway lined with battery-powered trolleys and with pipes overhead. After several turns, Prine entered a stairwell and took two flights up at a brisk pace as Eli hustled behind him. On the second floor, he opened the door and looked both ways. Looking over Prine's hunched shoulders, Eli saw Lisa behind the reception desk and realized they were in the lobby.

"Stay here," Prine said. He took a few steps and opened the bathroom door. After confirming it was empty, he motioned for Eli and mouthed, *Come on.*

At the front of Regency Biotech International, a ring of reporters stood behind yellow rope, a safe distance of thirty feet from the center of the press conference. The RBI logo, in bold metallic letters, embossed the front of the lectern. The lectern itself was centered so that the company name would be displayed from every angle. At the perimeter of the group of reporters, cameras poised on tripods waited for Sister Frances D'Aquila to emerge from the grand lobby. To capture live footage, cameramen coiled loops of black extension cord ready to be unraveled. Wherever Sister Frances might move, shoulder-mounted cameras could track her.

To the left of the podium, dressed in a long white lab coat and black high heels, Dr. Tsarina Anatolia stood smiling, and the cameras clicked off more than the usual number of test shots. The top button of her lab coat was unbuttoned, the lapel flaring to reveal ample cleavage.

At the right side of the podium, standing at attention in his tailor-made black suit, stood Vice President Alexander Zaboyan. He kept his hands clasped behind him, altering his stance only to wipe the sweat that ran from his forehead in a steady stream.

Like a schoolboy hiding from the teacher, Eli stood with his feet planted on the sides of a toilet seat and balanced himself with both hands against the walls. Just outside the stall, Prine kept watch with his usual flair. He had been waiting to set things right and would not let anyone discover Eli and foil the plan now.

Through a crack in the door, Prine saw Stone emerge from the side office, a wrinkled woman dressed in a blue habit at his side.

"They're heading out, Dr. B."

Eli stepped off the toilet, opened the stall door, and regarded himself briefly in the mirror. If all went as planned, in a few moments he would be on national television. He smoothed his white coat, still wrinkled from the cramped ride in Prine's trunk. Prine came up behind him, grabbed the hem, and gave it a firm yank straight down.

"You look a lot like Elizer Branch," Prine told him.

Eli froze at the mention of his father. "You knew him, didn't you?"

Prine nodded. "He was a good man. Don't let anyone tell you different."

Eli doubted that Prine knew of the illegal device testing on cadavers. And he hoped he never would.

Prine removed a black comb from a jar of blue, medicated solution, climbed up on the rungs of his stool, and administered three quick grooming strokes to Eli's hair.

Eli tried to dodge the last swipe. Surprisingly, he liked what he saw, strands of wavy gray hair pulled back.

Prine looked over Eli's shoulder and smiled. "Movie star doctor."

"Yeah, right." Eli moved to the door and left Prine balancing on his stool.

From the bathroom door, Eli had an unobstructed view of the entire lobby. Harvey Stone was escorting Sister Frances through the large glass doors, already dotted with the flash of cameras. Stone smiled as he offered his right arm, and the sister curled her forearm over his.

It's now or never, Eli thought.

He caught up with the couple before the doors had closed behind them. In a symmetrical approach, Eli slipped his arm in close to the sister's side.

Stone stopped abruptly.

Covered modestly in a blue habit, the sister gradually raised her head, a smile transforming her wrinkled face when she saw a young doctor sweeping in as her escort.

"It's so nice of you to visit us," Eli said and brought her thin hand to his lips.

"Dr. Branch," Stone said, his alarm evident. "What an unexpected surprise."

"Right where you told me to be, boss." Eli watched Bennie closing in, his arm in a sling and road rash across his face. Following Bennie were the same two guards who had chased Eli from the amphitheater at RBI on Friday evening. "Call off your boys," Eli said. "You don't need a ruckus on national TV."

Stone gave a wave and they stopped.

The featured trio kept moving toward the podium.

With a fake smile, Stone said, "Branch, I swear, if you screw this up, consider your brother dead." Stone motioned to Bennie, who reached inside his blue blazer and removed a very worn John Deere cap.

It was Eli who stopped the procession this time. Although it did not surprise him that RBI had taken Henry, its confirmation in the form of

Henry's cap came as a paralyzing blow. He would have to play by the rules, at least for now, especially after witnessing Jimmy in peril.

"That's not nice language in front of the sister," Eli told Stone.

The reporters began to sense a problem with Sister Frances's press conference. Someone from the crowd yelled, "Welcome to America," and grateful applause broke out.

Stone stepped up to the microphone.

"This is truly a historic day. I met Sister Frances D'Aquila over a decade ago in a small village in the African country of Lesotho. That morning she held the first child to receive our vaccination. Since that time, we have delivered over ten million vials of vaccines to that ravaged country."

Here we go, Eli thought. He glanced over his shoulder at Tsarina, who smiled and winked. Opposite her, Zaboyan looked like a mannequin in a clothing store.

Stone continued the accolades. "I have witnessed firsthand the miraculous work of this woman." He turned to Sister Frances, and, with a hand on her back, eased her toward the podium. This brought another round of applause, and the sister lowered her head in response. Then there was complete silence.

She raised her head briefly to a cascade of flash and said, with a slight accent, "I am honored by your kindness."

Hands shot up and the reporters vied for her attention, calling, "Sister, Sister!" But the press conference had been billed as a brief introduction to the international visitor, and Sister Frances retreated from the podium, a woman of few words. However, one TV reporter refused to let the trio escape, and stepped forward.

This woman is everywhere, Eli thought.

"Mr. Stone," Shontay Williams shouted, directing attention away from Sister Frances. "As CEO of RBI, can you explain recent deaths in patients with the aortic device manufactured by your company?"

Stone saw the CNN camera scan over to him. He made a stutter step toward the podium, but Eli intercepted.

"Ms. Williams," Eli said, addressing her directly. As he spoke into the microphone, Eli took command, both hands gripping the lectern.

"Sister Frances has traveled across the globe. This is her day. Let's not diminish it with talk of business."

Another reporter called out. "What's your name, doctor?"

Eli took his gaze off Shontay Williams and smiled. "Branch, Dr. Eli Branch."

The reporters scribbled his name in their notepads.

"I will escort the sister to Washington where she has an important meeting in —" Eli pulled back the sleeve of his coat, "less than two hours. Please be watching for her very important announcement."

Exactly what I wanted, Eli thought. Now the nation will be watching.

Stone was so relieved that Eli had fielded the question of the aortic device that this promise of an announcement went unnoticed and he said nothing. Another barrage of questions came forth.

"Will the sister endorse RBI's use of embryonic stem cells? Do you take responsibility for the recent deaths?"

But Eli had turned away in a position of escort for Sister Frances. His mission was accomplished and he wanted no part of any more sound bites.

CHAPTER FIFTY-FOUR

They left the press conference immediately and were whisked toward the company's Lear. Sister Frances leaned forward on the back seat of the RBI limousine, elbows against her knees. *This is a woman who prefers to kneel on the scorched earth,* Eli thought as he admired her. He poured a glass of water from the built-in bar and handed it to her. She accepted it graciously.

Eli had struck a deal with Stone — he would escort Sister Frances to Washington as long as a reporter accompanied them on the plane. This would keep Stone's plan intact, and the presence of the reporter would protect Eli from being detained by RBI security. Eli was surprised that Stone fell for it so easily.

The limousine quickly approached the Learjet parked in the center of the tarmac. They had little time before the plane would leave. Eli spoke directly to Sister Frances.

"RBI is promoting your visit as support for its stem cell program. Are you aware of this?"

Sister Frances looked confused.

"As we speak, Harvey Stone is informing the media about RBI's plan to conduct the first human embryonic stem cell transplant on U.S. soil," Eli said. "The operation is scheduled this morning at Gates Memorial Hospital. Stone will tell them that you support embryonic stem cell therapy."

Sister Frances was infuriated now. The sun-baked skin of her face flushed and she spoke in broken phrases.

"All life . . . from conception . . . is sacred."

On the opposite seat, Shontay Williams copied down every word.

The limousine stopped near the jet and the doors opened. While Eli escorted Sister Frances to the Lear, Prine pushed his food cart on the tarmac to the opposite side of the plane. Eli boarded with Sister Frances and the reporter. A few minutes later, the Lear was airborne toward Dulles Airport.

As the jet leveled out, the pilot spoke. "I thought Dr. Branch was accompanying us."

Sister Frances answered him. "It seems as though Dr. Branch has urgent business at his hospital."

Prine pushed the food cart across the tarmac toward his car. Although he had emptied it of food, the cart was much heavier than before. With the Lear's engine blast fading in the distance, Prine said, "Yeah, Dr. B, I was wrong. You are going to make it out of here."

When Prine reached the hangar where his Mustang was parked, Eli climbed out of the cart and assumed the fetal position again in Prine's trunk. Prine did a short turnaround on the tarmac and headed for Gates Memorial, just as Eli had instructed.

CHAPTER FIFTY-FIVE

Eli leaned into the open window of the Mustang. "Go home and lie low for a few days," he told Prine. "Let the dust settle."

Prine reached across the seat. His hand was bony and cold and the skin folded in on itself like wax paper as Eli shook it.

"Be careful, Doc."

Eli knew that entering Gates Memorial again could jeopardize his position in the field of medicine forever. He held to Prine's hand for a few seconds longer, this bridge to a former life. Then he turned and sprinted up the ramp of the loading dock.

Through the window of Operating Room One, Eli saw Korinsky, gowned and facing the operating table, his back toward Eli. Kanter was at the head, recording vital signs on his clipboard. It was a scene so similar to the one Eli had observed less than a week ago, in this same room, that he felt a sick sense of déjà vu. Except now, there appeared to be much less chaos.

That was about to change.

Eli did not see a patient on the operative table. There was no gurney inside the room from which to transfer a patient, no sound of a bed being pushed from the holding room around the corner. Eli glanced down the hall, empty except for a cleaning cart a few feet away. Yet, when he looked at the monitor above Kanter's head, there was clearly an EKG tracing and CO_2 waveforms returned from an endotracheal tube.

Roberta leaned over the table and handed a blue towel drape to Korinsky. As the surgeon moved forward to grasp the towel, Eli saw the patient's feet and the small frail knees of a child. To his right, Eli heard the activated hum of electric doors, and he ducked behind the cleaning cart. The doors opened and Karl Fisher lumbered into the hallway. He was struggling, both hands behind his head, to tie his surgical mask. Landers followed behind him. Fisher kicked open the door of Room One and yelled to Korinsky, "How we doing?"

"I'm about to cut her."

"Good," Fisher grumbled. "I'll have the donor tissue down here in ten minutes or less." He let the door close behind him and turned down the back hall of the operating suite, still fumbling with his mask.

Eli remained hidden behind the cart until Fisher was out of sight. He knew now the procedure-gone-bad that he had witnessed in RBI's amphitheater was just a test run for what was happening now. Crouching, his eyes came level with a collection of cleaning supplies inside the cart: old rags, jugs of ammonia, and a bottle of rubbing alcohol. He took the alcohol, slipped the bottle into the back pocket of his scrubs, and approached the window again.

The child's exposed body lay on the table. Before the final drape descended into place around the patient, Eli followed frail knees up to the rib cage and then the pale face of Margaret Daily. When Korinsky started to press his scalpel into the little girl's skin, Eli burst through the door.

Korinsky responded immediately. "Virginia, call security. Now! Dr. Branch no longer has privileges at this hospital."

"And you don't have privileges to endanger a child's life."

Virginia stood motionless and stared at Eli, uncertain of what to do.

"Call security, that's an order," Korinsky yelled again.

"What's going on here, Branch?" Kanter asked, stepping from behind the canopy. "You're out of line."

Eli moved toward the table as Virginia picked up the phone and began to dial. Korinsky cut the last few inches of incision on Margaret's abdomen, a line that snaked from her breastbone, around her navel, and was now oozing bright red blood.

There was a precipitous drop in both frequency and tone of Margaret's heart rate. Kanter looked back at his monitor. "Her pulse is dropping like mad."

"She's too sick, Korinsky," Eli said, and he continued to move closer. "She won't make it through the operation."

"Yeah, hold up," Kanter said. "She's bradycardic. I'm giving atropine."

Smoke from the electrocautery drifted above the table as Korinsky, on autopilot, sliced through Margaret's subcutaneous tissue. The smell of electrocautery filled the room and for the first time in his career, it made Eli sick. Korinsky was no longer making an attempt to control the bleeding.

"This is the future, Branch," Korinsky said. "If she doesn't make it, the next one will."

Kanter scrambled to infuse medicine and fluid. "Damn it, Korinsky, I said to hold up. Get me some blood, Virginia. This little girl needs blood, now."

Static crackled from the intercom and Fisher's voice boomed through. "The tissue's ready, I'm bringing it down."

"Back away from the table, Korinsky," Eli demanded.

Korinsky turned to face Eli, the scalpel out in front of him now with Margaret's blood wet on the tip.

"I can't let you kill a child just to save RBI."

Kanter hung a unit of blood. "RBI? What's this about?" Then he saw the scalpel pointed at Eli. "Virginia?"

"Security's on the way."

Eli extended his hand toward Korinsky. "Give me the knife."

Korinsky held his position and turned to look at Margaret. Then, he flipped the scalpel so he could present it to Eli handle first.

Eli reached for the knife but Korinsky cut a quick slice across Eli's forearm.

Eli felt a tendon snap and his blood splattered the floor.

"Stop it!" Virginia yelled and she pulled against Korinsky's arm. But Korinsky kept at him, swinging the scalpel.

Eli backed up against the electrocautery unit, stepping on the cord that ran along the floor to the handheld control on the operating table.

During the brief struggle, Eli pulled the bottle of alcohol from his back pocket, unscrewed the top, and dropped it at Korinsky's feet.

Korinsky pushed Virginia off and she crashed into a kick bucket on the floor. When he turned the scalpel back on Eli, Korinsky stopped. Eli held the electrocautery control in his hand. Korinsky glanced at the clear liquid beneath his shoes.

"Don't move," Eli said. "It can all stop right here."

With the smell of rubbing alcohol filling the room, Korinsky rushed forward, and Eli bent and touched the metal electrocautery tip to the expanding pool.

Flames shot up Korinsky's scrubs until his waist was engulfed. He fell against the table, pulled the sterile drapes that surrounded Margaret, and tried to extinguish the flames by wrapping himself in the cloth.

Eli grabbed the extinguisher from the side of the anesthesia machine and covered Korinsky in blasts of white powder and foam. He kicked the scalpel into the corner. But Korinsky was in no shape to use it again. He writhed in pain on the floor, his scrubs melted onto his back.

Fisher bumped the door open with his butt and turned, unaware, holding a metal specimen basin in front of him. He stopped at the smell of burning flesh and the sound of Korinsky screaming on the floor.

Over the intercom, a frantic voice called, "Code Blue, Room Eight, Dr. Fisher — Code Blue, Room Eight, Dr. Fisher."

The chairman of surgery looked at Eli. "Damn it," Fisher said. He dropped the basin and burst from the room.

Eli moved to Margaret's side and told Roberta to hold a sterile pad against the open incision.

"I have her stabilized for now," Kanter said. "What the hell, Branch?"

"I'll explain later." He turned to Virginia and said, "I'm going to Room Eight."

CHAPTER FIFTY-SIX

As a shortcut, Eli ran through the central supply area.

I should have known. I should have known.

When he entered Room Eight, Fisher was nowhere in sight. Landers stood over the patient, his hands submerged in an abdomen overflowing with blood. There were no drapes, no sterile gowns. The intern's scrub top was drenched, his eyes wild with fear.

Only Landers and a young female nurse-anesthetist were in the room. No scrub nurse or circulator. The monitors screeched a wild, erratic rhythm so fast that the beeps coalesced into one. Nothing was being done to correct the situation. The anesthetist stared at two bottles of medicine, her hand shaking, otherwise paralyzed. Eli looked down at the bleeding patient, Henry, his brother. Henry's face was mottled, the color drained from around the endotracheal tube in his mouth. For the first time before performing an operation, Eli did not take his extra moment. He did not close his eyes or bow his head. He did not even put on gloves.

Landers spoke, his voice cracking. "Dr. Fisher was out of control!"

With one hand, Eli pulled the instrument table close and ripped open a pack of laparotomy pads.

"I know," Eli said. "Listen to me, Landers. We're going to do the same maneuvers that we did with Scott Tynes. Evacuate the blood, find the bleeder, and stop it."

Landers nodded and stared at the deep, bleeding gash on Eli's arm. Two fingers on his mentor's hand hung limp from the severed tendon.

"But you have to tell me, what did Fisher do?"

Landers looked down at the pool of blood. "He cut out the pancreas, a big chunk of it, right out of the center. He didn't even try to stop the bleeding."

So that's it, Eli thought. *They're transplanting stem cells into Margaret to treat her diabetes, using my brother's pancreatic tissue to feed the cells and keep them alive until they become engrafted.*

Eli went straight to the source, sliding his hands over Landers's, deep into his brother's abdomen, until the laceration on Eli's arm submerged in the pool of blood.

Encased in a web of vessels and nerves, Henry's pancreas could be bleeding from any number of tributaries, Eli assumed. But the midsection of the pancreas lay on top of two major vessels, the portal vein and the superior mesenteric artery. If either one was injured, Eli knew he would likely not be able to save his brother.

Landers responded like an upper-level resident, scooping out partially clotted blood to gain the exposure Eli needed. From the rate at which blood refilled the abdominal space, Eli knew a major vessel had been torn. And from the darker maroon color, it was most likely the portal vein, a vessel that drained the entire blood return from the intestine to the liver.

"Call your staff now," Eli told the anesthetist, who immediately grabbed the phone. "And hang all the blood you can find."

He turned to Landers. "Where's the sucker?"

"Dr. Fisher said he didn't need one."

Eli glanced at the instrument tray and removed a large angled vascular clamp.

"We've got one shot," he told Landers.

Eli lifted Henry's mesentery from the wound. He inserted the clamp across the mesenteric neck where the veins joined the major portal system.

"If we can slow the inflow of blood, maybe we can see the hole."

Eli closed the ratcheted clamp with three metallic clicks.

"Won't that cut off supply to the bowel and cause ischemia?"

"Not if we're quick."

The clamp slowed the blood loss considerably. There was only back bleeding, and Landers managed to evacuate it. Eli reached up and positioned the overhead light to illuminate the wound. He extended an open hand toward the anesthetist.

"Give me your sucker."

"What?" she said. "It's been in his mouth, it's not sterile."

"Do I look sterile?" Eli responded, his patience gone. "Give it to me!"

She complied, and Eli suctioned the remaining pool of blood until he could see a tear in the side of the thin-walled portal vein.

At least it's not completely transected. Eli needed a small bit of fortune on his side.

He placed Landers's hands in the position of retraction and instinctively called out, "Four-O Prolene on an RB-one." Even as he said this, he knew there was no circulating nurse. He went to the suture cabinet, kicked it open with his foot, and selected the thin monofilament suture on a curved vascular needle.

"Hold the sucker just off the hole," he told Landers. "I'll close it primarily." But when Eli tried to clamp the needle with needle driver, the suture fell from his injured hand to the floor. He bent, clamped the needle directly off the tile, and inserted it at the apex of the bleeding hole, closing it with a running suture, over and over. In less than a minute, he was finished with the repair and released the clamp to allow return of flow to Henry's intestine.

"Wow," Landers said.

There was only minor residual oozing from the needle holes. The continuous beep from the monitor separated as Henry's accelerated heart rate slowly began to normalize.

Virginia opened the door and stepped into the room. During her span of thirty years at Gates Memorial, there was nothing she hadn't seen. But she brought her hand to her mask and gasped when she saw Eli, ungloved, with blood up to the level of the severed tendon in his arm.

She had no idea that it was the blood of Eli's brother. She pointed behind her in the direction of Operating Room One. "There's another surgeon operating on the little girl now."

Virginia's voice carried an urgency that was unfamiliar to Eli.

"Fisher?"

"No, a female surgeon. Something's wrong, Eli. I don't recognize her."

"It's all wrong, Virginia. All of it."

"Please come down there."

Eli knew that Virginia would not pull him away unless absolutely necessary. He looked at the monitor. The anesthesia staff had arrived and was hanging more blood. Even though he was still tachycardic, Henry's blood pressure had stabilized. Eli placed a pack of laparotomy pads over the site of Henry's vein repair. "Apply gentle pressure and let them catch up," he told Landers. "I'll be right back."

The intern watched as Eli left the room. He would hold pressure and wait for Dr. Branch, his mentor and friend, to return.

CHAPTER FIFTY-SEVEN

GATES MEMORIAL HOSPITAL
OPERATING SUITE
9:16 A.M.

Eli rushed into Operating Room One to find a tall female surgeon, her back to him, bent over Margaret, working diligently to close the little girl's abdominal incision. He had complete faith in the chief surgical resident, Susan Morris. Even though she was not a pediatric surgeon, Susan would adapt her skill to the delicate approach needed to handle the tissue of a child.

Eli walked up behind her. "Susan, glad you're here. How is she?"

But Susan did not turn around, nor did she speak.

From across the room, Virginia got Eli's attention and shook her head. He stepped to the end of the bed for a clear view of the operative field. Rather than closing the incision, the surgeon had opened the wound more. She held a large syringe filled with pink cell culture medium. At the end of the syringe, a long spinal needle pierced the portal vein adjacent to Margaret's pancreas.

"What are you doing?" Eli yelled.

Then he saw the aqua blue eyes above the rim of her mask.

"Live, my darling," Tsarina said. "Your mother tells you to live." She continued to inject as though Eli was not there.

"Stop," Eli demanded and pulled her arm away from the field.

A hospital security guard burst into the room. He wasn't alone. Lipsky walked straight at Tsarina with his pistol drawn. He looked at Eli, his left arm hanging limp, with blood running off his fingers.

Tsarina completed the injection of cells and turned to face Eli. "All I've ever wanted is a child," she said, pleading with him. "Now, all that remains of my daughter will live on in this little girl." Without warning, Tsarina pulled her hand out of Margaret's abdomen and drove the long needle deep into the base of Eli's neck.

The last thing Eli heard was the blast from Lipsky's gun.

CHAPTER FIFTY-EIGHT

Meg Daily stood over bed thirteen in the surgical ICU. The medical personnel had left the room, even the nurse, after stabilizing the post-operative patient.

This must be a good sign, she thought.

Outside the room, a policeman kept watch.

Meg had just returned from visiting her child in another intensive-care unit connected to the pediatric ward. There had been no internal damage, though a scar down the length of her daughter's abdomen would remain as a lifelong reminder.

Her scar will remind me every day, Meg thought, *of how foolish I was.*

Now she worried about what had been injected through the syringe. It was confiscated as evidence, and analysis of the fluid and cells was underway.

Dr. Korinsky had approached her after Margaret was admitted early Saturday morning in critical condition. Meg was told that a transplant was available for her daughter. It was a highly experimental combination of healthy donor pancreas and embryonic stem cells that would thrive in the transplant and produce insulin.

Highly experimental.

Yet there was a chance that her daughter would be cured forever. No more insulin shots, no more ambulance rides from day care. She had tried to contact Eli for his advice. After two hours of calling him with no answer, she became desperate and consented to the operation.

Now, that man she was standing over had saved her daughter's life. His eyes were open but unfocused. A long bandage applied to the left side of his neck had a line of blood seeping through.

Injury to the carotid, his doctors had told her.

His left arm was wrapped in a bulky bandage and elevated on two pillows. The tendons had been repaired simultaneously with the carotid artery repair in an operation that lasted over seven hours. The plastic surgeon said his strength would be fine, but he was unsure if Eli would ever regain the motor skills to be a surgeon.

Eli blinked.

"Hey," Meg said, her voice cracking. "Thought I was going to find you on my autopsy table."

"I'm pretty tough," he said, then had to clear his throat.

"Yeah, it's too bad. I was looking forward to seeing you naked."

"You're sick."

"I know." Meg leaned over and kissed him on the forehead. Her eyes were filled and wet.

"Pathologists aren't supposed to cry."

"A weak moment for me, I guess."

Eli waited for Meg to look at him again. "How's Margaret?"

"She's okay. She's going to be okay."

Then Eli was silent, hesitant to ask the next question. But his eyes sought the answer.

Meg grasped his uninjured hand. "Your brother's in critical condition, Eli. But they think Henry will live."

Relieved that his brother was still alive, Eli slept.

CHAPTER FIFTY-NINE

Eli kept his eyes shut and listened to the rhythm of normal beats from an overhead monitor. He could hear more distant monitors and the voices of nurses and respiratory therapists. His hearing seemed hyper-acute, and from the background noise, he picked out Rosie, the male ward clerk who was humming and singing along with the radio.

It was very tempting to continue lying this way, to play dead. All of the sounds swirled in his head, at once crisp and clear, then faded to static and back again.

He remembered another voice. Meg.

Margaret's okay. Henry's alive.

Eli opened his eyes. His neck hurt and a dull ache throbbed down his arm into his hand. But inside, he felt relaxed and strong, as though he had slept for days and was newly refreshed. He reached beside the bed and pressed a lever that allowed the railing to fall. It banged and bounced as it caught in the down position, and Eli waited for the disturbance to attract the nurse.

No such luck.

His room faced the central nurse's desk, where he could see an open-faced clock.

That's why none of the nurses are here. It's seven o'clock. Shift change. They're in the lounge giving report.

Beside the clock hung a white board with the roster of current surgical ICU patients written in bold black letters. The name Branch occupied the slot for bed thirteen. Rosie had written M.D. in tiny letters at the top right side, as though a trademark.

Henry's name will be coded, Eli thought. No one would know his identity.

He scanned the roster.

Two slots down, bed fifteen.

Stat Romeo.

Eli smiled at the random name they had chosen. *That fits Henry perfectly.*

He swung his legs beside the bed and sat upright. The move was too fast and his head spun. He waited for the nausea to pass. Then he unhooked the IV bag, cradled it like a football, and walked into the hallway. His hospital guard stopped him.

"My doctor has ordered me to ambulate," Eli said.

The guard looked confused about this but let him pass anyway. Eli walked to the open doors just two rooms from his.

Room fifteen was a double room with a curtain divider. Eli looked on the right side and his guess was correct. Henry was covered up to his neck with thick blankets. His eyes were taped shut, an ET tube hooked to the bedside ventilator that hissed with each breath. Henry's vital signs, as displayed by the monitor, were normal.

He is going to make it.

The patient on the other side of the curtain groaned. "Nurse." Then he called again, this time drawing it out, "Nurrrse."

Eli parted the curtain.

"Hey, man," the patient said. "Could you get my pillow?"

Eli saw that the patient's pillow had fallen to the side and was caught between the mattress and the bed rail. His head lay awkward and flat against the bed. Eli dislodged the pillow, gave it a fluff as best he could with one hand, and waited for the patient to lift his head.

"You'll have to do it for me," he said. "I can't move."

With his good arm, Eli lifted the patient's head until his chin rubbed against his tracheostomy tube. Eli nudged the pillow with his bandaged arm until it was wedged beneath the boy's head.

"Thanks."

Eli looked at the patient's swollen face for another moment.

"What's your name?" Eli asked.

The boy stared at the ceiling.

"Tynes. Scott Tynes."

CHAPTER SIXTY

The young nurse assigned to Eli was shocked to find his bed empty. Melissa Case blamed the guard, who then explained that Dr. Branch was ambulating. By then, the nurses were coming out of report, and they all went looking for the missing patient. One of the nurses knew that Scott Tynes had been Dr. Branch's patient. They clustered outside room fifteen.

"He's just a few hours post-op, and already he's checking on his patients?" Melissa asked.

"If I need a surgeon, I want Dr. Branch," another nurse said.

They watched the doctor leaning against the bed rail and talking with the young boy. Eli's gown was tied in the back, and it parted open below his waist. His nurse went into the room and pulled his gown together.

One of the nurses outside the door said, "Melissa girl thinks she needs a surgeon right now." This released a round of nervous laughter from the group. The nurse for Scott Tynes and Henry entered the room behind Melissa and the other nurses scattered to care for their own patients. But none of them knew that the other patient in room fifteen was Eli's brother.

When Eli returned to his room, escorted by his nurse, Lipsky was waiting for him. He was not alone. Two official-looking men in dark suits stood behind Lipsky, having passed by his hospital guard, who so far had proven ineffectual.

Eli stopped in the doorway and looked at Lipsky. "Are you going to shoot me too?"

"No, I thought I'd wait until after these fellows got through with you."

One of the suits stepped forward. "Dr. Branch, please, sit down."

Melissa helped Eli to a bedside chair and hung his bag of intravenous fluid on the pole.

"We know you've been through a lot, so we'll make this short and to the point." He flipped open his wallet. Eli didn't find the man's name because he was so focused on the words Federal Bureau of Investigation before the man slipped it back in his coat.

"We've been asked by the president to pay you a visit."

Melissa stopped writing in Eli's chart. Eli looked at Lipsky, who had a big grin on his face as if he was finally in the middle of something important.

The FBI doesn't mess around. They'll come after you straight from surgery.

"Let's just say the president was rather impressed with your actions this morning."

Eli looked at the stone-cold face of the other FBI agent and asked, "Impressed?"

Lipsky butted in. "Dr. Branch hasn't seen much television over the last few hours."

"Well, it doesn't matter," the agent continued. "We've been tracking suspicious activity within the biotech industry. RBI was at the top of our list. You just made our investigation much easier."

The second agent handed Eli a business card. "We need someone like you, with your skills, on the inside."

Eli felt a throbbing pain in his injured arm and wondered if he would ever be able to operate again. He studied the card a moment and looked up, his eyebrows raised. "You're telling me the president of the United States sent you down here to offer me a job?"

Both men turned toward the door. "You'll be hearing from us. Just take care of yourself."

Lipsky approached Eli's chair, removed a folded newspaper from his back pocket, and handed it to him. "Before you leave us small town boys behind, thought you might want to know what happened to your medical school buddies."

Eli opened the paper to front-page headlines:

RBI LINKED TO UNAUTHORIZED HUMAN EXPERIMENTS UNIVERSITY SURGEONS ARRESTED AFTER DEADLY GATES MEMORIAL SHOWDOWN

He scanned the article. It told of Sister Frances D'Aquila's television appearance in Washington, her denunciation of RBI's stem cell therapy, and the swarm of federal agents deployed to Memphis. Eli let the newspaper fall to his lap. He thought about Fisher and Korinsky, and he tried to grasp the magnitude of the events.

Lipsky waited to let the news sink in, until he couldn't hold it any longer. "Remember that wacko employee of yours and the skin we found under her fingernails?"

"Yeah?" Eli said, eager to know who had killed Vera, his lab tech.

"It matched the RBI scientist woman, Tsarina. She's the one who stole the cells from you; she had them tucked away in her lab."

Eli thought of the final moments in the OR before he lost consciousness, when Tsarina was standing at the operating table.

"She's the one sabotaging RBI's fancy little device," Lipsky told him. "Orchestrated the whole thing."

"The gunshot," Eli asked. "What happened?"

"It's a damn shame." Lipsky shook his head as he turned to leave. "She didn't make it."

CHAPTER SIXTY-ONE

Meg Daily pushed the wheelchair out of Eli's room in intensive care. After a single night's stay, he was being transferred to the ward and was expected to be discharged in a couple of days.

"There's no reason I can't walk to the elevator."

Melissa scolded him. "You know the policy. We don't have many patients that can just walk out of the ICU."

Meg joined in. "You're starting a fight after all the nurses have done for you?"

"What did they do?" Eli asked. "Let me walk around with my bum hanging out?"

A group of nurses had gathered at the central desk to say good-bye. They all heard Eli's last statement and started cheering and clapping. Meg stopped the wheelchair in front of them and they cheered even louder.

"I thank each and every one of you." Then Eli tilted his head sideways and said, under his breath, "Now get me out of here."

As Meg wheeled him by the door to the nurse's lounge, Eli noticed that it was empty. "Stop a second."

"I thought you wanted out of here?"

Eli raised himself from the wheelchair. "I left something."

He walked to the cabinet beneath the coffeemaker, pulled out the oversized envelope, and returned to the wheelchair. "The next thing I have to do is hire a lawyer," Eli said. He turned the envelope so that Meg could see the legal address as she pushed toward the elevator.

"The Tyneses are suing me."

"I thought you said the boy was alive. That you talked to him."

"Doesn't matter, he's still paralyzed."

Meg backed the wheelchair inside the elevator next to an elderly couple. The man held onto his wife, who was hunched over with severe osteoporosis. Eli greeted them, then opened the envelope. He dreaded what he was about to read.

> To Eli Branch, M.D.
>
> From the Law Offices of Belosi and McCrumb
>
> As the attorneys representing Mr. Roger Tynes, we are contacting you based on his request dated 14 July. Mr. Tynes has informed us that on the night of July 13, you assumed care of his son, Scott, who was critically injured in a motorcycle accident. Mr. Tynes likewise informed us of his son's life-threatening injuries and certain paralysis. Mr. Tynes is convinced that your surgical skill was crucial in saving his son's life.
>
> Based on this information and Mr. Tynes's urgent request, we initiate the following:

Here it comes, Eli thought.

> A gift in amount equal to one million dollars will be given to the University of the Mid-South Medical School in your honor.

Eli read the sentence again before going to the next line.

> These monies will be restricted for the purpose of research, programmatic enhancement, or faculty endowment. Further use of this financial gift, within these categories, will be at your discretion.
>
> As per Mr. Tynes's instruction, we are contacting you privately to avoid further media intrusion during this difficult time for the Tynes family. We ask that you honor his request for silence until Mr. Tynes desires to come forth with a public announcement. Please contact our office to arrange transfer of funds at your earliest convenience.

The elevator stopped and the elderly couple slowly walked off.

"Did you see that old man?" Meg asked. "How sweet."

Eli finished reading the letter and looked up at Meg, who was still going on about the sweet old couple. "You won't believe this."

"That bad, huh?"

Eli decided to skip the million dollar part, for the moment.

"He wants me to take his yacht for a cruise."

"Yacht? Who's he?"

"Roger Tynes." Eli reread the lines out loud.

> On a more personal note of his gratitude and appreciation, Mr. Tynes would like you, and a guest, to make full use of his private yacht, which is docked in Miami Beach, Florida. We will arrange a flight for two according to your schedule.

Meg grabbed the piece of paper. "What?"

"Read for yourself."

The elevator doors opened to the ninth floor. Eli had to roll himself out because Meg was completely absorbed in the letter.

In the hall, Eli wheeled around to face her. Meg's mouth was half open with a developing smile.

"Something about a sailing partner," Eli said, "or am I mistaken?"

Meg read the lines verbatim. "You and a guest."

Eli smiled. "I've never seen a pathologist in a string bikini."

Meg threw the letter in his lap. "If you don't take me on this trip, you never will."